THE SILENT DAUGHTER

CLAIRE AMARTI

FIRST EDITION

For Mum and Dad

Prologue

The wind has a moan in it, and a mournful shiver shakes the trees. I hate October.

The cemetery is almost empty today, even emptier than usual. It's just me, Jan, and up in the grey sky a bird of prey making its wide circles. Fiona would have been able to tell us what kind of bird. She could point to any tree or bird and say *that's a whatever-it-is,* even though she grew up just like I did in a little Connecticut town. Fiona was passionate about nature for some reason, she even had a bird almanac beside her bed. And she had one of the best memories I've ever seen. That was in the old days, when we were still kids. Before she grew up, and replaced birds with other things. More dangerous things.

The bird overhead wheels and drops. I wonder what it's spotted. Rabbit? Squirrel? There's no point running, little creature. Nowhere to hide now. Life's not fair, right? Sometimes the cards just aren't stacked in your favor. We should know by now, it's always the more powerful animals that win.

I lower my gaze to the grey headstone before us.

Kennedy, Fiona.

Beloved daughter.

Loyal friend.

The familiar nausea churns in my stomach. Beside me, Jan kneels down and starts pulling small weeds from the headstone. The weeds are only ever small ones, because Jan comes here regularly. She watches over this little patch of earth. The lettering on the headstone is sharp and clear -

1

I hear they carve them with lasers these days. I think for a moment what it might be like to be a gravestone carver. Quiet, I decide. Peaceful. The right kind of life for someone like me, the hermit I've become.

Satisfied with her weeding, Jan places the little clump of pink freesias underneath the stone. She's always calm and matter-of-fact when we visit her daughter's grave, no tears. She just sees to the weeds and clucks her tongue whenever there are signs of youths drinking in the cemetery, empty cans or cigarette butts. She treats it like a living room that needs cleaning but it's hard to know what she really feels - how much she's recovered or ever will recover from the loss. Ten years ago now, which is hard to believe. It's the one thing - okay, one of the two things - that I will never talk to Jan about. I just don't have the words. And if I'm honest I probably don't want to know what exactly she feels now. I can't bear the guilt.

'Okay love, we'll be off now.'

I don't know if it's me or Fiona she's talking to. The wind whips around her words, moving across the grass and shaking the spruce trees by the cemetery wall. Jan plants her hands on her thighs and levers herself back up from the ground. We link arms and I steer us back towards the parking lot.

'You mustn't worry about the job thing, Sadie,' Jan says. 'You know you can stay with me for as long as you like.'

'I know,' I say, and give her arm a squeeze through the raincoat.

'Everybody needs a break sometimes,' she goes on. 'It's nothing to be ashamed of.'

A break is a nice way to put it. She's conveniently

leaving out how I was asked to leave Horton College, and how I've been having periodic panic attacks since arriving back, jobless, to Milham. It's frankly embarrassing. Jan's house has always been a second home to me though. As for my actual home, Mom's house is only a three-minute drive from Jan's, but that door is closed to me these days.

'I sometimes think that -' Jan pauses. 'I sometimes think it was my fault, Sadie.'

I stop walking, taken by surprise.

'What do you mean? What was your fault?'

She sighs. 'Well, you know. Driving you so hard. Pushing you. You never did 'have a break' growing up, did you? I was always pushing you to do more. You and Fiona. But Fiona was different. She never worked as hard as you did.'

She didn't have to. Fiona was smart, smarter than me. Smarter than almost anybody. I touch the locket I always wear around my neck.

It's true, Jan coached us, pushed us. But I always wanted to be pushed. I wanted to escape little Milham town every bit as much as Jan wanted me to. Everything she dreamed for us, I dreamed too. Harder than she knows.

I squeeze Jan's arm again.

'You were my fairy godmother. You still are. Don't second guess yourself. And don't worry about me. I'm keeping an eye out for substitute teacher gigs to tide me over for now. Something will come up.'

She turns her head just enough to look me in the face; her raincoat squeaks. She smiles at me.

'You're a good girl, Sadie.' Her voice is kind, protective, loving. 'You always were.'

I drop my eyes from hers, focus on the parking lot. The drops are coming down thick now, enough that nobody could tell if it's rain on my face or tears. I glance back. The wind is strong and the flowers are cheap, and there's already a flutter of pink petals come loose, whipped up in the air like morbid confetti.

A good girl.

If only she knew.

One

The doctor's waiting room hasn't changed much since I was a little girl. Whiskery old Doctor Harrison died years ago, but the chenille sofas, the sad-looking potted plants, and the popcorn ceiling are all pretty much the same. What's changed is me. It's twenty years later and I'm not here for an earache or a sore throat any more. I wish I were.

The ancient television set thrums in the corner, and in front of me is a chipped coffee table with a big spread of dog-eared magazines promising crash diets and inside scoops on royal babies. The only other people here are a mother and son - the kid's playing on his mother's phone while she flips through *People.* I rub my sweating palms on my jeans. I hope Dr Jamil won't have a problem with refilling my prescription. From the way she spoke to me when she filled it, I think she meant for the Klonopin to last me a couple of months, not a few weeks. I know it's not great. I know I should slow down. But it feels so easy, so instant, when the anti-anxiety meds kick in and take over. Besides, I think, if Dr Jamil knew the full extent of what I'm carrying, she'd understand. Hell, she'd probably skip the benzos and go straight to a tranquilizer.

I glance out the window to the steady October drizzle. The bonnet of Jan's car is already slick with rain. Hopefully she's left an umbrella inside it. At Horton right now, the horse chestnut trees will be full to bursting, ready to drop. The girls will be changing out their early-Fall blazers for their winter coats. Those redbrick buildings will be growing dull in the winter light.

I hadn't been teaching there long - just a year. It hadn't been part of my plan to come back to the U.S. but Jan had been having a bout of poor health and deep down I was thinking maybe Mom and I could start to heal those old rifts if I finally came home. I was homesick I guess. I'd left Connecticut at eighteen and never looked back. Stanford, and then England, then Singapore, Holland, Hong Kong. I'd been teaching on the International School circuit, fulfilling my teenage promise to myself and Jan to get out and never come back. After everything that happened with Fiona, all I wanted was to be as far away as possible, somewhere where nobody knew me, and nobody could point fingers or make suggestions about my past. And then the opening came up at Horton. I saw it posted online. *Girls' second-level academy in Northern Connecticut.* It was strange seeing it posted there in black and white, that familiar name. It was even stranger that I applied, considering how things turned out the first time: I'd been at Horton before. My first time, I was sixteen years old. Fiona and I were regional scholarship students, coached to within an inch of our sanity by Fiona's mother, Jan, who taught at our local high school and had got wind of the scholarship incentive.

We graduated from Horton College, Fiona and I, starry-eyed and ready for the wave of upward mobility that everyone had promised us. A few months later, I was at Stanford, and Fiona was dead.

I still can't say with certainty what made Thorpe take me into her office less than a month ago and have her 'discussion', basically letting me know that my one year of teaching at Horton was all there was going to be. She talked about 'fit'. Granted, there had been a few... episodes, in the recent months. There were things she didn't know about, things I couldn't possibly tell her, and as a result I'm sure my behavior had been a little off. And I know that my teaching methods hadn't been to everybody's tastes. Thorpe had failed to warn me that some of the Horton parents were highly religious, and that my reading list was too provocative for some of them to tolerate. Never mind 'the customer is always right': at Horton, it was the parents who were always right. *We're not really teachers,* my colleague Simone, the history teacher, had said wryly to me one day. *Basically we're customer service reps.*

Or maybe it wasn't my reading list. Maybe it was that despite my résumé, despite my Stanford degree, despite my years abroad, my accent still wasn't quite a 'fit', just like it hadn't been a fit when I was a scholarship girl.

But I still didn't expect to be let go just a few weeks into the new year. They couldn't fire me outright, not without proper legal standing. But a 'discussion' with Thorpe only goes one way - hers.

The doctor's door swings open and the receptionist comes out.

'Mrs Gonzalez?'

The woman across from me snaps the phone from her son's hand and ushers him in front of her through to the examining room. The door closes again and the receptionist resumes her place at the desk. Surreptitiously, I take my phone from my pocket and check it. It's stupid that I'm acting so secretive about it. It's stupid that I'm checking it at all - deep down, I know all I'll see is a blank screen. But some part of me is still waiting. It's been weeks.

Everything in me itches to text that number - *one more time,* my brain urges, *just one more time* - but I swallow, and slip the phone back in my pocket.

'Would you like a glass of water, Miss Kelly?' the receptionist chirps.

'Oh, um. Sure. Thank you,' I say, because she's smiling so brightly that I feel I ought to accept.

She disappears through the door again, and in the empty room the television seems louder. An ad for diabetes medication with its million-and-one legal disclaimers finally segues back to the local news station. I rub my eyes - I barely slept last night, again - and tune in to the newscaster, who has her serious face on.

Schoolgirl missing, the ticker reads.

Huh. I wonder if it's somewhere local. There are plenty of wealthier communities around here, but Milham isn't one of them. We provide the gardeners, cleaners, plumbers and mechanics to this little patch of Connecticut's wealthier families. After all, they need somebody to mow their pristine lawns, service their Land Rovers, wipe their kids' noses, and dust their homes. Something tells me that if a girl from around here has gone missing, it's not one of those girls, with their helicopter parents and nannies. More likely it's a girl from somewhere like Milham - some kid from the wrong side of the tracks who never stood a chance.

After some more solemn words from the newscaster which I can't hear, the studio camera cuts to an outdoor scene. A scene I could draw from memory. A scene I know like the back of my hand, like the cracks in the ceiling I stare at when I can't sleep. A scene that all too often, on my sleepless nights, I *do* draw from memory in my head.

The camera pans round a sprawl of redbrick buildings, neat lawns, chestnut trees. Tall black gates and a long gravel drive.

Horton.

A Horton girl has gone missing.

I don't realize I'm holding my breath until the camera cuts again. And now I'm no longer looking at those redbrick walls, those Harry Potter turrets. Now I'm looking at the face of a sixteen-year-old girl. Blonde hair waterfalling over her shoulders, either side of an oval face. Shrewd eyes, serious mouth, lips a little parted like she's about to speak. That's when I realize I've been holding my breath, because the gasp when I inhale almost chokes me. If I had that glass of water, it would have fallen right from my hand.

The girl on the screen is Devon Hundley.

Two

'Miss Kelly? Are you all right, Miss Kelly?'

The receptionist is looking at me with concern. I stand up, swallowing. I realize I've dropped my phone on the ground and bend to get it. I stumble a little.

'Miss Kelly...'

'It's okay,' I say. 'I'll - I'll come back later.'

'But the doctor's free now.' The receptionist knits her brows. 'She's ready for you -'

I wave my hand, trying to make a reassuring gesture. 'It's - I'm sorry. Very sorry. I'll come back later.'

I leave her by the door, staring at me, and step outside into the cold air.

Breathe, Sadie.

I draw the Fall chill into my lungs, trying to jerk myself back to reality. Drizzle coats my hair. I make it to the car and immediately turn the radio dial.

'...her parents, Angela and Philip Hundley, are appealing to anyone with information to call the dedicated police hotline -'

I snap the radio off. Already my phone is starting to buzz, I can feel it vibrating in my pocket.

Devon, what have you done?

*

Devon Hundley.

She looks like money, that was my thought when I saw her for the first time. At Horton, most of the girls would almost make a show of being scruffy and bed-headed at breakfast, if they appeared at breakfast at all. They'd come through the doors yawning elaborately, slouching in designer loungewear, messy buns, slept-in makeup. Thorpe hated it of course. I figured they cultivated the look on purpose, a combination of rebellious and slatternly that they found exciting. It doesn't take having boys around to make teenage girls compete for sex appeal. It was unnerving, the wall of raw hormones you could feel coming off them. Sometimes I felt we were running a modern-day convent, locking up young maidens at the request of their parents, stamping out unmentionable urges, and keeping their bodies safe from the hands of marauding boys.

But the Hundley sisters weren't like that. They were like princesses or something - not modern princesses, running about town and getting into trouble in the tabloids - more the medieval kind, dainty but hard-edged, imperious. Unlike the girls who would flop through the doors looking barely out of bed, Devon always appeared with her hair neatly combed, held back with the thin velvet band she always wore. She had a clean look about her somehow, as though her shirt was just a shade whiter, her shoes just a touch more polished than the other girls'. Perfect skin, perfect teeth. Her older sister Lucy was much the same, just as groomed and put-together, if a little more bored-looking. Devon reminded me of a sphinx. That blank expression, where you were never really sure what she was thinking. I never saw her angry or sulking - or giddy or impatient or out of control. She didn't talk much to other girls in her year from what I saw. It was hard to tell if she had friends.

It wasn't long before I knew she was Horton's top swimmer - swimming was a very big deal at Horton. It hadn't been when I was there - Fiona had been on the swim team, and she'd been an indifferent swimmer; - but apparently in the years since I'd been there, they'd had a student a year or more get a swimming scholarship to college. And Devon, judging by the trophies lined up in the hall outside of Thorpe's office, was the best they'd had in a while. Nessa Rath was the school's 'silver medal' swimmer, and she was the year above Devon, and Devon's roommate as well - but she didn't come close to beating Devon. Swimming prodigy, that was the one thing everybody at Horton knew about Devon.

And now she was gone.

*

The red brake lights of cars in front of me cut through the early dusk. The windscreen wiper squeals against the glass and the streets of Milham pass in a blur. This town that I used to hate, and then started to miss, and that right now, suddenly, I feel almost afraid of. I glance in my rearview for no good reason, as though Devon Hundley could somehow be there, an arm's reach away, waiting to be discovered.

She'll turn up, I tell myself. A couple of years ago we had two girls "disappear" who, it turned out, had plotted a getaway to New York City. It was all a stunt. The school went crazy, so did the parents, and then the students confessed and showed us the pictures on instagram, the girls making fish-pout faces in front of Saks Fifth Avenue, giant shopping bags in hand courtesy of Daddy's, or Mommy's, credit card.

But Devon's not like that.

Be quiet, I tell the voice in my head. She'll turn up. Of

course she will. What happened to me has nothing to do with -

I slam the brakes as the hazard lights of the car in front suddenly loom out of the fog. I shake my head, pull around the obstruction, and almost miss the turn-off for Jan's road. Two squares of light beam out from the kitchen. She's home. Jan's retired now, but she used to teach at Milham High School. I park, open the squeaky, side-heavy gate, and let myself in. I can hear her moving around in the kitchen, the clink of a spoon in a mug. She puts her head round the door.

'I was just listening to the news.' She clicks her tongue. 'There's a girl missing. They said she goes to Horton.'

I suppress the shiver and focus on wiping my feet on the mat. It's shaped like a hedgehog, as are a lot of things in this house, because Jan loves hedgehogs. The coat-rack has a sign that reads *Pobody's Nerfect*.

'Devon Something,' Jan goes on as I walk into the kitchen.

'Hundley,' I say, not meeting her eyes.

'Hundley, that's right. Did you know her?'

'She's Horton's top swimmer.' I have a flash of being back at Horton, the viewing area above the new pool where I used to go sometimes in the evenings for some peace and quiet. I see Devon and Nessa practicing lengths below me, their arms slicing through the water, silent behind glass.

'Her poor parents, they must be near-dead with worry.' Jan tsks, plumping up a cushion on the sofa before she settles into it, mug of tea in hand. 'What are they like, the parents?' She looks at me, eyes big, waiting for details. Rich girls going missing: even Jan, who isn't a gossipy sort of person, wants the scoop. If she's like this, just imagine what the media is going to be like.

So I describe Angela and Philip, their wealth and business standing, the McMansion they have in the Connecticut countryside just thirty minutes from here. I don't tell her that I know exactly what it looks like - down to the chandeliers in the hallway, the marble chequerboard pattern of the Carrara tiles, or how the whole house always smells of lilies. No, I keep all that to myself, and my hands folded across my chest, in case something in them gives me away. I tell her that Philip's a doctor, and that Angela runs a company.

Jan clicks her tongue again. 'Well, God willing, she'll turn up soon.' She grips her mug and I wonder if she's thinking about Fiona. I feel a familiar twinge in my chest. Old guilt, the guilt I get whenever Jan mentions Fiona.

'How did the appointment go?' Jan says, suddenly her brisk self again, as if trying to sweep the topic away.

'Oh...fine,' I lie.

'You'll be careful with that medicine, won't you, love? You mustn't go eating it like candy, you know.'

I roll my eyes. 'Yeah. I know.'

'Have you been getting any more of those...' she waves her hand, not wanting to say *panic attack* even if we both know that's the right label.

'Not for a while,' I say, which is the truth, but also probably the reason my prescription only lasted three weeks.

Jan nods, sips her tea.

'And no word on that new post you applied for, Sade?'

I actually got a 'no thank you' from them this

morning - a maternity cover position that I was hoping I might get. I guess no matter what spin you put on it, my abrupt departure from Horton just doesn't look good. They're reading between the lines and they don't like what they see.

'Not yet,' I say.

'Well never mind, love. They'd be lucky to have you, but remember what I said. You're welcome here as long as you like. It's nice for me, having you around.' She swirls her spoon around the mug, looking thoughtfully down at the brew. 'You know,' she hesitates. 'I saw your mom at church today.'

'Jan-'

'You don't think it's worth a try, Sade?'

I drop my eyes from her hopeful ones. 'I just... you don't understand.'

'She's your mother.'

As far as I'm concerned, it's bad luck coming from a single-parent family where your single parent has never liked you all that much. Mom grew up in a strict Irish Catholic family in the suburbs of Providence, Rhode Island - all her neighbors were Murphys and O'Neills - and got pregnant in her teens. Some guy whose family was in town for the summer and she never saw again. Mom got by. She worked, and managed to support us, and eventually buy a little house not far from here - maybe not exactly the American Dream but testament to her grit for sure. With the right kind of opportunities I'm sure she could have done much more - run a company, run for office, who knows - and I guess she's never let go of imagining 'what if' and blaming me for it.

Jan downs the last of her tea and pats me on the

16

shoulder as she pads back into the kitchen.

'One day you two will figure it out.'

Jan is an optimist, and she believes the best about people. That's one of the many reasons I adore her. Jan's no fool, though. She doesn't believe the world is all sunshine and rainbows. She works at a hotline for troubled youth, and that alone means her eyes are always wide open to how cruel the world can be. I've seen her get pessimistic about society, especially when she hears about some fresh tragedy in the news, but when it comes to the people she loves her reserves of faith are endless. It's like there's nothing we can do to let her down, no matter how many times we mess up and give her cause to doubt us. I don't know what I did to get admitted into that special category of people, but it's one of the best gifts in my life. I know Jan would throw every inch of her five-foot frame like a tiger at anyone who tried to hurt someone she loved.

As for me, I'm no hero - I'd like to imagine I'd throw myself in front of a bus to save some innocent passerby, but I guess I probably wouldn't - but Jan is one person I'd do anything to protect.

'Have you eaten, Sadie?' She bobs around in the kitchen, pulling tupperwares from the fridge, rice from a cabinet. Jan is also a dab hand in the kitchen. Moving around so busily, with her sandy grey pixie cut and irrepressible energy, she makes me think of a storybook elf.

'Thanks, but I'm not really hungry,' I say.

'You sure?'

I nod.

'I think I'll just get an early night.'

She looks at me sympathetically.

'Okay, pumpkin. Sweet dreams.'

I turn to head upstairs, then impulsively turn back and wrap my arms around her, plant a kiss on her cheek. She laughs.

'What was that for?'

'No reason.' The reason is that I'm scared suddenly. Scared of what it means to lose someone. I know I won't be able to get the story of Devon Hundley out of my mind. I hear Jan switch on the television as I climb the stairs, and the burble of a newsreader's voice follows me up. I know what will be on that screen. *Who* will be on that screen.

Sweet dreams.

Yeah right.

*

It wasn't a lie when I told Jan I was exhausted, but once I hit the pillow my head won't stop churning and let me sleep. Finally I pick up my phone. I scroll through the news updates. Horton is going to come under fire for this. Apparently Devon simply wasn't there yesterday morning at breakfast, and Horton doesn't have many security cameras on its heritage redbrick. They have them at the main gates of course, but if Devon didn't leave in a car, then she could quite easily have bypassed the cameras on foot. I watch an appeal online that Angela and Philip Hundley have made, speaking earnestly into the camera, asking for information and promoting a hotline number. You can already see what two days have done to them. Philip has wrinkles he didn't have a few months ago, and Angela's face is as pale as if she's been dipped in talc.

I text Simone Bailey, the history teacher at Horton

who became a friend during last year. It's a pretty immersive way of living there. Some teachers live off-campus, but there's a few that have accommodation - free accommodation - on the grounds, which means you sleep, eat, and breathe Horton except for holidays and, if you want, weekends. Simone has a little cottage there - her husband Richard mostly travels for work - but the most junior teachers like me also served as R.A.s on the dorms - which means I slept in a cold little bedroom in the East Wing, among the ninth-graders.

Saw the news, I text.

She texts back straightaway.

Jesus, Sadie. It's a shit-show here. Girls weeping in the stairwells. Hysterics. Thorpe is going NUTS.

I'm not surprised if Thorpe is going nuts. Something like this could skewer enrollment at Horton for the next five years. Who's going to send their precious daughter to a school that might accidentally misplace her?

I close my eyes, imagining myself back in that viewing balcony, my evening refuge when I didn't want to return to the chaos of the dorms. The muffled sounds and fug of damp, chlorinated air drifting up towards me, so comforting somehow. Devon and Nessa practiced most evenings, it seemed. Sometimes I'd put down my book or the papers I was grading to watch them. They were mesmerizing. It was like a transformation. During the day, outside of the water, they were just normal teenage girls. In the water, they could do anything. They were fierce, fearless.

As for the rest of the Hundley family - the parents - I'd met them for the first time last Fall, at my first Horton Parent Teacher evening. Horton's PTA evenings were kind of fancy compared to what I was used to. First we all gathered in the dining hall for Thorpe to make her welcome speech, and staff passed hors d'oeuvres and poured drinks while parents 'mingled'. Teachers were expected to be available but not obtrusive. The schmoozing - and particularly the boozing - was for the parents to chat and network with each other. Snippets of conversation drifted to the corner that Simone and I had colonized: the stock market, recent divorces, alimony settlements, and holidays abroad. Simone rolled her eyes at me and swiped another flute of Prosecco from a passing waiter, not even caring if Thorpe saw. I was sticking with water. After a half-hour of 'mingling' the teachers took up residence in the first-floor classrooms and parents moved from one to the other. The Hundleys were the very first set on my schedule.

Angela Hundley was wearing Vera Wang, which I knew because I'd been watching Fashion Week on YouTube a few nights ago. Who turns up to a PTA meeting with style fresh off the runway? Horton mothers, that's who. Although as I found out, the *really* upper-crust ones, the "my great great grandmother rode in on the Mayflower" types, were more prone to frumpy cardigans and hair that hadn't been near a stylist in years. Those women were so confident they belonged that they didn't even bother with their appearance. Apparently, beauty and fashion were for the "new money" types - like Angela, with her glossy hair, understated manicure, and couture suit. And Philip - tall, boyish, designer-stubble chin. He was a doctor, an ex-army medic, I'd heard. I had a tray of water on my desk but Angela waved it away when I offered. Philip Hundley looked me up and down, crossed his arms and grinned.

'So you're the new girl.'

My eyebrows shot up involuntarily. *New girl?* What did he think I was, a teenager on her first babysitting gig? Philip Hundley was still grinning at me. So he'd meant it as a tease. *Easy to be a joker when your audience is paid to smile.*

I obviously wasn't the only one who'd noticed. Angela shot him a look, and Philip held up his hands.

'What?' he said. '"New woman"? That sounds even worse.'

I was blushing, and annoyed that I was blushing. Angela made an exasperated noise.

'She's not a *woman*, Philip, she's a *teacher*.'

I waited, my eyes widening further, assuming she'd realize what she'd just said and correct herself - or at least try and laugh it off. But no. She just looked back at me and asked about the scheduled class trips for the year ahead. I tried to keep the information straight in my head and my voice calm as I answered her questions, while her outrageous comment went round my head like a carousel. *I can't wait to tell Simone this one.*

Out of the corner of my eye, as I answered her, I saw that Philip Hundley was laughing. It was silent laughter, and he was leaning back, out of Angela's line of vision. She didn't turn his way once as she spoke, so she didn't know. But I could see it clearly, and he wasn't trying to hide it from me. In fact he kept trying to catch my eye, like a naughty kid in class. He shook his head.

'Sorry,' he mouthed, then went back to his silent mirth. A faint snort finally caused Angela to look around. Philip adopted an impressive poker face and made a show of looking at his watch.

'My dear, should we...?'

'Well, welcome to Horton, Ms Kelly,' Angela said as she stood from her chair - as though she were my employer, or an immigration officer admitting me to her country, which in a way, she was.

I watched them disappear out of my office and along the corridor, their tailored blazers swinging, and prayed I wouldn't have to see much more of them.

If I'd known where all this would end, I'd have prayed a lot harder.

Three

A shriek wakes me. Heart thumping, I leap out of bed, dash to the landing, to the sound of Jan's voice.

But as I reach the staircase the shriek comes again and I realize - no, it's not a shriek of fear. It's laughter. Jan's laughing. I guess - this is a painful thing to realize - I guess it's a while since I really heard Jan laugh. Jan's a merry person by nature but I guess in the past weeks I just haven't been very merry company for her.

Jan and I get along better than ever these days, now that she doesn't feel the need to be a stand-in parent any more. We like a lot of the same things. We're both addicted to reading and crossword puzzles - Jan goes through a new book every three days, she reads five times faster than I ever could - and she's always got something new to share with me, a story or some quirky little fact she heard, like *Sadie, did you know that Boston cream pie is the official state dessert of Massachusetts?* She was the one who taught me to have a curious mind. So yes, we get along great. But despite all that, I guess there's been something sitting between us for a while. I guess carrying too many secrets can tire a person out.

I'm out on the landing now, where the open staircase gives a view down to the kitchen. I peer over, wanting to know what's making her laugh so loudly and raucously.

But it's not a what, it's a who. A man, my age or so. He's scruffy, not in an on-purpose way, more in an I-play-videogames-for-a-living kind of way. Then again, I'm wearing pajama shorts and a sweater at eleven a.m. on a weekday, so who am I to judge.

'Sadie!' Jan spots me. 'I was just talking to Rob, our new neighbor. The one I told you about?'

I do remember, sort of. She told me a 'young guy' had moved in down the road, and that he was 'very handy about the house'. Apparently he's been fixing a few things up for her, which I guess is good, seeing as Jan's idea of home safety is not the same as most people's. She has windows that don't seal, a burglar alarm that doesn't work, and an electrical wiring system that is well below code.

'Come down and say hello.'

I'd much rather go back to bed - my head is throbbing, from flickers of Devon Hundley and Fiona merging into each other, haunting me all night - but I shamble down the stairs and paste on a smile.

'Rob.' He puts out his hand and gives me a bland smile.

'I'm Sadie,' I say. 'I'm, um -'

Jan fills in smoothly for me. 'Sadie's staying with me for a bit while she sorts a few things out.' She looks at me warmly. 'I've known her since she was yea high.' The pride in her eyes makes my stomach rumble with that old, guilty feeling once more.

Rob nods, oblivious. 'I'm new round here. Used to work in Hartford, but I'm in IT and I mainly work remotely, so I can kind of go anywhere.'

And you came here? I have to stop myself from asking. As far as I'm concerned, Milham has exactly zero attractions, except for in my case, Jan.

'How're you finding Milham?' I say.

He shrugs, which is almost as bland as his smile. 'Oh,

you know. Rent's cheap.'

Maybe this Rob guy isn't very good at his remote job.

'Well,' Rob looks at Jan. 'Did you want to show me that -?'

'Oh yes, the gutters.' She snaps her fingers as if she's just remembered something delightful. This new guy sure makes her cheery.

'All right then, let's take a look.' Rob nods at me. 'Nice meeting you, Sadie.'

I hear them outside, Jan's perky voice and Rob's lower one, as I trudge back up the stairs. I just hope he isn't charging her an arm and a leg for this handyman work he's doing. I get dressed, pop one more of my dwindling supply of Klonopin, and shuffle back downstairs to the television. I turn to the news channel and wait for the twelve o'clock news and an update on Devon Hundley.

*

By afternoon it seems like yesterday's "breaking news" has become today's lead story. It's been established that Devon's bike is missing from the school grounds too. I'm glued to it all, I can't look away. Jan has a volunteer shift at the hotline, and when she comes back she joins me on the couch, touching her hand to her mouth and softly shaking her head.

'Sixteen years old. They say the first 24 hours are the most crucial, don't they?' She bites her lip. 'Did you see anything - I mean, any signs, you know? Anything that suggested she might do something like this?'

'I can't say that I did. I didn't think that much about her, I suppose,' I lie. 'She was just one pupil among many.'

Jan nods. 'There's so much we only see in hindsight, isn't there?'

I swallow, not trusting myself to speak. I know who she's thinking of. And sure, we all have blind spots. And then there are people like me - the ones desperately trying to stay in other people's blind spots. The ones pulling the wool over everyone's eyes.

I imagine viewers all around the country asking the same question. Why would a girl like *that* run away? I know what they'll see. A pretty sixteen year old who lives like a princess; who has everything money can buy. An athlete, talented, bright future, has it all.

If anything, I'd have said her sister Lucy was the one who needed watching. Lucy had spent a good chunk of last year at a clinic for eating disorders, all hush-hush of course. Everyone thought she'd been on an exchange program. But meanwhile Devon, the younger one, seemed to be doing just fine. Now I wonder what I didn't see.

Devon, what have you done?

Jan sighs and turns off the news. To her it's just one more sad headline.She pushes aside a stack of *Reader's Digests* - she's had a subscription ever since I've known her, and once a year she purges the back issues - and puts her feet up on the coffee table. Her slippers are cosy and bright, just like Jan. She's always been a study in contrasts to my mother. Mom is tall, poised and severe as a ballet dancer. Her house never has a whisper of clutter in it. Everything is put away as soon as it's been used, and she has an honest-to-God feather duster that she breaks out a couple of times a month. Jan's house is always messy, but in the most comfortable way. Her taste is kitsch, her clothes are hippy-ish, and when she laughs she tends to snort. In other words, being around Jan is a comfortable place to be.

But even Jan's spell can't quite erase the anxious voice in my head tonight.

She yawns and turns to me. 'Fancy a tea?'

Jan says it's her Irish blood that means she only likes strong black tea: *none of that fruity business for me*, she says with a laugh. She must be caffeine-resistant or something, because she drinks it late into the night and sleeps like a baby.

'You stay there, I'll make it.'

In the kitchen I succumb to temptation and take out my phone, scroll to Contacts. The number I promised myself I wouldn't text. The voice in my head is telling me to put my phone down, leave all this alone. I open a message and type:

Are you okay?

The phone pings in my hand, making me jump, but when I check it's just Simone.

You coming to the vigil? she's written.

Apparently they're holding one tonight at the Horton chapel. Aren't you supposed to do vigils for the dead, not the Missing? Maybe they want to televise it - maybe everyone will be standing in front of the camera begging her to "come home". The thought of being there turns my stomach in ways I don't want to analyze. I dread the idea, but also some part of me needs, wants, to be there. To be part of it. To see *them*.

Please come, she texts when I don't respond.

I text her back that I will, and as soon as the decision is made, take a deep breath. As I let it out my phone chirps again. I swipe it open, but the message isn't from

Simone this time.

I told you, Sadie. Delete this number. Delete everything. I won't ask again.

Four

The car purrs along the Litchfield County roads. I drive carefully, steadily below the speed limit - the way I always drive since that night. The last night I saw Fiona. In my memories I'm eighteen again, dressed in black again, and it's another teenage girl that holds our attention. I see it all: the church, the cemetery, Jan white-faced, dropping a rose onto the coffin before they begin to shovel in the earth. My mother, her pinched face and the way she didn't meet my eyes.

I swallow, and realize I've taken a wrong turn. I turn the car around, forcing myself to focus. I turn off the highway and take a smaller road, twisting and turning, and finally there they are, the black gates looming up in front of me in the dusk. Inside, the car park is fuller than I've ever seen it, with flickers of movement as shadowy figures ahead of me flow into the chapel. It's a minute to six; my detour delayed me. I hurry up the avenue, the chestnut trees rising up in black shapes either side of me. Outside the chapel there's still a small crowd and I fall into step with a familiar face. Ned Ogden, the swimming coach. He nods somberly at me, and it obviously doesn't register with him that I haven't been around for the last weeks, and don't teach here anymore. He looks disbelieving, hollow-eyed. Devon's his star swimmer.

'Sadie. Good to see you,' he croaks.

Ned's not that much older than me. Back when I was at Horton he was an assistant coach that most of the girls had a crush on. He gave me a vague look when I met him

29

again last year and told him I remembered him. No wonder. I was terrible at gym; shot-put was probably the only thing I was actually good at. He's stuck around at Horton though, and now Ned's the head of the athletics program. He's aging well, except for right now, when the anxiety on his face makes him look gaunt, and at least ten years older.

We edge through the chapel doors and already I'm thinking I shouldn't have come here. Then I see Simone, and her eyes flash relief as she waves me over. I'm moving her way when a hand grabs my arm and I startle.

Thorpe. I look into the face of our head teacher, my boss until the tight-lipped session last month where she dismissed me. She looks like a different woman now. She looks washed-out, almost vulnerable.

'Ms Kelly. Please stay after this is over. We need to speak.'

My throat dries instantly. Speak about what? *She knows,* a voice whispers. *Somehow she knows.* I push the voice down. She's probably just annoyed that I came to this without her permission. I don't represent Horton any more, maybe that's what she wants to remind me.

'Yes, Mrs Thorpe.' Old habits die hard and something about this woman still scares me. Once she releases me I slide into Simone's aisle.

'What was that about?' She obviously saw the interaction.

'Nothing,' I say, trying to believe it.

Simone sighs and leans into me. 'God, Sadie. What a day. Everyone's going crazy. And the media...'

I nod, still looking around me. I know the Hundleys must be here, but they'll be right at the front, where

Thorpe disappeared to. There are too many bodies stacked between here and there, I can't see anything. Hunger and dread flow through me again, all mixed together.

'Packed, isn't it?' Simone says. It is. We're mostly surrounded by other Horton staff, in this little corner at the back. Simone to my right, Ned to my left, and there's Ms Denoel, Ms Gupta, old Hirschfield. Most of them only know me as Ms. Kelly, the teacher; they weren't here for my first go-round as a Horton scholarship girl. I think the three women to Simone's right work in the cafeteria. And then beyond our little cluster of staff are the schoolgirls. I'd almost forgotten the intensity of them, the group energy they have that seems to pulse through a room: hormones, body spray, whispers. Some of them have rubbed-raw eyes, some are openly crying. They look so young tonight, all of them. There is a whimper from somewhere in the back of the room and it ripples through the crowd like fear has a shape. I catch Ned's eye and he grimaces. I wonder how many teachers as well as pupils Horton is going to lose because of this. *I* wouldn't want to take a job in a school making headlines for losing its students.

There's a rustling and the sound of someone stepping onto the dais. Thorpe has taken the stage.

'Girls,' she says.

Someone hiccups.

'Parents. Friends.'

Suddenly I'm hit by a powerful wave of memory. Suddenly all I can see is Fiona's face. I see her running down the road towards me, eight years old. I see her at eighteen, lurching down a staircase, drunk, lipstick smeared, eyes full of contempt. I push the images down.

Thorpe's voice carries over the heads, like she's speaking directly to me.

'We're here tonight to come together, to pray, to join in asking that our friend, sister, and daughter, Devon Hundley, will soon be returned to us. Our hearts are with Devon's family. We lift up our hearts to ask that wherever she is right now, Devon is safe and healthy, and that her path home to family and friends will be swift.'

The crowd shuffles, murmurs. I feel my chest contracting into a hard ball. It's like my lungs are fighting for air. This is too much.

'I'm sure I don't need to remind any of you girls that if you have *any* information, or any reason to suspect you know *anything* about Devon's disappearance, to speak immediately to myself or to another teacher. The importance of doing so cannot be overstated. At Horton we are a family, and we will do anything and everything we can to protect a child of our family. We're appealing to everyone - everyone in this room today, everyone in the county, in the state, in the nation - to help bring Devon home.'

There's more murmuring, and Thorpe continues to speak, but I zone out, feeling my mind starting to float like a ghost above us all, looking down at bowed heads, lighted candles. It's hot in here. Too hot. I feel fuzzy suddenly, like I might faint. I can't. I can't faint. But the tingling in the back of my brain gets worse, a darkness eating its way round the edges of my vision. I grip the back of the pew.

'Excuse me,' I whisper at Ned, and he looks at me in alarm and shuffles to let me pass.

'Excuse me,' I say again, and the blurry shapes behind

Ned part, more bodies moving, and I edge a little closer to the door. I can feel a breeze start to trickle towards me and my head starts to clear. I notice who's on the stage now. For a moment I almost think it's Devon, but no, it's the older sister, Lucy. She's white-faced, grim. Her voice comes out halting but fierce. Her grief is like a tiger waiting to get out.

'The Horton Family,' she's saying. She pauses. 'You say that, but what kind of family are you, really?'

There's something in her voice, we can all hear it. I freeze, breathing through my nose, the door still three feet away.

'Family protect each other. You were supposed to protect her.' Her voice rises. 'You were supposed to protect my sister.'

I see Thorpe scuffling in a corner, obviously trying to take the stage again, or do something about this disruption. Lucy Hundley sees it too and backs away from Thorpe, not wanting to be silenced. Her eyes roam from Thorpe out over the stage, the crowd.

'You were supposed to keep her safe.'

Then Thorpe is on the stage and so is another teacher, ushering Lucy down. Girls are crying. I lurch towards the door, into the bleak night. The sound of raised voices drifts after me from inside the chapel as I stumble down the drive.

*

The morning is blustery and dark. I wake groggy, my head filled with the panicky feelings and half-images that haunted me all night. I rub my sleep-crusted eyes, check the time on my phone, and drag myself from the warmth, scuffing my feet into slippers. Jan's already out, her bedroom door's wide open and the house is silent. I pass the third door on the landing, Fiona's door. It's bigger than the tiny guest room I'm sleeping in now, but I could never sleep in there.

My vision blurs again for a moment and I grip the banister. I feel in the pocket of my robe. Yes, the little bottle of benzos is still there. Still not empty.

I remember the day Fiona and Jan arrived in Milham. Mom told me we were having visitors and to be welcoming. We *never* had people around to the house. Not even my school friends. Mom avoided my friend's parents at the school gates. I was used to her ways by then.

'Jan is somebody I knew in Providence,' she'd explained. 'An old friend, you could say.' My eyes widened. We almost *never* went back to where Mom was from. Grandma had dementia, and said things that weren't very nice. Mom had a couple of brothers that didn't live there any more, and only occasionally spoke to on the phone. She never spoke very warmly of the Irish-Catholic township where she'd grown up.

'She just got a job teaching history at the high school,' Mom went on. 'And she has a little girl almost your age. I suppose you'll be in school together.'

I spent the morning tidying my bedroom to perfection, arranging my stuffed animals and dolls so they sat in neat straight lines, and the flimsy books on my bookshelf so that none of them toppled over or stuck out. I smoothed my duvet so that there wasn't a single wrinkle. I waited on the low wall that bordered our little front yard. Cars passed by but none of them were the right one. And then one came down our road, slowed, stopped. A door cracked open and a little girl exploded out of the back seat. Curls, freckles, denim; she had a couple of inches on me. A wide grin and fearless eyes.

'Hi,' I said shyly.

That was my first glimpse of Fiona.

*

I pull my robe tighter around myself and throw some toasting bread under the grill. There's mail open on the counter and it catches my eye as I close the oven door.

Bills.

There are way too many red, bolded words there. I lift the paper, reading it more closely. Jan's gas and electricity are in arrears. I swallow. That's not from absent-mindedness. Jan is the type to always pay her bills on time. I'm pretty sure if she hasn't, it means she wasn't able to. Guilt rattles through my chest. I didn't realize she was struggling - not like this. She never said.

Of course she didn't.

This whole time she's been supporting me, acting like it was nothing to feed an extra mouth - but meanwhile she has troubles of her own. It's like a shock of cold water. This can't go on. I need to move out of here.

I need a job. And when I have one, I can help *her*.

The charred smell coming out of the grill brings me back to my senses. *Dammit.* I fling the oven door open and smoke wafts out. I fan it out of the way and go open the front door - and jump as I see a figure in front of me.

'Holy -!' I steady myself. 'Rob. What are you doing here?'

The neighbor looms in front of me against the blustery sky.

35

'Oh, I just - I brought these back for Jan.' He looks at me with his same blank expression. I see then he's holding a set of keys.

'You have her keys?' There's something about this guy. He's not bad-looking, actually, but there's something about the way he looks at me, like he's watching, or waiting for something.

'She had me make a spare set,' he says.

She did? I wonder if my face is showing my disapproval. I don't know why Jan would give her keys to a man she barely knows.

'Sorry to startle you,' he says. 'I was just about to ring the bell.'

Huh. I pocket the keys he was holding. I expect him to turn away but he doesn't.

'You were teaching at that school, weren't you?' he says. 'The one on the news. With the missing girl.'

My stomach drops a little. I didn't realize Jan had told him all that. I don't want to have this conversation. I just nod, as noncommittal as possible.

'Shocking, isn't it?' he says.

'Yeah,' I say and end there, signaling that's all the statement I'll be making. He can just read the gossip headlines like everybody else.

As if on cue, my phone starts ringing from indoors.

'I have to get that,' I say, pretending it's not another robo-call trying to spam me into a fake insurance payment or something like that.

But by the time I get to my phone, the ringing stops. When I scoop the phone from the table it's not an unknown number. Instead it reads: Lucinda Thorpe. I breathe deep, and sit down. *Last night.* She told me to stay.

I remind myself whatever it is, she can't hurt me now. I'm already unemployed, and apparently unemployable. She can't make it much worse than this.

Of course she can, the voice says. *You know she can. If she* knows, *Sadie, it's all over for you.*

Five

Jan comes home with an Amazon package under her arm.

'What'd you buy this time?' I ask. Jan has a bit of an Amazon habit. I think it makes her feel modern.

'A camera,' she says, going over to the kettle, always her first stop on entering the house.

'You're taking up photography?' I follow behind her, trying hard to put Thorpe's phone call out of my mind. No voicemail, of course. I checked - twice.

'Not that kind of camera,' Jan says, waving her hand. She settles the kettle back on the stove and lights the gas. 'A whatchamacallit, a security camera. I've noticed a few things recently in the front yard, I don't know... a flowerpot got smashed somehow. Someone moved Henry' - Henry's the gnome - 'And I just thought it would make me feel more comfortable.'

'Well,' I say slowly. 'That makes sense.'

But I don't like the idea of someone sniffing around in Jan's garden. And what for? It's not like her house screams *wealthy inhabitant*. It's not like any houses on this road do. Probably just some kids with a football, or someone's unruly dog.

'You should get that gate fixed, too,' I add. 'So it closes properly, you know?'

She nods. 'Rob's going to do it for me. He said he could install something on my phone too, a security thing, for all those phone calls I've been getting. It can screen by location and everything,' she says, obviously impressed.

Him again. 'This Rob guy is pretty handy, isn't he?'

She looks at me, eyes narrowing slightly. 'What's that supposed to mean, Sade?'

'It's just...' I guess I sound petty now, maybe even jealous. And maybe I am. Maybe I don't want him muscling in on my territory. Maybe I don't want Jan taking him under her wing.

'I just think you should be careful who you trust. You barely know this guy and he has keys to your house already.'

She sighs, then looks at me and taps her nose.

'Instincts, Sade,' she says. 'You know the first stranger I invited into my home here, when Fiona and I arrived? *You.*' Her eyes soften and I know she's picturing us, two little girls flying in and out of the rooms of this house. Day after day, year after year.

'And I wasn't wrong about you, was I?' She takes the kettle off the ring and pours a steaming cup.

I bite my lip. There are things Jan doesn't know. And if she knew them, she might very well say that she was wrong, all wrong, about me.

My phone rings again. *Saved by the bell,* I think. I change my mind though as soon as I hear the voice on the other end.

'Ms Kelly.' The clear contralto fills my ears. I clench the phone, trying not to drop it.

'Ms Kelly,' Thorpe goes on. 'You'll recall I wanted to speak to you yesterday. At the - at the vigil.'

'Yes,' I murmur. I can't help noticing how even the word *vigil* sticks in her throat, like she still can't accept any of this.

'I wanted to -' she pauses. 'I wanted to invite you, Ms Kelly, to rejoin us here at Horton. Should you wish to, that is.'

I sit frozen. *What?* This is not, not at all, what I had expected.

'To resume your old position,' she clarifies, when I don't speak.

Say something, Sadie.

'Oh,' is what I manage.

'I need hardly mention,' she goes on, 'That this is a vulnerable time for the institution, and having your support at such a time would be, well, appreciated.'

'I see,' I say. My brain is starting to tick again, catching up, or trying to. But I still don't understand. Why the about-face? What about before?

'I don't quite understand,' I say. 'You- I mean, before...'

There's a pause.

'Ms Kelly, whatever... concerns, may have arisen earlier in the year, would mean very little to us in light of recent events.' She breathes out. Her voice changes and the high-and-mighty notes go right out of it. 'Let's speak frankly. You must know as well as I do that this...upset -' *So that's what she's calling it* '-While devastating for Devon's family and all of us, is also likely to be very damaging for the school. I've been notified this morning by three sets of parents who are pulling their daughters out of Horton and I'm praying it stops there. This sort of thing can be contagious.' She stops. 'And staff, you know, are not immune to a school's branding, either.'

Oh. I see. Whoever she got to replace me, or had lined up to replace me, has pulled out. And now she's stuck. I guess I appreciate that she's giving it to me straight, not bothering to flatter me.

Thorpe clears her throat. 'Ms Kelly, I realize this is rather short notice for you. Horton would be glad to, um, recognize that, with an increase to your original salary.' There's a pause. 'We'd like you to start Monday, if possible.'

Monday. Forty-eight hours.

'Think about it,' she says.

*

There's not much to think about. Monday morning, I grab my suitcase and hug Jan with my free arm. She's trying to keep the skeptical look out of her eyes. She didn't really want me to go back to Horton. She reminded me about Dr Jamil; about the panic attacks that I returned home with, and of how I haven't been 'myself' for a while. She's concerned that going back there is triggering all the wrong memories for me.

'And now all that stuff with that poor girl,' she'd said. 'It's going to be a very different place, Sadie. Something like this casts a very long shadow.'

I know. Believe me, I know.

But I thought of the red-lettered bills, and the rejection letters from the jobs I'd applied to, and the prospect of months of unemployment in Milham stretching ahead of me. Yes, part of me felt nauseated at the idea of returning to Horton. But it was for the best. It was necessary.

Over the weekend the search for Devon Hundley has continued. Police officers were being interviewed on the news, urging the public to report anything, anything at all, to the tips hotline they've set up for this case. The Hundleys appeared on a special TV appeal, side by side on a red sofa, looking into the camera with pleading eyes. A reward has been offered for any information leading to their daughter's safe return.

Now, in the car, the radio's on but I don't hear it. I watch the buildings melt by, and drive past the road where Mom's house - my old house - stands. I turn away. At a red light I unscrew my tube of Klonopin and wonder about internet prescriptions. I'm definitely going to need *something* in the days ahead, if Horton is anything like how it was when I left. Although honestly, I believe the same thing Jan does: it won't be the same. It's going to be worse.

*

I remember so clearly, Fiona's and my first day there. The nose of Jan's car pushing through those tall black gates - in my memory they're impossibly tall, fairy-tale tall. The September sky was all scudding clouds and cold sun. It looked like I'd imagined Pemberley might look when I'd read *Pride and Prejudice* the year before. So dignified and noble, the kind of place nobody would ever raise their voices in. I gasped, instantly in love.

The Head was a headmaster then, Mr Lewis. He had a droopy mustache and large knuckles that dwarfed my hand when he shook it. It was the first time I could remember an adult shaking my hand. A guide brought us round the campus: me, Fiona, Jan and Mom. I remember standing in the dining hall - it was between meals, so it was empty except for the five of us. I remember the beams in the barrel-vaulted ceiling, which seemed considerably higher than a reasonable ceiling needed to be. I remember seeing from the side of my eye how Fiona cupped her hands around her mouth, and I knew, just knew, what she was about to do - shout *echo* like she did every time we cycled through Milham's abandoned railway tunnel - but then I saw her think better of it and drop her hands. It startled me, because it seemed like the first time I had seen Fiona - oh-so irrepressible Fiona - think better of something. Adults always adored Fiona, even at her most mischievous. She could get away with murder.

We came back a few weeks later, after all the papers were signed and the nominal fees - thank you, scholarship - paid, to begin term. There was chapel on the first day, before class. Horton was historically a Catholic school even though you didn't have to be Catholic to go there now, and they were very proud of their private chapel. I remember how it felt to walk through the doors, the tile beneath my new shoes, the cool click of it underfoot. The service had already started by the time our teacher shepherded Fiona and me in. The girls were singing, and an avenue of song seemed to rise up around us on all sides. I shivered. It was like we had come to a school full of angels. Terrible, shining angels. I had seen the gleaming cars in the parking lot as we arrived and now I saw the faces that went with them, polished and confident and serene. The whitest of white socks pulled over golden calves. Cheekbones that caught the light. Their hair, gleaming like it had been brushed to a thousand strokes. Everything clipped and groomed: these were the pedigree dogs.

Yes, a voice inside me said. *Pedigree greyhounds. Bred to kill.*

Six

The autumn sun makes everything stand out in sharp color, and Horton looks handsomer than ever. Deep green lawns flawless as a golf course. Ahead is the original main building, its broad redbrick face with long wings on each side like arms reaching towards me. The chestnut trees cast leaf-patterns on the grass. It's horse-chestnut season now but even horse-chestnuts hardly dare to drop in a place like this, under Thorpe's beady eye. Nothing can be out of control at Horton. Nothing can be less than perfect. I buzz down the window and hit the intercom, and soon the huge iron gates shudder and swing open.

.I park the car and bump the case over the cobbles, my shoulder twinging in its socket. I leave the case in the hall as I clack down the stone tiles towards Thorpe's office. Past the closed wooden doors, past the sparkling trophy cases dominated by Devon Hundley's trophies. I pass just one student in the corridor and she doesn't even look up. It's like a hush has fallen over the place.

Thorpe's door is ajar and I stand there a moment, deciding whether to knock.

'Ms Kelly. Come on in.'

I startle. She's watching - actually, more like glaring - from inside, her red-framed bifocals hanging on a chain below her jowls. I push the door wider and go in.

'Good morning, Mrs Thorpe.' Lucinda Thorpe goes by "Mrs". Most of the other female teachers use "Ms". But Thorpe is a traditionalist.

'Ms Kelly. Here you are. Good to have you back,' she

says unconvincingly.

I nod.

'So how are the girls?' I ask.

'Well, so far no others have been pulled out, so that's something. We'll see how the enrollment figures fare in due course.'

That wasn't exactly what I meant. But trust Thorpe to be looking at the bottom line.

'We're on damage control, Ms Kelly,' she says. 'I probably don't need to say so, but I can't emphasize it enough: we really don't want anyone or anything to rock the boat right now.'

I nod, not sure exactly what she has in mind. Just making sure none of the kids have reason to call home and complain, I suppose.

'How are the Hundleys?' I say, even though I probably shouldn't.

She blinks at me from over her glasses. 'They're much as one would expect, Ms Kelly.'

I wonder what that means. Are they holding it together, or falling apart?

'And I suppose Lucy has gone home?'

Thorpe's lips tighten. 'Lucy Hundley is still here with us, Ms Kelly.'

I'm surprised. 'She doesn't want to be home with her family?'

Thorpe stays impassive. 'I assume that both she and her parents felt that stability, continuity of routine and so on, would be beneficial for her.'

I hate when she talks in this high-and-mighty way, like she's somebody's publicist instead of a real person. I also wonder what the hell the Hundleys are thinking, letting their older daughter walk the halls of a school where her sister's name will be on everyone's lips, where everyone will be whispering and staring and pretending not to. Devon's been missing almost a week now.

Thorpe briefs me on what the various classes have been covering over the last few weeks. It should be easy to pick up where I left off.

'I'll go upstairs and unpack before dinner. I'm back in the ninth-grade dorms, I suppose?'

'Well, in fact...' Thorpe drops her eyes for an instant, which sets an alarm bell ringing in my head. Thorpe is never embarrassed, never sheepish. Something must be up. 'You're, ah, not an over-sensitive sort I think, Ms Kelly?'

I narrow my eyes, failing to see where this is going, but I can tell it's nowhere good.

She sighs. 'The thing is, Nessa Rath - you know, Devon's roommate - she's been, well naturally she's been rather *troubled* by this whole sequence of events. As you can imagine we sought to accommodate her in a new room. It was all very short notice. We put her in what used to be your room.'

I see where this is heading.

'We thought perhaps you would take up residence in the vacated room.'

Devon's old room. *Perfect*. That won't feel creepy at all.

Thorpe ducks her eyes again but only for the briefest moment. I wonder if she's thinking what I'm thinking: *what if Devon comes back?* Maybe Thorpe is only suggesting this because she doesn't expect to see Devon again.

Then again, even if Devon is still alive, it's not likely

she'll come back *here*, is it?

'It's a very nice room,' Thorpe says, having recovered enough to sound defensive.

Oh, I'm sure it is. Devon wasn't a scholarship girl, or an ex-scholarship junior teacher. No doubt it's far nicer than the one I'm used to.

But still.

'What about her things - Devon's things?'

Thorpe's eyes shift sideways. 'The Hundleys, um, removed them. After they took inventory with the police, of course. They decided they preferred to have her things at home.' She looks up. 'We thought it would be advisable for the girls to have somebody in that room, Ms Kelly - not to leave it empty. Girls can be so... impressionable at that age.' She clears her throat. 'I mean, you don't *mind*, do you?'

I stare at her, and she has the decency to flinch just the tiniest bit.

'I suppose I'd better start unpacking,' I say, and hold out my hand for the key.

*

The wooden staircase gleams back at me. The afternoon sun is at just the right angle, and the stained-glass panel on the half-landing casts colored patterns along the wood. The dorms are empty and silent; all the girls are in class.

Memories flood over me as I walk along. Memories of last year and before that, what feels like long ago, as a student - the girls flocking from their bedroom doors, the rustling of skirts and sweaters as they funnel down the stairs, breakfast gong ringing. Elbows jostling, bumping each other, teasing, laughing, mocking.

And another memory: Fiona and me, timid fifteen-year-olds on our very first day. I was clutching the orientation map the secretary had given us. We'd made it through our first half-day of classes. I'd unpacked already, and Fiona was bringing me upstairs to show me her room. I'd been carrying a lump in my stomach all day, a mix of regret and fear and shame - but I'd made it! I was at Horton! Jan was so proud, and I was here with my best friend. What was I worried about? I felt like I was losing my voice, my throat was so dry and scratchy. Maybe I was sick. Maybe it was a fever. Maybe I'd have to stay in the infirmary for the rest of the week, or be sent home.

Fiona, though, seemed to be walking on air. She trailed her hand dreamily along the wooden banister as we climbed the stairs. She seemed almost to be dancing. She turned towards me and shot me that wide grin of hers, two impish little canines on display, her summer dusting of freckles bright in the refracted sunshine.

'Isn't it *glorious*?' she said. She'd always loved beautiful things. Glamour, celebrity, all of it. She adored beauty magazines, even though Jan rolled her eyes at such 'frivolous' reading. I remembered how for her thirteen birthday she'd begged Jan for a pair of oversize sunglasses she'd set her heart on. Jan bought them in the end. They'd actually suited Fiona perfectly. No one else would have pulled them off like that.

'Her name's *Octavia*,' Fiona confided, her eyes big with admiration. She'd already met her roommate earlier that day - all the girls at Horton had roommates, no matter how wealthy, because it was *character building*.

Octavia. We came from a world of Jennys and

Stephanies. I could tell from the admiration dripping from Fiona's voice that Octavia was something special. The knot in my stomach tightened even more, and I had to stop a moment to breathe deep. Between Fiona and me I was the babyish one, the shy one, the one who still wanted to climb trees and keep my best friend all to myself. But that had been getting harder to do in Milham, because everyone loved Fiona. The girls in our neighborhood wanted to hang out with her, and the boys jostled and pranked each other for her attention. I guess I'd been waiting to be replaced. But I didn't think it would happen here, so soon, on our very first day at Horton.

'Here we are.' Fiona opened the door and nudged me through. There was a girl on the bed by the window. *Octavia.* I saw straightaway what Fiona meant. She was... well, she was perfect. She lay back on the bed like a bored aristocrat, long legs in front of her and one hand behind her head. Her honey-colored hair flowed over her shoulders and over the bedspread. Sharp cheekbones, long limbs, skin a white-girl-bronze that made me think of places I'd read about but didn't know how to pronounce. *Turks and Caicos, Cannes, St. Tropez.* There was another girl there too, sitting on the bed beside Octavia, pretty too in a meaner kind of way.

'This is my friend Sadie,' Fiona said, ushering me forward. I tried not to feel like a human sacrifice.

'Hi, *Sadie*,' the friend drawled.

Fiona grinned at me. It worried me, how happy she seemed. But Fiona was better at this kind of thing than me. It made sense she wasn't sick with nerves the way I was. Come to think of it, I didn't think I'd ever seen her nervous in my life.

I sat on Fiona's bed, where she'd dumped her suitcase, unzipped. I watched her start to unpack, taking out an armful of things and lugging them over to the shared closet. I saw Octavia and her friend exchange a quick glance which I pretended not to notice.

'Wow.' Fiona's voice came from inside the closet. She pulled out a fur coat on a hanger, staring at it with a kind of awe.

'This is *yours?*' Fiona said, turning her head to the figure on the bed. I followed her glance then looked away.

'She'd let you borrow it, wouldn't you Tavi?' the friend said. She eased herself off the bed and sauntered towards the closet. My stomach tightened again and I glanced towards Octavia, but her head was turned, gazing out the window, like all of us already bored her.

'And maybe Tavi could borrow some of *your* things,' the girl said, and dipped her hand into Fiona's suitcase like I wasn't even there sitting next to it. She pulled out a velour hoodie, grinned and held it up in front of her, then swung round to show Octavia, whose mouth crooked up in the corners. She dropped the hoodie and dove back into Fiona's things, rummaging and then taking out a t-shirt, and next a pink top with a diamanté pattern. The air was shifting in the room. I didn't want to look up.

'Sure. You can borrow whatever you like.' Fiona's voice wavered, hitting me like a stone in the chest.

No, I wanted to say. *Stand up to them. Fight back. Say something.*

I'd never seen Fiona stuck for words. I'd never seen her struggle to please anybody. With our friends it was the other way round. Fiona was always the one whose attention we wanted, the one we wanted at birthday parties, the one the boys liked best. I remember that day the gong ringing, the weirdly bright way Fiona said *oh good, dinner,* and how she and I walked down the corridor without looking at each other, avoiding each other's eyes all the way through the meal.

*

The same gong rings now, and soon I hear the doors opening and closing on the corridor, the students in the neighboring rooms leaving, moving down the stairs towards the dining hall. Second gong rings. I wait in my room till it's quiet again. I push the memories down. The ghosts. The guilt. I don't think about those days anymore. For good reason.

My suitcase sits at the foot of the bed, still full. I can't quite bring myself to unpack it. The other bed - what I know from my room inspections is Devon's bed - stares back at me from across the room. I make a mental note to ask for it to be removed. Thorpe can complain all she likes about me being 'over-sensitive'. She was right about it being a nice room though. Compared to the room I was in before, this is positively palatial. I go to the window, examining the view, which is in the opposite direction to my last room. These are the views that donor parents pay for. I can see out over the quad; the main gates down to the right, and straight ahead of me the new gymnasium with its floor-to-ceiling glass windows. But it's winter now and the nights start early. The dark is rolling in.

Third gong.

I take a deep breath, and open the door.

Seven

When I step through the wide oak doors into the Dining Hall, I can feel it in the room - a Devon-shaped shadow over everything. A thinness to the air. The girls sit in the same places, eating the same food, but they're different than before. They look paler, faint and limp like flowers without sun. No one is throwing things around or laughing. If you were new to this school you might think what nice manners they had. But I know better. I glance around, taking it all in, and feel eyes on me. From across the room, Simone Bailey is walking my way.

'What. The. Fuck.' She draws me into a quick side-hug. 'You didn't tell me you were coming back.' She shakes her head. 'I mean, you're crazy, right? You got out, and now after everything that just happened, you come back?'

Simone still thinks my departure from Horton was entirely voluntary. Thorpe, I guess, is the only one that knows the full story. Not even *I* know the full story.

I shrug.

'Well, it's good to have you back,' she says. We glance around the room together, taking it all in. 'It's like a morgue in here or something, isn't it?' Her eyes settle on a girl across the room, eating alone.

'Nessa Rath's been given the third degree, poor kid. I don't think she can stand much more of it.' She looks at me.

'She didn't see anything?' I try and picture sneaking out of a dorm room without waking your roommate. If you're well prepared, it wouldn't be so hard.

I see Lucy Hundley across the room, carrying a glass back from the water fountain. She's walking alone, eyes down. I think of myself at her age, and Fiona, and what I lost.

But did you lose it, Sadie? Or did you destroy it?

'I figured she'd be home by now,' I say. Simone follows my eyes and sees who I'm talking about.

'Lucy? Yeah. Hope she doesn't relapse.' She's obviously remembering Lucy's struggle with eating disorders last year.

I rub the back of my neck. The noise in the room dies to a quieter murmur as the food emerges.

'Come on,' Simone nudges me towards the tables. 'We can't keep talking about this, it's too depressing. I'm famished.'

Weeknights at Horton, each table has one member of the faculty at it to keep some kind of order. So instead of chatting with Simone through dinner, I suck in a breath and get ready to take my seat among the eleventh-graders. They look up as I approach.

'Hi Ms Kelly.'

'Evening Ms Kelly.'

Only a couple of the faces register any surprise at seeing me, and in the next moment they're back to their meal. If it were normal times, no doubt they'd be full of curiosity and gossip, wondering about why one of the teachers left for a month and suddenly reappeared. But Devon's disappearance seems to have knocked that right out of them.

I reach for my napkin, and an involuntary shiver goes through me. It's a memory - a memory of last term, and the first evening I reached towards my side plate and found something there that shouldn't have been there. It's not something I'll ever tell Dr Jamil about, let alone Jan, but that was the beginning of the panic attacks, those letters. If you can call them letters. At least tonight there's no little white envelope waiting to ambush me.

'All right, Miss?' a quiet voice says. I look up. It's Nessa Rath.

'Yes, thank you Nessa,' I say crisply, reminding myself of Thorpe for a second. It's unfair, but Nessa Rath unsettles me. There's something about those big, peeled-open eyes, pale and unblinking, that bothers me. She seems so vulnerable all the time, that rabbit-in-headlights gaze.

It's because she reminds you of yourself, the voice inside me says, and I glare at my plate and push the thought down. But it's probably true. That was me as a student here: jumpy, always watching, unsure of myself all the time. I'd like to think I've changed since. But maybe I haven't.

'Are you sure, Miss?' Nessa's thin voice asks again. Her face is flushed a mottled pink.

'*Yes*, Nessa.' I don't quite manage to keep the irritation out of my voice and she ducks her head, her near-white hair falling in front of her face. I immediately feel a pang of guilt, and then in the silence a voice carries down from the middle of the table.

'The *real* question is what, or *who*, was she running away from?'

It's Kaylan Reese, one of the more outspoken girls in the eleventh grade. Her eyes travel down the table towards Nessa. They're in the same grade but opposite ends of the spectrum: Kaylan is a queen bee, Nessa is an outsider.

'Maybe she was just sick of her creepy friends.'

'Kaylan,' I say sharply. I see Nessa's head has ducked further, the whitish strands now almost brushing her plate. I feel a wave of guilt at being harsh on her. I'll have to keep my eye on Kaylan and her friends. Horton has a decent reputation these days for anti-bullying measures, but in my experience too much can pass unnoticed.

Outside the wind rises, throwing itself against the walls of the dining hall like it wants to get in. *Ghosts*, I think. Some restless spirits, jealous of our living, breathing bodies. Maybe Jan was right about coming back. Maybe it was a terrible mistake.

But it's too late now.

*

After dinner, back in my room, I finally unzip my suitcase, open the closet, and start moving my clothes in. Prim, 'appropriate' teacher-clothes. High necks, opaque tights. The girls are the ones with a uniform, but staff have one too, just less official. The aim is pretty much the same: snuff out any hint of sex appeal.

And is it working, Sadie? The sarcastic voice is teasing, mocking. Fiona's voice. I hear it in my ear still, sometimes. Since I first came back to Horton I've been hearing it more and more. Which reminds me... I fumble around in the suitcase. Yes, there they are. I put my meds in the bathroom cabinet.

I unpack the few personal items I brought with me. A photograph of one of my favorite views from Hong Kong. A picture of Fiona and me from when we were ten years old. I used to keep that in my office downstairs; I'll put it back there tomorrow. As I think it a shiver runs over my neck, down my back. I straighten and turn around. It wasn't just in my mind. There's a breeze in here, a chilly gust where there wasn't one before. I go to the windows, pull back the curtain. The window's open. I could have sworn they were all closed when I left the room for dinner.

Maybe the fastening is loose. As I close it I glance out one more time at the tree-lined drive, and the tall black gates visible at the end.

Like a prison.

In the darkness, I fumble my way to bed. Between the cool sheets I could forget where I am, I could close my eyes and travel back in time, almost to the beginning.

I let the memories rewind, and for a moment I'm eight again, my first sleepover in Fiona's house. Our whispers travel in the dark, across the divide of two narrow twin beds.

'Sadie's not your real name though,' Fiona bounced up from her pillow to say.

'Of course it's my real name,' I said.

'No it's not. Sadie's short for Sarah, Mom told me.'

I was about to say *not me, I'm just Sadie,* until Fiona said: *'My* middle name's Sarah, too.'

I shut my mouth and swallowed my retort, smiling to myself in the dark. Sarah and Sadie. She was a Kennedy, mom and I were Kelly.

I snuggled deeper into the covers, under the spell of my new best friend. 'Yeah,' I smiled up at the ceiling. 'We're almost the same, aren't we? Almost like twins.'

*

What was that? I dredge myself up from sleep, looking around blindly in the dark. The panicky feeling of being in the wrong bed. Then the knowledge seeps in.

Horton. You're back at Horton, Sadie.

But what was it that woke me? My ears are pricked, on high alert. There it is. A scratching at the door, like fingernails. My heart pounds. I hesitate, then get out of bed and tip-toe across the chilly floor to the door and whip it open. No one.

Of course no one, Sadie.

I go back to bed, pulling the covers to my chin. Outside the wind lifts. A tree, probably. Probably that was all I heard. The branches of a tree, scratching against brick. Yes. That was it. That must have been it.

As I force myself to go back to sleep, another image comes to mind. Another windy day - the day I left Horton. The file boxes and suitcases I carried to the taxi in the buffeting wind, cobblestones catching underfoot. And a girl's face watching me from a second-floor window, a girl who was supposed to be in class but wasn't. A girl who, it seemed to me, was smiling as she watched me go. Yellow hair held back with a velvet band.

Devon Hundley's face.

Eight

I wake to the sound of the gong and realize I'm shivering with the cold, covers bunched at the foot of the bed. I yank them round me with a groan. Morning already... it feels like I was up all night. The pipes clunk. How is this room so freezing? I huddle deeper into the covers for a last minute of warmth. Chilblains may sound quaint in the pages of *Little Women* or *Jane Eyre*, but there'd probably be a lawsuit if any of Horton's students came down with any. I must not have turned the radiators on last night. The bells in the chapel ring out the hour. I glance across the room at Devon's empty bed.

I push back the covers and fish for my slippers, and in the little en suite I splash water on my face, then stand in front of my closet feeling dazed. I'm like someone who's fallen off her horse and now is too scared to get back on. *In the deep end*, I murmur to myself. *Come on, Sadie. Don't be a wimp.*

The corridor is almost empty. I get a few wan *good morning miss*es from the girls I pass. They shuffle past me, not really speaking, even to each other. I look at their pale, washed-out faces. Devon's disappearance has changed us all.

I let the cluster of girls pass ahead of me down the stairs. I catch a glimpse of myself in the window's reflection as I follow them. My silhouette is skinny - too skinny - and tensed up, my shoulders showing the anxiety that's followed me from my dreams back to waking hours. On the half-landing there's a large poster for swim

Regionals. Thorpe is all into 'school spirit' when it comes to supporting the swim team. But I don't think anyone will want to think about swim team now.

Near the dining hall I hear raised voices, and see the students ahead of me stop, gawking. There's a group of girls in a circle, and whatever's going on is escalating fast. One of them shrieks like her hair's being pulled.

What on earth?

'Stop it. Stop it!' another voice shrills.

'Girls!' I stride forward, arms out. Heads spin my way. Young, hostile eyes. The girls move apart, slow and sullen.

'What is going *on* here?' I try and sound like Thorpe, sharp and no-nonsense.

'Nothing, miss,' somebody mumbles.

'Good. That's what I thought. Don't let me see this again.'

I glimpse Nessa Rath among the crowd, her pale face sleepless and hollowed-out. She catches my eye and turns away. This isn't like the Horton girls. They can be vicious little cats if they want to be - but they're the well-bred kind of vicious, which means they keep their claws in check until they're behind closed doors. Or to put it Thorpe's way: they're *young ladies.*

We all move in to breakfast. Simone catches my eye across the hall and raises an eyebrow.

And the day has barely started.

*

My first class of the day is the twelfth-graders. They take their usual seats, and I move through the lesson keeping my eyes averted from the seat on the back left, where Lucy Hundley sits. I stop myself from glancing her way because if I do, I might stare. It's hard to imagine what she's going through.

But I *can* imagine. Because when I was her age, I lost my best friend, a friend who was like a sister to me. I lost her for good. At least Lucy still has hope.

When the bell rings for second period I nod to them to pack up. My eyes slide towards the back left of the class where Lucy's packing in a hurry, like she wants to be first out the door - but in her haste she drops a file of papers, and they scatter all round the feet of her chair. A couple of girls ask if she needs help but she waves them on. The last girl brushes past and then it's just Lucy left in the room, glaring at the floor as she collects the papers. Just her - and me.

'Lucy?'

She glances up. Something tells me if I say something too personal, too soft, it'll break her. I keep my voice neutral.

'If there's anything you need, anything I can do... extra time on a paper, or some take-home work if you don't want to be at school just now -'

Her fierce eyes meet mine.

'We just want to help,' I say lamely.

'You can't help.' She slides her bag over her arm.

'Lucy -'

She spins round. 'Do you know where she is, Ms Kelly? Do you know where my sister is?'

I shake my head wordlessly.

'Then there's nothing you can do to help.'

I want to say something more, something that might get through to her, but I can't. She's right: I have nothing. Lucy stands there a second longer, eyes bright and angry, then flounces out of the room. I wince in advance, waiting for the door to slam. But it just hangs open, quivering: quivering like me, like the trees, like the autumn leaves outside.

*

Two periods later it's the tenth-graders: Devon's old class. I shut the classroom door, not making eye contact till I reach the front of the room, dump my bag on my desk and turn around. There's something about them that chills me - how hostile they look, arms folded, staring at me.

'Good morning, class,' I say.

They shuffle, some cough. They look back at me with sullen faces. No one says good morning, like some kind of protest. But what are they protesting?

They're protesting your failure. You're the adults, and you failed them. Now one of them is gone.

'So.' I decide to carry on as normal. 'I gather you had got up to Act Four in *Romeo and Juliet*.' I open my copy and thumb through it. 'Nasreen, could you catch us up?'

Nasreen Elliot clears her throat but doesn't look up at me.

'Um. We'd got to the bit where Juliet's dad - Capulet - he's yelling at all the servants to get the house ready, because Juliet's fiancé - not Romeo, the other guy - he's about to turn up.'

I nod along. 'Scene Five. Right where the drama starts. Would you like to read it aloud for us, Nasreen?'

She shakes her head, looking down at her desk. I don't push. Everything's like walking on eggshells right now.

'Any volunteers?' I say. Nobody looks up.

So I start to read it myself. Only a couple of lines in, I realize the mistake. It's where Lady Capulet and the nurse discover Juliet's body, lying cold.

Her blood is settled, and her joints are stiff.

By the time I reach *Death lies on her like an untimely frost,* there's a kind of whimpering gasp from someone in the second row. It's Nicola Harkness, a little mouse of a girl, and I know she's not doing it for effect. I make a decision, and close the textbook.

'Girls.'

They stop staring at their desks and look up at me.

'We don't know yet what's happened to your friend. Nobody knows. We're all hoping to hear good news, but this period of not-knowing is very difficult. I'm sure you feel a lot of anxiety. But you don't have to deal with these feelings alone. You can speak to an adult, your parents, a teacher. We're here for you.'

I don't know who says it, but somebody does: it's low but clear. *Like you were here for Devon.*

My mouth drops open a little. I tighten it and scan the back row, looking for a pair of angry, rebellious eyes that would belong to the speaker. But everyone's looking away again, at their hands or at the floor. Only a few pairs of eyes meet mine, and with such a bruised, vulnerable look that I find myself wondering if I imagined it after all.

*

I ask Thorpe if the girls have been talking to anyone about what happened to Devon. The late afternoon light slants through her office, highlighting the creases as she frowns.

'Obviously we've tried to keep the media at bay so far as possible -'

'No,' I say. 'I mean like a grief counselor or something. A therapist.'

She eyeballs me. 'Ms Kelly, I appreciate your concern for our students. But this is not....' She gestures wildly - '*California.* Bringing in a therapist would mean we're suggesting that the girls are damaged. That they need *fixing.* We can't afford to make such suggestions to their parents.'

To our donors, is what I hear.

I walk back down the corridor as the bell rings. Class is over, and I stand for a moment at the top of the staircase, watching over the banister as the girls flood out of the classrooms, joining into little groups, hoisting bags, tossing their hair. Horton girls tend to come from a certain kind of gene pool, the gene pool of society power-couples: ruthless man, gorgeous wife. And sometimes the wife is ruthless too. All in all, most of these girls are young woman to be scared of.

'Sadie!'

I let out a sharp breath - I didn't know there was anyone near me - and turn to Simone.

'How did you sneak up on me like that?'

'Regretting coming back yet?' she says. I shrug rather than admit how true that feels.

'Come over for a drink at my place,' she offers.

Simone's married, so according to Horton's accommodation hierarchy, she and her husband get one of the converted staff cottages on the grounds. Never mind that her husband, Richard, works in the air force and is almost never here.

I nod. 'Go on then. I could use a drink.'

She grins and we swing back along the corridor, past Thorpe's office.

'Just let me check the mail real quick.' She ducks into the mailroom a few doors down. I follow her in, and find myself staring at my own cubby, which of course is empty. The label with my name on it is new - a reminder that I was thoroughly erased from here just weeks ago.

The white envelope that was waiting by my side-plate at the dinner table last term - it was just the first. More came later. I remember the sick feeling in my stomach when I came to pick up my mail and found another blank, sealed envelope waiting for me in my mail cubby. I'd almost come to expect them. They all said the same thing, more or less. *We don't want you here.*

*

It's freezing in Simone's cottage. The single-glaze windows haven't been repaired in probably decades and there are gaps in the seal. She pulls a woolen throw from where it's draped over the sofa and tosses it my way, then goes to the kitchenette where I hear the bottle of wine pop.

Simone's always been a saving grace at Horton. She's irreverent and outspoken - much more so than I've ever dared to be - and she seems like the kind of person who *should* get in trouble all the time, but she never does. The students love her, and even Thorpe seems to quite like her. Simone has a wild mane of red hair, long dangly earrings in a million different colors, and always has a tousled look about her somehow like she's just come back from a rousing walk on a windy beach. She tends to say exactly what she thinks, and although with some people that

65

would put me on edge, with Simone it's something I appreciate.

'Sauvignon blanc okay?' she hollers from the kitchen, and I yell back that it's great.

Something's different about this place - I've been here before a few times last term. I can't quite put my finger on what's changed, and then I realize. The photos. There used to be photos of Simone and Richard all around the room. Now all the photos are gone.

Strange.

I'm not a fan of Simone's husband, if I'm honest. I haven't seen all that much of him - because he travels so much, they live pretty separate lives - but I remember vividly when Simone and he hosted a little end-of-term party last year and he drank far too much. At least I assume he drank too much. That's what I'm putting it down to, that he followed me outside for "fresh air" and then proceeded to try and kiss me. I lay awake worrying about whether to tell Simone, but I didn't know her that well at that stage, and I'd only met Richard a handful of times; I didn't know the first thing about their marriage. For all I knew it was an open marriage - they spent so little time living in the same place. Besides, the punch had been awfully strong. Enough to make anyone lose their head for a minute or two.

Simone reappears with two very large, very full glasses. She's the eldest in her family and has three younger brothers, which I always find kind of amazing - I can't imagine what that would be like. She likes to say she learned to fight and drink early in life, thanks to them. One thing is for sure, she has a much higher tolerance than I do.

'Handy how much they hold, isn't it? Basically a soup-bowl on a stem,' she winks, and hands me one of the super-size glasses. We clink and she settles in the armchair across from me, pulling another throw over her knees.

She sits back in her chair. 'So how does it *really* feel? Being back?'

I take a large swallow of wine, and exhale. 'Honestly? Intense. It feels like I've been out of the saddle way longer than a few weeks. The girls are so....'

'Awful?' Simone suggests, and grins.

I shake my head and force a smile. 'Everything just feels so strange, after Devon...'

'Yeah.' Simone swigs from her fishbowl of wine. 'It's turning everybody a bit crazy. And did you hear about Ned and his car?'

I shake my head.

'When they found she was gone, a few of us went out looking for her, driving around the roads here, you know? It was raining hard, and we figured on her bike maybe she wouldn't have got far. But Ned, I guess he hit some slippery piece of road or something, and-'

I wince. I hate hearing about car accidents. It brings everything flooding back.

'I mean, he's fine, obviously. Just a huge mechanic's bill and he's been on a bunch of painkillers.' Simone takes another sip. 'But, I don't know - it's like everyone's being affected by this somehow. All these little ripples...' She trails off. 'You have to wonder, don't you? Why she ran away, I mean.'

The million-dollar question. Everything in Devon's life seemed fine, as far as we could see. Thorpe has a very strong anti-bullying policy, and I never saw or heard anything to make me worry Devon was having trouble with her peers. It was true that for a pretty, talented girl she didn't seem to have a lot of friends - I rarely saw her with other girls besides Nessa - but being pretty and talented didn't mean you had to be an extrovert.

I look up over my glass at Simone. 'Why, do you have a theory?'

She gives me a searching look.

'There's something weird about that family, don't you think?'

I keep my eyes on my wine. My heart thumps faster. 'Weird how?'

She shrugs. 'Well, you were the one who reported Lucy, remember?'

Reported makes it sound like a crime. I was just worried about her. I didn't think Thorpe was happy with me for bringing it up, but the girl's collarbones were jutting out of her shoulders. The uniform hid it, but I'd seen her in a tank top enough in the warm Spring months, sitting out in the grounds, to know that there was something going on.

'Eating disorders aren't that rare,' I point out. 'I mean, she's a teenager…'

'Whose mother used to weigh them every morning,' Simone interjects.

I raise my eyebrows. 'Angela did?'

We definitely have some controlling parents here at Horton, but that's a new one on me.

Simone gives me a knowing look. 'And, you know, that *marriage*.' She screws up her nose as if just thinking about Philip and Angela is distasteful to her.

I didn't think Simone would be such a snob about it.

Philip and Angela Hundley come from very different backgrounds. Angela is a very wealthy business owner, and Philip is just a regular guy. I gather some people said some nasty things about it when they tied the knot. I don't know why Simone is so disapproving though. If it were the other way round - a rich guy, and an "ordinary" girl - people would probably think it was a cute Cinderella story. Somehow when it's the woman who's rich, people think she's a cougar and he's a gigolo.

'You have to wonder, is all I'm saying,' Simone goes on, swirling her glass. 'What goes on in that home. Devon didn't have a reason to run away from *us*.'

I feel chilly suddenly, and twitch Simone's wool blanket closer.

Devon, Devon, Devon. She's all anybody wants to talk about these days. Today, she's been missing for a week.

'I keep remembering last Halloween,' Simone says. 'The party, you remember?'

I remember it all right. Horton did its usual school dance for the students and Simone, Coach Ned and I ended up chaperoning. We decorated the new gym with orange and purple streamers, cutouts, spooky-but-cute props for the girls to pose with. We were basically there to police the event for alcohol, cigarettes, or anything stronger, but Simone had snuck some vodka miniatures into her own handbag to help get us through the night. She and I did shots in the staff bathroom - poor Ned is kind of a square, but I think he guessed from the way we were giggling by nine o'clock.

I'd promised my students extra credit if they came as a character from a novel, and I'd made myself a case in point, dressing as Jane Eyre: I bought a Victorian-looking black dress online, with a high lace collar; tiny, Beatles-era wire spectacles, and sculpted my hair up into a severe-looking bun. I had Simone pin a sign to my back that said *Poor, plain and little.* It was only afterwards that I realized how close to the bone the whole costume was - I had dressed as an underpaid, overworked governess to the rich. Now, suddenly, it comes back to me in a flash. Devon Hundley - she'd dressed as Ophelia, Hamlet's drowned sweetheart. She'd got hold of some marvelous-looking old gown and draped fake strands of seaweed around herself, with little glass sea-creatures, crabs and tiny fishes, pinned to her dress. She'd painted her face a chalky, greenish color, and altogether the effect was unnerving.

'You remember?' Simone's voice takes me back to the present.

I nod.

Simone sips from her wine. 'You heard about all that hullabaloo over the diary?' she says.

'Diary?' I echo.

'When they came to search her room? The Hundleys were hell-bent on finding it. They thought it might have "answers", you know? Apparently Nessa said she thought Devon had a hiding place for it, but Nessa didn't know where it was. They turned her room upside down looking for it.'

'Maybe she took it with her?' I say.

Simone shrugs. 'I guess. I passed by the room when they were searching for it. Philip Hundley was *shouting.* I mean, really bellowing.'

I feel chilly again. 'It makes sense,' I say, ignoring the

damp sweat beading on my neck. 'They wanted to know where she'd gone. They must have been desperate.'

'Yeah,' Simone says, like she's ready to change the subject at last. Which to me is a relief. I search for something easy.

'So,' I say. 'How's Richard?' But apparently this isn't the right topic either. There's a change in the atmosphere. The smile on Simone's face wavers.

'What do you mean?'

'Well, what's he up to these days?' I keep my voice light, not sure why this suddenly seems like dangerous territory.

Simone takes a large swig of wine. 'You know how it is. He's a busy guy.'

I nod. 'Where's he stationed now?'

'Jesus, Sadie, what's with all the questions?' She slams her glass down and I wince, waiting for it to crack.

'Look,' Simone draws a breath. 'Sorry. I just... I guess everything that's been going on has been stressing me out too. Maybe we should call it a night.'

'Yeah.' I don't meet her eyes, putting my half-finished wine on the table and gingerly removing the throw and draping it back over the sofa. 'Maybe we should.'

Outside the wind whistles through the trees, and even the three-minute walk to the East Wing feels further than I'd like. It's so dark these days, with winter setting in. Dark and cold. I focus on the warmth of the wine inside me, and try not to think about Simone's sudden weirdness, or about those memories of Devon.

Something cracks behind me, making me whip around. There it comes again, a crunching sound. A twig snapping underfoot? But who would be out here at this hour?

Don't be silly, Sadie. Stop imagining things.

Fiona was always the queen of make-believe, the one with all the imagination. But lately, it seems, I've got her share.

Nine

There's someone sitting in Thorpe's office when I walk by in the morning. A slender figure, ramrod-straight back, tailored suit, golden hair. From the back it could be Lucy Hundley, only better-groomed.

Angela.

I hover outside Thorpe's door, waiting, and then sure enough the woman moves her head just a fraction to the side. I breathe in sharply. It's her. My nerves tingle, telling me to step back from the door, though rationally I know she can't see me. I'm much too far behind her to be in her peripheral vision. I take a steadying breath and lean closer. What are they discussing?

Angela pauses, then, mid-speech, and I freeze. Just as she swivels her head my way I step back from the door.

Did she see me?

But what does it matter if she does?

The bell goes again and I realize I'm going to be late for my eleventh-graders. I scuttle down the corridor, slow my step just before I reach the door, and try not to sound breathless as I enter.

'Class. Good morning.'

The hollow chorus bounces back at me.

'Lauren, would you please pass out these worksheets here and we'll get started?' I tap the pile on my desk that I dropped off in the classroom before going to bed. Questions on Toni Morrison's *Sula.*

The worksheet's distributed to about half of them before the giggles start. Nervous giggles. I look up.

They're looking at each other, then at the floor, and definitely not at me. A fleeting glance to my right - the morning's young and it's still dark outside, the electric lights making a mirror of the windows - tells me I don't have food on my face or a stain on my blouse.

Lauren Sterling is frozen in the middle of the aisle, cheeks pink, grasping the rest of the stack of worksheets. She's fixed on me with a panicked sort of look in her eyes.

'Lauren?'

She drops her gaze and silently walks to my desk. Without looking at me, she lets the stack thud down, and I see it: instead of the discussion questions I'd printed out, six bullet points on the page, there's just one thin sentence printed across the middle of a blank sheet.

Sadie Kelly is a dirty liar.

I swallow, lift the page. The one below it is the same. And the one below that. I don't need to investigate further to know that that's what's written on each of the papers half my class are staring at now.

'Thank you Lauren,' I say quietly. 'You may sit down.'

She gulps, and scurries back to her seat. I stand up and walk round the front of my desk. No one is laughing now.

'Who's responsible for this?' I say.

There's no answer, not that I was really expecting one.

'*Who*,' I say, my voice a tone steelier, 'wrote this?'

'Right,' I say, after the silence has reached a count of ten. 'Pass them back to the front, please.'

They do, and I snap the sheaves from each girl in the front row and stuff them into my bag. I'll get rid of them later.

'Since we're done with kindergarten for the day, let's move on.' I make a show of dusting my hands, and then flip open to where I've left my bookmark. 'Sula and Nel,' I remind the class. ' Best friends. But even best friends can betray each other.' I look around the classroom, clearing my throat. They're all staring at me, wide eyes locked on mine.

'I want you to contrast two examples of loyalty, and two examples of betrayal in the novel. Go.'

I leave them working on their essays as I slip out of the room, door left open, to check over the photocopier. Nothing's amiss. No signs of anyone being in here who shouldn't have been. I take the discards out of the recycling, bury the stack of *liar* sheets underneath it, and drop the rest back on top.

I walk back towards the classroom, ears pricked, waiting for the sound of some disruption inside. But the sound that catches my ears is a faint click-clack from the other end of the corridor. Beside Thorpe's office, Angela Hundley is sweeping down the hall, black trench coat swirling about her like a cape. At the main doors she pauses, her head moves in my direction.

Her eyes take me in in one bite - quickly, easily, the way a tiger would swallow a mouse. She blinks and - am I imagining it? - smiles a little.

And then she's gone.

Liar liar, you're on fire.

*

The first of the envelopes came during the Spring term. The cherry blossoms were in full bloom, gnarled

75

ogres that clustered round the East Wing, and for just those couple of weeks transformed into a playground of pink and white. It made me think of Fiona when we were very young, leaping around in a swimming costume, pretending it was a tutu.

The envelope on my side-plate was the first one. Nothing written on it, no name. But it was on my place setting, so it had to be for me. I ignored the teasing smell of coffee from the urn on the sideboard and looked around, wondering who had left it there. A few girls had already sat down at our table, but none of them were looking my way or seemed in the least aware. I picked up my butter-knife and slid it through the fold. Just one flimsy bit of paper inside. I tipped it into my hand.

It was handwritten, boldly lettered. It was just one line.

You don't belong here.

I froze, and forced a laugh. It was bizarre, after all. What a ridiculous thing to leave on my side-plate. I turned it over. Blank on the other side.

Two seats away, Devon Hundley blinked at me with her serious, dark eyes. I startled. She'd been watching me this whole time.

'Everything all right, Miss?'

'Fine, thank you, Devon.'

She blinked, a slow, unhurried blink, then drew her lips together and smiled. I couldn't quite put my finger on it, why that look she gave me made me stuff the note, envelope and all, into a ball in my pocket, and abruptly stand up from the table. *Coffee*, I told myself, marching over to the steaming urn. I waited for Coach Ned to finish pouring his, and as I waited my hand drifted to my pocket.

It pressed down, stuffing that little ball tighter and tighter.

More came later. The words changed but the theme was the same. *You're not welcome here.* I didn't know what to do. I couldn't bring them to Thorpe, she'd just wonder what it was I'd done to bring this on myself. It would make me look suspicious. It would make people want to ask questions, dig deeper.

And that was the last thing I wanted.

*

That night I hear it again, the scratching at the door. I wake up, wonder if I've imagined it.

'Hello?' I hiss into the darkness, and it seems like the scratching stops. But then, after a few minutes, it starts again. This time instead of calling out I get out of bed quietly and inch my way to the door. I fling it open, hand coiled back, ready to grab whoever it is before they can run, and give them a piece of my mind.

But there's nobody.

I stand there, a stray breeze wafting down the corridor, playing around my ankles, my bare feet. Instinctively I glance at the ground, looking for another of those envelopes.

Nothing. The corridor's empty, except for me.

Me, and my memories. Horton's like an animal, I think: a great, sleeping beast, inhaling, exhaling. A monster sleeping in the dark woods. And when it wakes, it will pounce.

Liar, liar, you're on fire.

I shake my head. *No dreams tonight, Sadie,* I decide. The last of my Klonopin are sitting by my bed. Two down, and sixty seconds later, I'm out for the count.

*

I'm back in Mrs Drake's English class, that first time Fiona and I walked in. We'd had trouble finding the room, there were only two free seats left, one at the back of the class, one at the front. Fiona didn't skip a beat, just headed straight to the back, leaving me to take the front seat. The rule applied at Horton just as much as it had in Milham: cool kids at the back, nerds at the front. I lowered myself into the chair. Back home the boys had liked to make a special nerd-face for me which involved sticking out their front teeth like a squirrel and pushing imaginary glasses up their noses, never mind that I had perfectly normal teeth and had never worn glasses. But for some reason with Fiona it was never that way. Her super-smarts didn't make her weird - maybe because she didn't even seem to notice them herself. They were like a party trick to her: she'd perform it if you asked, but she didn't really care. She belonged at the back of the class.

I took out my books, pencil case, fountain pen, and Miss Drake tossed a couple of extra reading copies at our desks - *The Turn of the Screw*. Everything went fine until half way through the lesson when Fiona piped up with a comment- she hadn't been called on, but waiting to be called on was never one of Fiona's strong suits.

I saw the way Miss Drake scrunched up her face ·as Fiona spoke.

'Say that again, Miss Kennedy?'

I heard the hushed, embarrassed-but-not-really giggles. I looked back to Miss Drake, but she seemed oblivious.

Fiona repeated herself but it still wasn't enough.

'Once more time, dear?'

We came from a place less than an hour away, but Miss Drake acted like Fiona was speaking a foreign language. I looked around.

Fion-er, somebody whispered, and more giggles erupted. *Fion-er drives a kah.*

I didn't turn around as Fiona repeated, slowly, what she had said. I heard how her voice changed. The tremor in it.

Everything had always come easy to Fiona, always. I think *that* was the moment - the moment when the confidence she'd had her whole life fall away like a chunk of mortar falling off a wall. I didn't turn around. I couldn't. I sat frozen, eyes front.

I think we should go home I said to Fiona a couple of weeks later. She ignored me, because we both knew that wasn't going to happen.

But if it had? Sometimes I still think about that. If it had, maybe she'd be alive right now.

*

It's morning, and the last bell for class rings as I'm walking down the corridor. Through the panel in the door I can see the girls are all already seated, waiting.

'Good morning, class.'

'Good morning, Ms Kelly.'

And then I notice one empty seat among the rows. I know instantly whose it is.

'Astrid,' I ask the girl who sits next to her; they're friendly I think. 'Have you seen Lucy this morning?'

Astrid shakes her head. 'I think she's sick, Miss?'

Why do these girls make everything into a question?

'Well, did she go to the infirmary?'

'I don't... know, Miss?' Astrid fidgets under my stare. 'I mean, she wasn't at breakfast?'

I look around at the rest of the class. 'Has anyone seen Lucy Hundley this morning?'

Eyes look blankly back at me, or duck down to the floor.

So that's a no, then.

I pick up the phone and hit the quick-dial button for the infirmary. Carmen, the school nurse, picks up on the second ring. She hasn't seen anyone this morning. I tell the class to read the first four stanzas and read over the discussion questions on the worksheet. I tell Nasreen Elliot she's in charge, leave the door open, and knock on Mme Denoel's door across the hall to let her know. Then I beat it upstairs. The Seniors don't share rooms, and they're at the top of the main building instead of over on the East Wing.

She's fine, I tell myself. *She's just skipping class.* But some terrified part of me is still expecting the worst. I tap on Lucy's door, get no answer, rap harder.

'Lucy? It's Ms Kelly. Can I come in?' My heart pounds again. 'Lucy?'

I push on the door. It's unlocked.

Ten

'Lucy.'

A wave of relief comes over me. She's here. She's awake. Everything's fine.

She turns her head away, exposing a pale, slender neck. Her blonde hair is matted against the pillow. She looks like an invalid in an old-fashioned book. She and Devon both had this quality, this fine-boned, fragile air to them. Like despite all that money, there was something inside them pulling them down, something they had to fight.

'You're supposed to be in class right now, Lucy,' I say. 'Can you tell me why you're not?'

At first I think I'll get no response but after a few moments her face crumples, like a sheet of paper in someone's fist. There are no tears, no sound. Just this spasm, and then her face straightens again like it never happened.

'Lucy?'

'I can't,' she whispers. It's a fierce, angry whisper.

'Lucy, if something's wrong, you should go to the infirmary.'

She glares down. Shakes her head. 'I can't.' She looks back at me. 'I tried to get out of bed this morning - I did try. I just can't.'

I don't have to be a genius to know that whatever's going on here is psychological.

'Should I call your parents, and have them come get you?'

I say it gently, but it gets an instant reaction. She juts her head up from her pillow.

'No! You're not to call them.'

I try to keep my face neutral, as though this reaction isn't shocking.

'It's not a punishment, Lucy. You can come back to Horton as soon as you feel better. But if you can't come to class, or to the infirmary, then we have to call your parents so they can look after you at home.' I pause. 'It's okay to leave Horton, you know. Staying here... it won't bring her back.'

Lucy flinches, then sets her mouth tight. 'I'm not *stupid*.' She lets her head fall back against the pillows and speaks in the direction of the window.

'Don't call them, Ms Kelly. I'll be fine. I just want to stay here today.'

I wish I were qualified for this kind of thing.

'I suppose we can let you rest a little longer. We'll see you at dinner though, won't we, Lucy?'

Looking out the window, I think she doesn't hear me. But then her sharp little chin dips, a silent nod.

'Okay,' I say, and close the door.

But Lucy isn't at dinner. When I get there I glance around the room, verifying. And I wait a few minutes to be sure she's not just late or in the bathroom. But soon her place is cleared away and it's clear she's not coming down. Thorpe isn't here; *we're* expected to eat with the students, but she often dines privately. I excuse myself and go back to Lucy's dorm. She's sleeping - if not peacefully then at least deeply - in her bed. I creep closer, listening to her breathing. It's steady. Even. I check her bedside table, looking for anything worrying. Pills. A note.

No. I push that voice down. There's nothing like that here. She's just a sad girl, asleep.

I go back down to Thorpe's office and tap on the door, but it's empty. I lean over her desk and pull the home phone directory from its place. Deep breath.

...D, E, F, G...

There it is.

'Hundley residence?' A woman's voice, not Angela's, answers. It must be the housekeeper, Mathilde. I shouldn't know her name, but I do. There are a lot of things I shouldn't know about the Hundleys, but do.

'I'm calling from the Horton school. Is Mrs Hundley available?'

There's a pause, overly long.

'Mrs Hundley is not in,' she says finally.

'Do you know when she'll be back?'

Another long silence. I guess this woman is used to screening a lot of nuisance calls.

'Hello?' I say, impatient.

'I can't say.'

'You mean you don't *know,* or -?'

The phone rustles, and her voice tightens. 'Mrs Hundley is not at home.'

I roll my eyes. 'Yes, we've established that.' I hesitate. I don't really want to say the next part, but I do. 'How about Mr Hundley, then?'

'Mr Hundley is not available either,' the woman says, her primness fully recovered.

'Is he out with Mrs Hundley? Will they be back this evening?'

'I'm sorry, Ma'am. We - I - I can't say.'

And she puts down the phone before I have a chance

to say anything more, leaving me staring in disbelief at the receiver in my hand.

What was *that* about?

*

I swing by my office after dinner to pick up some materials for class. The door's open, which surprises me. I usually lock it. When we were students at Horton we weren't allowed to lock our rooms - fire risk, we were told. I always thought it was more of a power-move, just to remind us that privacy was a privilege we didn't have. As a teacher, of course, we're encouraged to lock all offices and classrooms when not in use. But I've been distracted lately.

I flick the light on, and go to my desk to gather up the papers - I go through them carefully, making sure there've been no nasty tricks or switches this time. But they're just as they should be. And then I notice something. A rectangle of perfectly clean, dust-free wood. A space where something used to be. A photograph - my photograph. The one I keep here, the one of me and Fiona as kids. I finger the locket round my neck, a nervous habit.

Maybe it just got knocked over. I check to see if it's on the floor somewhere, or got tipped into a drawer. But even as I go through the motions of looking for it I know I'm fooling myself. That neat little rectangle on my desk proves it. It didn't slide off or fall over. The photo was plucked, neatly, from its place. And wherever it is right now, it's not in this room.

The photograph frame is silver, but no one here is hurting for money - and I refuse to blame it on the cleaning staff. One of the girls must have snuck in and snatched it. I guess a lot of thefts aren't about value. They're about mischief and knowing you can get away with it. Someone wanting to show off to her friends. That's all it was.

It must be.

*

I decide to have an early night to rest my head, but sometimes sleep is worse than being awake.

In the dream I'm back in Milham, sixteen again. Thumping bass sounds outside the bathroom doors. Blue light shines down from above as Fiona peers into the bathroom mirror. It's the weekend, we're out dancing, fake IDs in our tiny purses. I look in the mirror too. My sixteen-year-old face is nothing like Fiona's. Mine is round, bland, boring.

'Here.' Fiona's hand, a tube of lipstick open, offering it to me. I take it, draw it over my lips. A red smear grows wider.

Ugly, I think. *Ugly, ugly.* I raise an angry hand to rub it off.

When I turn to hand the lipstick back no one is there.

'Fiona?' My arm holds the lipstick in front of me, in the empty air. I'm suddenly afraid. I'm suddenly so alone.

'Who are you looking for?' A voice says, and I spin round. It's a girl. My age. Where did she come from?

'I know you,' I whisper. Long shiny hair, a black Alice band.

Dream-Devon ignores me. She turns away from me, watching herself in the mirror. She likes what she sees: she smiles, and there's blood between her teeth.

I start awake, about to cry out. Not from the dream -

from something else. Something loud. Wind whistles round me, enveloping me in the dark. *Am I outside?* my sleep-dull brain says. But I feel the bed beneath me; I fumble for the light. It snaps on.

There's glass like crystals all over the floor, catching the light. Shards of it everywhere, winking at me. The wind rushes, the curtains billow. There's a gaping hole in the window. Beneath the window, the stone that caused it.

*

Simone answers her door, stares at me.

'Sadie? What on earth's the matter? It's almost midnight...' She looks at my face. 'Come in. Come sit down.'

I hold the glass of whiskey she's poured for me. Now that I'm not in my room any more, I'm wondering if I overreacted.

I describe it again. She drops into a chair opposite me. 'But why - who would do that?'

'I don't know.'

Simone blinks. 'Sade, maybe it was just, you know, girls being stupid.'

But I can hear the doubt even in her voice. It's a nasty trick, there's no getting around it.

She gets up, goes to the window, her woolen throw still draped over her shoulders.

'Sleep here tonight,' she says. 'I'll make up the couch.'

Eleven

In the morning I see a pair of uniformed police officers walking out of Thorpe's office. When I pass by, Thorpe's not at her desk as usual. She's standing at the window with her back turned, feet planted on the floor, that haughty stance like a queen looking down on her kingdom. But then I see how tightly her hands are clasped, how the nails are gripping so hard they're stippled pink and white, and the veins are standing out on her arms.

'Mrs Thorpe?' I say, and she spins around.

'I just saw the police... any news?'

She grimaces.

'No credit card use. No phone use. No transport booked in her name. No evidence she's still alive.'

I hesitate, then tell her about the damage to my window. She looks appalled.

'I'll ask Omar to go up and have a look at it right away,' she says. Omar's the janitor. 'I can't *believe* one of our girls would be so - so reckless.'

Reckless isn't exactly the word I'd use, but I guess as long as I get the window fixed. These October nights aren't going to be pleasant.

Lucy's back in the corridors at least, which is somewhat reassuring. I figure Thorpe won't want to see Lucy's "day off" as a problem worth talking about, but I make a mental note to go see her anyway. Meanwhile I put the rest of last night out of my head as best I can. It all feels like a strange dream now, when everything is so normal again.

Or as normal as it gets, these days.

At lunch Coach Ned catches Simone and me as we take our plates to join the line. 'Simone, Sadie, I was wondering - would either of you be willing to co-chaperone at the swim meet tomorrow?'

Simone grins. 'Oh no. You got me last time, Ned. I'm not sitting on a stinky bus of bickering girls for two hours again.'

I see Ned's jaw working. This meet is going to be a difficult one, the first without Devon.

'I'll do it,' I say.

It's like everything leads back to her. Our conversations are booby-trapped, and *Devon, Devon, Devon,* are the words waiting to explode.

'Thanks, Sadie,' he nods.

Simone nudges me. 'Come on. Before they take my coffee away.'

As we eat quickly, Simone asks me if I've seen the latest.

'The Hundleys are offering a reward for information about Devon's whereabouts.'

I think of the last ad, where the language was about Devon's "safe return", not just "whereabouts".

It seems like our expectations are getting lower and lower; like hope is shrinking.

I have the juniors for the last class of the day. Nessa Rath's at the back, trailing the louder girls, but when she goes to take her seat I see one of her eyes has a shadowy bruise round it. She's covered it with makeup, badly.

During class she seems her usual, barely-there self, and keeps her nose buried in the book. I ask her to clean the whiteboard for me when class finishes, so that the room empties out and I can speak to her alone.

'Nessa -' I point. 'What happened here?'

She flushes and looks away.

'Swim practice. I smacked myself on one of the lockers. Someone had left it hanging open, and I bent down to pick up my bag, and -well.' She shrugs.

I wince. 'Does it hurt?'

'No miss,' she says firmly, unusually firm for Nessa. 'It's fine. Everything's fine.'

Accidents do happen. Fiona was on the swim team, and on the track team too - not that it helped her popularity. I remember plenty of nights she'd complain about bruises, pulled muscles, and the like. But she never got a black eye from slamming into her swim locker.

I bite my lip. 'You might think of calling into the nurse, just see if she has anything for the bruising.'

'Yes, Miss.'

'Nessa, would you tell me, if something was going on? If you needed... help, of any kind?'

'Yes, Miss.'

Her eyes are flat, hiding whatever's behind them. Is it my imagination, or is there something else - something impatient, a little sneering, underneath all that mildness?

She couldn't have been running around throwing rocks last night - could she?

I glance again from the corner of my eyes, but she's slipped from the room, like a pale fish slicing through black water.

Liar, liar.

I run my thumb over the side of my phone in my pocket. Thinking of the number that I swore I wouldn't text.

Leave it, Sadie.

But I don't leave it. I wait until classes are over, then go upstairs to my room and change. Jeans, a sweater. Dark clothes. Outside I pull my hood up and close the door of the East Wing behind me. Walking down the path to my car in the dark drizzle, the feeling only deepens: of being drawn, inevitably, to a place I should avoid.

It's half an hour before I get there.

People all over New England send their daughters to Horton, but the Hundleys don't have far to go. They're only a little Connecticut drive away. I trawl around the neighbourhood for a while, eyeing the grand houses peeking out over hedges and trees. I slow the car as I approach the one that I know belongs to Angela and Philip. There's a black car parked outside - police. There's a news van further down the road, too. Somehow all this hadn't occurred to me. I can't just park and walk in. I can't stand there in the courtyard and look up at those windows and remember.

I slow the car as I drive by.

The driveway is lit with old carriage lights. At the far end of it, the house rears up in the dusk, black gables against the sky. There's a light on. Is that a person, silhouetted in the window? Or just a shadow?

Then it's gone, and I keep driving. I pass the unmarked car on the road and my neck prickles. Do they see me? Are they watching me?

The roads feel deserted as I drive back to Horton. I touch the locket at my neck and glance in the passenger seat; for a moment the past is so real I'm expecting to see Fiona there. She lingers there, somewhere between imagination and memory, ready to tease me.

Well, that was a nice little outing, her sarcastic voice says as I steer the car back onto the grounds of Horton. The parking area is dimly lit. In the shadows lie thicker shadows, the black columns of trees all the way up the drive. I wish they'd light the lot better.

It's almost midnight, past lights-out, and the windows of the dorms are mostly dark. I cut the engine, step out and slam the doors. The wind is low, and everything is strangely quiet. I gather my coat tighter round myself and tell my brain firmly to be quiet and get moving. The East Wing is far ahead of me, tall and black. My feet move quietly across the cobblestones - and then a man's voice right beside me says '*Sadie.*'

I let out a shriek and my keys drop on the wet ground.

A hand closes over my shoulder. Another sound comes out of me, a kind of whimper. The hand - a vice - grips harder.

'*Sadie.* It's me.'

I look up. Holy...

'What are *you* doing here?'

It's Philip Hundley.

Twelve

We sit in his car, staring at each other. The bags under his eyes are deep. His hair is ruffled, like he can't stop running his hands through it. He looks awful. And yet -

'I didn't mean to startle you,' he says again. 'I just, I had to see you.'

I focus out the window. It's a struggle to look at him. 'I thought you didn't want me to contact you. You told me to delete your number.'

He gives me a pained look. 'You know why, Sadie. I was trying to do the right thing - for everybody.'

I nod, staring through the windscreen.

'And then -' His voice constricts and I feel a dart of pain in my chest. I'm being selfish. How could I expect him to be thinking of *my* feelings, after what has happened to Devon? He looks at me with those haunted eyes.

'Angela's falling apart. I don't know what to do.'

'You shouldn't be here,' I say.

He lowers his eyes. 'I just... needed to see you, Sadie.'

I sit there, breathing shallowly. That used to be all I wanted to hear. But then everything changed. And now...

He keeps speaking. 'I just... I don't know what to do, and I'm - I'm afraid.'

I look at him. 'What are you afraid of?'

He pauses, then shakes his head.

Ahead of us, through the windscreen, a light blinks on in Simone's cottage then dies again. It's late, she shouldn't still be up.

'Sadie?' His voice falls into the silence like a stone hitting water. I stare out the windshield.

'I'm sorry,' he says.

The trees wave darkly around us. We sit for a while in silence, and then he begins to speak again in a low voice.

'When Thorpe called I thought nothing of it, you know? I thought it was a stunt... I thought she'd be ringing our doorbell any second. But then, we called her and called, but her phone was off. Not even one ring. Straight to voicemail. Devon's phone is *never* off. And we waited. Called the police. But... nothing. No trace of her. No credit card use, no online bookings, nothing.'

The wind dies again. The trees are still. I feel like I'm holding my breath.

'Angela...she was like a stone. Like a statue. I still haven't seen her cry. I go into the bedroom sometimes, and things are broken, smashed. Like a madman broke in. But she doesn't say anything about it.' He passes a hand over his face. 'She scares me, Sadie.'

A hush falls over us again. Though he's turned towards the window, I see a hand go up to his face, wiping his eye. His hand lies on the gearbox between us. He looks so lonely. I want to touch it; to comfort him - but not like this. He and Angela had been divorcing when I started seeing him. He told me so. *I'm as good as single*, he said.

But then all that changed. And now Devon is gone, and I can't get away from this fear seeping into my bones. A fear I don't fully understand.

Philip turns back, looking at me. His hand moves towards mine, clasps it, bridging the distance I hadn't. And then he pulls me towards him, and all I can see is his eyes in the dark, his mouth. The touch of his stubble. His lips.

'I've missed you,' he says.

My eyes snap open. The car is dark. Everything is dark.

'I can't.' My voice comes out a whisper. 'We can't. Not any more.' *Not like this.*

'Sadie, please-'

'No, Philip.'

I pull myself from the car and off into the cold, dark night. After a while there's the soft sound of an engine starting. He doesn't put his lights on until his car is at the gate. I watch the beams pierce the dark as the car swings round onto the road.

I watch until the lights are gone.

*

It all began last year, Spring term. I was grading papers late into the evening. My office was a poky little room on the ground floor, not far from the office where the School Board, apparently, were having one of their monthly meetings. Occasional bursts of voices drifted down the corridor, making it harder to concentrate. I looked up from the papers and rubbed my eyes. The photograph of Fiona and me that I kept framed on my desk looked back at me. I sighed and cracked into another confused essay about Hamlet's ghost, when I heard footsteps and humming. I glanced up and immediately recognized the tall figure crossing in front of my door.

Impeccably dressed, thick hair swept back, and even from where I sat he had an air of looking for trouble, like a teenager in a man's body. I felt myself blush slightly and duck my head back down to the paper in front of me. I remembered him instantly, from that parent teacher evening. Him, smirking, and his oblivious wife.

Then the whistling stopped and the steps backtracked, and he was looking in my door. He was grinning slightly, as if amused. His tie was askew.

'I *thought* it was you,' he said.

There wasn't much to say to that.

'New girl.' He grinned. 'So what's your real name?'

'Sadie,' I said. 'Sadie Kelly,' I added, because just my first name sounded naked, too intimate. *Ms Kelly* was what the students called me, it was even what Thorpe called me - our head was formal like that - but I couldn't exactly suggest it to him.

'Sadie,' he said, and smiled. There was something unexpected about the smile. The pompousness fell away, like he wasn't performing any more.

'Grading homework?' He nodded at my desk. 'What nonsense have they produced this time?'

The smart-ass facade was back again.

'Essays,' I said. 'On Hamlet.'

He came into the room, closing the door behind him. I noticed that he had closed it, but it was harmless. Probably.

He sat down in the chair across from me - the chair Angela had sat in at the Parent Teacher evening.

'May I?' he said, mischievously. I didn't know what he was talking about, until he'd twitched the paper from the top of the stack towards him. I put my hand out and snatched it back. I wasn't even thinking, it was pure instinct. He looked at me, and I frowned.

'That's between my students and me.'

He blinked, amused, and gave the paper another

slight tug as though to test me. I didn't budge, just looked him in the eye.

He drew his hand back from the pile. The mischief left his eyes, but he wasn't upset. Instead of the coldness I'd have expected, there was a new, faint warmth.

'Who's this?' He gestured at the photo of me and Fiona.

'No one.' I angled it away from him. She actually looked a little bit like the Hundley girls in that picture, come to think of it - that golden hair, the wide eyes.

There was a light clack of branches against the window. It was dark outside and there was a little wind; the trees were dancing. I loved the view at this time of evening. It was always my private view. Not something I shared with strangers.

'Hamlet.' Philip Hundley drummed the table, enjoying himself. 'He's Indecision, right?'

I waited. I wasn't about to applaud his *Shakespeare 101*. But he was unfazed. He grinned back at me and continued, ticking them off on his fingers.

'Macbeth: Ambition. Lear: Pride. Hamlet's supposed to be Indecision. Right?'

'That's the general opinion,' I said.

He grinned. 'I'm an expert on fatal flaws.'

I wondered where this was going; if he really wanted to have a conversation about this, or if it was all some sort of tease.

'I suppose they taught you all about them at Andover,' I said, with a good dose of sarcasm.

He laughed in a way that sounded genuinely surprised. '*Andover?* Oh no. Run-of-the-mill middle class, me. Can't you tell?'

Despite myself, I was surprised, and it must have shown on my face.

Philip nodded, seeing my interest. 'Angela's the pedigree one. I'm just a blow-in. No Ivy League here.' He glanced at the door and back, pretended to whisper furtively. '*Community college*. Don't tell anybody.' He paused. 'And don't you think they let me forget it.'

I asked myself who *They* was. Angela's family? The people he golfed with? Who was I kidding - I knew who *They* were. I was surrounded by *Them*. *They* were the ones Mrs Thorpe fretted about morning till night, the ones we all jumped to attention for. The ones who pulled our strings.

He tapped his fingers on the back of the chair and there was the faint whoosh of wind outside, shivering in the branches.

'The thing about fatal flaws, though... Fatal flaws means it's all *fate*, doesn't it. Not free will.'

I folded my arms and plastered a polite smile across my face. I'd heard this one before. 'You mean, you don't have free will if you can't escape who you are.'

He pointed a finger at me as if to say *bingo*.

Despite myself a chill passed through me. *If you can't escape who you are.* He had no idea. *I* was the expert on that.

'You're quite the philosopher,' I said instead, stiffly.

He grinned, then opened the door and saluted me with his other hand resting on the doorknob.

'Thank you for letting me drop in, Sadie Kelly.'

'Good night, Mr Hundley.'

He strode off down the corridor leaving me to the darkened room, red pen lying abandoned on the desk.

Outside, the wind was dead. The trees were finally silent. I went back to my essays, telling myself I was happy that that Philip Hundley, smooth-talking, intrusive, had finally left me in peace. But for some reason, now when I tried to re-read the paragraph in front of me, I couldn't concentrate. Finally I gave up, threw the pen down in frustration, locked my office door, and went to bed.

Two days later Thorpe called me into her office and said I was to give Philip Hundley a tour of the new gymnasium. The huge indoor pool was the big draw of course. There was going to be an official opening, with ribbon-cutting and all that jazz, in a couple of weeks, but apparently Philip Hundley was getting a sneak preview. As donors with a daughter who was Horton's swimming star, it wasn't a request Thorpe was about to turn down.

'Why me?' I said.

She sniffed. 'He asked for you.'

I hated the nervous energy that spiked in me when she said it, and instinctively moved my glance in case my eyes would give something away. When I looked back I saw she'd made herself busy rifling through some papers on her desk. It occurred to me that she didn't want to meet *my* eyes. If Philip Hundley had taken a shine to me, she didn't want to know about it. And I realized that whatever I thought about being alone in a room with him didn't matter to her. I was there to be an asset to Horton. And if my assets were in the shape of a chest that a donor wanted to ogle, so be it.

I shook my head, putting the thought out of my mind. I was making too big a deal out of this. It was just a tour.

It was early evening, before dinner had quite finished, but I excused myself from the table early. I met Philip

Hundley at the entrance to the main wing - I saw his car pull up, and I trotted down the sweeping flight of stone steps to greet him. Greeting him in the open air felt safer. It was autumn, but not as cold as it should have been. He was in a suit, I saw as he extracted himself from the car, but it was wrinkled and disheveled, like he'd just stepped off a flight. When he saw me he raised an eyebrow and didn't quite smile. I felt a swell of irritation, like he was holding back, like I was supposed to work for his smiles. *Well, that's not happening.* I fought the urge to drop a sarcastic curtsy.

'How did those essays work out, Ms Kelly?' he said, slamming the car door behind him. He hit the bleeper without looking back, and there was the clunk of four doors locking shut. 'I trust Devon's was outstanding?'

Devon's *had* been good. But it was up to Philip to know that; I wasn't about to tell him and sound like I was flattering him.

'So,' he gestured, and this time smiled. 'Lead the way, Ms Kelly.'

I led him past the main house, past the dining hall, where all the lights were on and the sound of hundreds of chattering girls drifted from inside.

I punched in the code and we went in. The gym still had that new-house smell, glue and tile and metal, and a top-note of chlorine. There was an indoor running track, rooms of weight machines, a few of which the janitor had already had a tough job removing chewing gum from. I gave him a whistle-stop tour, keeping a couple of paces ahead of him at all times, and my eyes away from his.

'Annoying for you, having to show me around like this,' he said.

I stopped awkwardly. I couldn't say *yes* but I didn't feel like making a show of reassuring him either.

'Angela wanted me to, you see.' His voice tightened. 'She wants to do a press release about it for the board of directors, but she's traveling for the next couple of weeks. So I'm here to stand in.'

'Oh.' I felt a little silly then, though I wasn't quite sure why.

'I know what you're thinking,' he said, and I blushed.

No you don't. I hope you don't. I realized now that the anger I'd been feeling at him was partly at myself. The anger had been a kind of excitement, and a kind of fear. And now that he'd given me his reasons for being here, the fear had died down and I felt unexpectedly hollow.

'You're thinking I shouldn't be on the board. That this is all a charade, when I'm only here because of my wife's money.' He pushed open the door of the weight room, and I saw his reflection bouncing back at me everywhere in the angled mirrors. He smiled, and there was no bitterness in it. 'And you'd be right, Sadie Kelly.'

He closed the door and looked at me.

'Well, I won't have it for long.' He shrugged. 'The money.'

I had no idea what he meant by that. I turned away, led him quickly down the corridor. The smell of chlorine tickled my nose, mixing with his cologne.

'I hope your daughters have been enjoying the new facilities,' I said in the blandest voice I could manage.

'Stepdaughters,' he said, eyeing me. 'Technically.'

I looked at him, not understanding.

'Your pupils, Ms Kelly. I'm their stepfather, I'm Angela's second husband. You didn't know?'

I shook my head.

'I'm devoted to them,' he said. 'I call them my daughters. But...' he shrugged.

He was watching me, waiting to see how it shifted my impressions of him. And it was true: he seemed less untouchable now. I saw the wrinkles in his clothes again, and the patch where he'd forgotten to shave. He seemed a lot less like a god. The house, the money, the clothes, the daughters, it was just a life he'd married into.

I realized that he was looking at me too, that he'd been staring at me just as frankly as I'd been staring at him. Before I could think about it any longer, I pushed the door open to the swim hall and marched through.

The huge, vaulted ceiling loomed above us, and the only sound was the soft hum of the pool's heating system, and the lap of the filter. The floor-to-ceiling windows flooded the place with sun during the daytime, but now it was almost dark, and the light was grey, and the pool's surface was inky. I looked around for the light switch and swept my hand across the wall to find it, but couldn't.

'Leave it,' Philip said. And even though he'd just told me all the reasons he was just a regular Joe like me, that he wasn't someone to take orders from, I still felt like that was what I was doing, taking orders, and despite myself, a little thrill ran over my shoulders. I let my hand drop by my side. The heating system abruptly clicked off, and the silence thickened. We glanced at each other. He moved forward, to the edge of the pool, and stooped and dipped his hand in.

'It's warm.'

'Oh,' I said, and my voice sounded odd.

He looked around at me, examining my face. His own

was unreadable in the shadows by the water's edge. He straightened, and when he stood up again I realized how close he was standing, just an arm's length away. He reached out the hand he'd dipped in the pool, reaching towards my bare arm, just where the sleeve of my t-shirt ended. His hand glided, just grazing my skin, then drew back. I stepped back, and shivered.

'See?' he said. 'Warm.'

Outside, the moon was coming up.

. *

After things between us began, I existed in only two states: being with Philip, and thinking about being with him. It was hormones and energy and a rush like skydiving when he put his hand on me. When people say *I lost my head* I'd never understood how literal it feels. I felt like I had no logic any more, no sense of consequence, no awareness of tomorrow.

He'd told me the situation with him and Angela. How they hadn't been living as a couple for years now, but she wanted the "stability" of having him around for the girls on the couple of weekends per month that they came home from school, since Angela travelled all the time for business and was rarely home. How when she was, they slept in separate rooms. How they'd already filed for divorce, but weren't telling the girls until this summer, when it was all complete.

I heard it all hungrily. I didn't want to play the role of other woman; I wasn't breaking up a home. I was just doing something crazy, stupid, unhealthy, where the only person I could really hurt was myself. At least that's what I thought then.

I began to see the different sides to Philip, and each side I saw fascinated me more than the last. He was changeable as the weather. Quiet and pensive some days, and on other days jolly and full of stories. I admired how he'd kept his career as a doctor and how much he cared about it, even though Angela - so he told me - said he'd be better off giving it up and just drawing a salary from her company. But he hated being bored, and he wanted to keep doing something with his life that he cared about. I liked his moodiness, too, the way he'd be lost in thought and far away, and then suddenly bright as if the sun had come out. There was so much going on it was like being in the eddy of a whirlpool, and I was whirled along. There was something vulnerable, too, about the way he changed and shifted, as if like his energy told all his secrets. He couldn't hide himself away like I could.

I wasn't focusing at my job but no one complained. I'd start reading a paragraph from one of the student essays, and have to reread it ten times - or I'd stop at the end of a paper and realize I'd absorbed nothing.

The week seemed long until I saw him. Sometimes he'd surprise me, texting me that he was here, in the car park, waiting. Other times he'd give me notice and I'd wait for him on the road, outside the gates, under the chestnut trees. I felt I could hear the car coming, that I could tell its particular sound from a distance, and at the first glimpse of the shining metalwork round the corner I didn't bother to hide from myself how my heart leapt. I'd fling myself into the passenger seat and he'd give me just a sideways glance and half-smile and keep driving, but it was never long until we pulled over, because the air in the car was too thick with desire, we both knew I couldn't wait that long to get my hands on him.

It was five days after the swimming pool tour when I walked out of the dorms on a Sunday afternoon and found him smoking a cigarette. I wasn't even surprised. I stepped out onto the cobbled square, not closing the door all the way. We weren't in a private space. A student could have appeared at any moment. But it was a quiet, February Sunday. No one was around.

'The girls were home for the weekend. I just dropped them back,' he said, shrugging.

'Their dorm is the other side,' I pointed out. He was at the wrong corner of the East Wing.

He just smiled at that, didn't respond. He dropped the cigarette and ground it out causally.

'Want to go for a drive?' he said.

And just like that, I got in. I didn't even think about if anyone was watching. As we crunched along the gravel through the grounds, out towards the black gates, I didn't look anywhere but straight ahead. I think I barely realized I'd actually climbed in, that I was really here, sitting in his car, my knees inches from his hand on the clutch. We passed through the gates. I found myself studying that hand. Its golden skin, its faint blond hairs.

He laughed, then, startling me. I found my gaze darting upwards, finding his. His eyes weren't on the road where they should have been.

'I don't bite,' he said. His eyes slid sideways, taking me in.

'That's what I thought,' I said, not looking at him. 'All bark and no bite.'

His laugh seemed to come all the way up from his feet, and it made my toes curl with a strange pleasure.

'Where are we going?' I said, though it was just out of curiosity. I felt strangely unworried; free.

'We can go anywhere you like,' he said, then glanced at me again. 'Within reason.'

I didn't have anywhere I wanted to go. I didn't *want* to go anywhere. I just wanted to stay in this car, beside this man, feeling the whir of the engine carrying us into an unnamed future. I rolled down the window, taking in the cool, drizzly air. It cut through my lungs like a drug.

'I shouldn't be here,' I said. But it didn't sound like an objection, just a fact.

He glanced at me. 'Probably not.'

I looked out the window, the roads whipping by. 'I don't have anywhere to be,' I said.

I saw him in profile, the side of his mouth tucking a small smile.

'I know where I'll take you,' he said.

I watched him, left hand on the wheel at seven-o-clock, so sure and calm. His right hung loosely over the gear-stick. From the side of my eye I watched his baby finger, the calloused edge of it, and how close, how very close, it seemed to my bare skin.

We were driving towards Bantam Lake, I realized, back in the direction of Milham, almost. We glimpsed the water, darting in and out from between the trees, and then we took a side turn onto a smaller road and drove on until we pulled in at a marina. He parked, got out, slammed the door. I had a brief reality check and felt for my phone through the pocket of my skirt - *it's fine, Sadie* - then popped the door, not wanting to show my confusion. Philip held up a finger to say *wait*, then clicked the controls and the trunk opened. He pulled out a picnic basket, one of those wicker ones. He'd planned this.

'Come on,' he said over his shoulder, snapping the button so the trunk eased shut, made its smug clicking noise.

I followed him down the pier.

'This is it,' he gestured.

So the Hundleys had a boat. Of course they did. I squinted at the name written across the bow.

'The Dolores.'

He climbed aboard, but I didn't follow. He turned, raised an eyebrow. I hesitated.

'I'm a very good sailor,' he said. 'You needn't be worried.'

That's not why I'm worried.

He looked at me and put out a hand. There was something natural about it, and confident and vulnerable at the same time. I put my hand in his like we both knew I would. His palm was warm, not too dry, not damp either. It wrapped round mine.

On the boat he threw me a life jacket and busied himself with the ropes, securing things, loosening things, I couldn't tell. He freed the rope from the moorings, started the engine, and cut it when we were out in the water, picking up wind. I'd been glad for the sound of the motor, it had made it impossible to talk. Now in the relative silence it felt very quiet, and we seemed very alone. Was this crazy? Surely only a crazy woman would go out into open water - farther from shore, much farther, than I could possibly swim - with a strange man. I surreptitiously pulled my phone from my pocket and checked it.

'No signal,' Philip said. I started. Obviously I hadn't

been as surreptitious as I thought. He was looking at me with a small smile playing on his face. 'Am I right? No signal - we're in a dead zone here.'

'Oh,' I swallowed, putting it away.

'Don't worry,' he tapped the space by the tiller. 'Coastguard radio. You get in trouble, you call for help. You're not as alone as you feel, on the water.'

'So.' I cleared my throat. 'How'd you learn to sail?'

He smiled. 'I've always loved messing about on boats. It runs in the family. My dad was in the navy. I thought I would be too, but I ended up in the army. For a while.'

'Really?'

He nodded. 'Made good friends there. Lost some, too.' He glanced my way. The humor had left his eyes. He looked older now, sadder.

'Who did you lose?' I asked, thinking of Fiona.

He sighed. 'Someone I served under in Iraq. We became friends. I couldn't believe it when I heard he'd died.'

I felt a rush of something then, a sense of belonging. Here was someone who would understand. I hadn't expected something like this, not from this man who seemed to have everything, and a life so unlike mine.

'I lost someone too,' I said. 'My best friend. When we were eighteen.'

He turned from the tiller, eyes fully on me, taking me all in. 'What happened?'

'Car accident,' I said, as though that was the full truth.

'I'm sorry,' Philip said softly. I felt my face was probably red, so I turned it into the offshore breeze.

'Ms Kelly.'

I looked at him, my cheeks definitely warm now, the teasing way he'd used my name.

'Open that.' He nodded to the picnic basket parked on the bench beside me. I lifted the flaps. Champagne. Strawberries.

'Are we celebrating?' I said.

He turned and the light came out from behind the clouds and caught him. I admired how the shaft of sun fell on him, on his cheekbones; his straight, slim nose, his jaw.

'My divorce, if you must know.'

I blinked. 'Your *divorce*?'

'We filed the first part today.' He glanced at me. 'Open it.' He nodded to the champagne.

When the foam spilled over my hands I looked up to see him giving me a devilish grin. He checked the lines quickly and, seeming satisfied to leave the boat steady for a few minutes, flopped down on the seat beside me. I took a breath. Suddenly so close. I thought, *you're like a frog in boiling water, Sadie.* He'd given me just enough space that at each moment I had felt just on the safe edge of the cliff. A couple of hours ago I could never have pictured myself here, inches from him, like this. And yet I'd been complicit in every small choice along the way. Into the car, onto the dock, aboard the boat - I'd been inching further and further without noticing. Or telling myself I wasn't noticing.

With his head flung back on the white leather upholstery, his easy grin, he seemed so youthful. He wasn't like Angela at all. He was so boyish, more of a teenager than a dad.

'Your style doesn't really suit you, you know. Those-' I gestured at his trousers, starched and knife-pleated down the middle. They were like what I imagined old men wear to the country club.

'These?' Philip pulled at the fabric. 'Our housekeeper does these.' He said the word *housekeeper* like it was ironic.

'Don't act like you don't enjoy having one,' I smirked.

He grinned, then swiveled his head to look at me. 'Don't worry, Ms Kelly, I know what I like.'

My throat felt warm. The smooth way the words rolled out of him

He reached for the champagne. A breeze cut through the air, playing with the curls above his forehead. He brought one of the glasses to the neck of the bottle, waited for the foam to die down, and filled it again to the brim then passed it to me.

'Carpe diem, Ms Kelly.'

It was a cliché of course, but a self-aware one, and his grin was so irresistible. A thrill passed through me and then a wave of something else, an excitement that was more like panic. What was I doing here?

You didn't do anything, a soothing voice in my head said. *You only agreed to go for a drive.*

I hadn't *done much* with men in general. When Fiona was around, she was always the one they were interested in. And after Fiona - well, after everything that happened, I didn't feel like I deserved to be with someone. I didn't want anyone to know the truth, the real truth, about me.

He was looking at me. My face must have turned serious.

'Want to learn to sail?'

I wished he'd drop his eyes from mine. I felt like he could read me too easily. I cleared my throat.

'That depends.' I kept my voice light.

He smiled. 'On what?'

'On how good of an instructor you are.'

The smile broadened. His hand, lying on the upholstery right beside me, tweaked the hem of my skirt. It was a teasing move, but more than that. I tried not to let him see my breath catch. My leg had been inches from his hand for the whole drive but he hadn't touched me at all. Now it felt like something had been acknowledged that I couldn't go back from. A line crossed.

He tugged again, moving me closer, then took the glass from my hand and refilled it. Then he took a strawberry and bit off the stalk, dropped the berry into the glass and handed it to me. He didn't smile, just watched me drink. When I stopped he smiled a little, and motioned with his hand in a way that said *go on.* I sipped again. And again. When the glass was finished he took it from me, very gently.

This time I couldn't hold back the gasp, and his palm was cool and rough as it grazed my thigh. He smiled.

'I think you'll find I'm a very good instructor,' he said as he leaned in, sliding my skirt an inch higher.

It was all I could do to keep breathing.

Thirteen

If there were any noises in the corridor last night, I couldn't tell - I was too busy tossing and turning, images of Philip Hundley and me, half-memory half-dream, flooding my sleep. Now it's morning and still I can't get Philip Hundley out of my head. The shock of him last night, waiting for me, grabbing me in the dark... our talk in the car. It all seems like a dream now. A strange dream. Except I know it's not. Because I have a text from him this morning.

See you soon, Sadie, it says. Didn't he hear what I said last night? But Philip Hundley isn't used to being told no. Is this sick feeling in my stomach excitement or fear? I realize that this is what I've always felt around him, a kind of excitement that can't quite tell the difference between pleasure and danger.

At two o'clock we meet out front to take the bus to the swim meet. I take an empty seat near the front and hear a shocked hiss from one of the girls. When I turn around and see her face it clicks: it's Devon's seat, they'd all been leaving it empty on purpose. It's silent except for the radio. In the seat across from me, Nessa sits looking wretched. Coach Ned gives a little pep talk as we arrive at the venue but it doesn't help.

'Devon would want you to do your best,' he says at one point, and I see Nessa grimace like his words make her want to throw up. Yeah, me too.

When the bus pulls up and we all start filing out, it's worse. It was like they'd been waiting for us. All these heads turning in our direction. There must have been eight or ten other private buses all pulled up, the coaches pretending to shuffle their students along and not to stare but in reality staring more than anyone.

'Ned,' one of the other male coaches strides up towards us. He clasps Ned's shoulder in a gesture of support that looks fake. 'What a terrible thing. So sorry to hear it.'

He steers Ned off to the side then, obviously wanting to hear all the gory details.

Now here we are in the hot, clammy hall that smells like chlorine. I pat my pockets for the Klonopin, wondering how subtly I can pop a tablet without the girls noticing me. We're sitting on the bleachers about half-way up. There are boys' teams here as well as girls'. Apparently the boys' teams go first and then the girls. *Big surprise,* I want to say, *when do we ever put girls first?* When they finally vanish, apparently.

Another whistle blows, and the figures lined up at water's edge dive in. There's shouting and cheering, and the claps bounce off the tiled walls and seem to be coming from everywhere.

Nessa's eye is recovering pretty well. I watch her go down for her race, looking awkward and pale. But then as soon as she hits the water all the awkwardness disappears. In the water she's beautiful.

Beside me I hear a deep sigh from Ned. I turn and he gives me a shaky smile. Devon's absence is probably as painfully obvious to him as it is to the girls.

'I heard about the thing with your car,' I remember. 'Did you get it fixed yet?'

He looks embarrassed.

'I feel pretty stupid about that. I'm fine. I was really lucky, honestly.' He clears his throat and glances back down towards the pool. 'It's just hard to believe, isn't it? How she's just...gone. I mean, what *happened* to her? Shouldn't they have found her by now? Even if it was... you know. Bad news...'

I flash back to Devon's narrow face watching as I left Horton that day, dragging my belongings out to the taxi in disgrace. I saw it, I know I saw it. The tiny smile before she dropped the curtain back in place.

I feel a little light-headed suddenly, dry in the mouth. I grab my canteen from my bag and stand up, inch down the bleachers. Near the end of the row Nessa sits with her chin in her hands, white-blonde hair gathered under a swimming cap, just one pale baby-fine streak escaping out the back. She doesn't look at me as I pass.

There's no water fountain in the corridors outside, so I follow the signs for the women's bathroom. There are voices talking as I walk in, coming from the stalls. The door swings silently closed behind me.

'I hear her mom is kinda nuts,' one says. It's a younger voice. I can't put a face to it but I recognize it as a Horton student. 'It was her dad - stepdad I mean - who ran the show,' the voice continues.

I'd like to think they're talking about someone else, but there's only one obvious topic of conversation for today.

'Yeah,' the other voice chimes in. 'I remember hearing her mom was weird. *Him*, though,' the voice says slyly. 'Yum-*my*, right?'

'I know, right?' the first one laughs. 'He's totally hot.'

I go red to my roots. *But it wasn't like that,* I think. He wasn't betraying his wife. I remember the boat, us toasting his divorce papers. Then the cisterns flush, and I'm busying myself filling up the canteen when the girls come out. Ella Schmidt and Drew Hearne.

'Hi, Ms Kelly,' they say, blithely.

You're only fifteen, I want to scream at them. But so what? Devon was only sixteen, and apparently she was old enough to get on her bike and vanish into thin air.

We're on the coach home when my phone pings again.

Philip: *What's going on, Sadie?*

I silence it and put it in my pocket.

*

What's going on, my imps? That was what Jan would always say to us as kids, when she found us in Fiona's room, making a fort under her bed or mummifying the Barbie dolls. *Little imps, what are you up to?*

I could have told her some of what her daughter was up to. I could have told her about the mystery boyfriend that Fiona had recently begun boasting about - but then I didn't know much about him. When she started getting sent chocolates or flowers, at first I honestly thought she must have sent them to herself. I ran through in my head the boys we knew, but I couldn't see any of them making a gesture like this. But apparently he wasn't one of them. He didn't go to Milham High; he was older, Fiona said, already graduated.

I met him at The Reef, Fiona said. The Reef was a club night near Milham where some of the gang liked to go. I'd only gone once or twice. That crowd had always been more Fiona's friends than mine, and now that we were growing apart I was starting to feel like an outsider. An outsider in Milham, and an outsider at Horton.

They could have been worse to us, at Horton. They didn't make up songs about us, didn't empty trash cans on our beds, there weren't rituals of public humiliation. They mostly just ignored us, like they ignored the women in the cafeteria who wheeled the trolleys of dirty dishes back to the kitchens. But there were moments. Like when I saw a few girls from my Calculus class giggling in the gym over Fiona's brand of body spray, and if they didn't say the words *white trash* I heard it anyway. They thought the same about Fiona's sneakers, about her hair-ties that had rhinestones in them, about her book bag with fake-Burberry trim. It had never occurred to me that those things spoke a language, that you could be betrayed by the things you held your hair up with. And still, every time Fiona was asked to repeat in class, there'd be a shifting like leaves rustling behind us, faint but perceptible, single drops of suppressed laughter like raindrops. I thought I knew what girls were like, until I met those girls.

It changed how Fiona was back in Milham, the weekends or holidays when we went home. The Milham group hadn't changed, and now Fiona leaned into their admiration in a way she never had before. Before, where she'd just accepted the boys' attention, now she seemed to breathe it like air. The other girls started to like her a little bit less.

We started going out to clubs with fake IDs. Boys, strangers, liked chatting to her, offering to buy her a drink. She was still Fiona, she was still a smart girl, too smart to get into a stranger's car, but I worried sometimes that the smart girl would get buried, just long enough for one terrible thing to happen. A guy who says *wanna smoke outside* or *let's take a walk*, and then they're out the side door and in a back alley, a hand over her mouth and her back against a wall. It could happen. It does happen.

That's why I'd wanted to stay part of that world, at first - to watch over her. But she'd made it clear she didn't need me for that.

I looked up from my composition paper, over to Fiona's bed where she was admiring the recent delivery of flowers, her finger moving softly over the petals of a pink rose. She'd put the arrangement on her nightstand, still in its cellophane.

'Sadie, what's a selkie?' she said out of nowhere.

There was something in the way she said it that made me feel like we were kids again. She'd always been the whiz in school but I was the one who knew the long words and always wanted to use them. The question caught me off-guard but I smiled.

'Don't you remember?' I said. I pictured Fiona and me in her house, a sleepover, Jan reading us bedtime stories. Jan was part-Irish too, she'd always liked the Celtic myths. I can still see the big volume she owned with its dark, swirling illustrations. I told Fiona about the selkie story, the woman under an enchantment, a seal-woman who's trapped on land, blending in with the humans; who can't go back to the ocean.

She looked thoughtful when I said that. Her hands stopped their motion. She eyed the rose, then pinched her fingers and pulled a petal until it snapped off.

'That's us,' she said, and across the room her eyes met mine. I knew what she meant of course. I knew it instantly. We were trapped here, trying to walk and talk like the

Horton humans, but inside we longed for the sea. The ocean we couldn't go back to.

I asked her why she'd brought it up and she shrugged, but I saw the way her eyes slid from mine, like there was something she wanted to hide. She went back to examining her roses and from the corner of my eye I saw another petal snap off, and flutter to the floor.

Fourteen

Omar's fixed the window, and my room looks normal again, but I'm having trouble falling asleep. My brain's running too fast, unable to shut down. I get up and take one of the Klonopin. It's Philip - the thoughts of him are what's keeping me from sleep tonight. He's messaged me twice since last night, and I'm having trouble ignoring the messages. But I don't know what to do *but* ignore them.

I'm remembering, though. The days last term when we'd drive off somewhere, or go out to the boat. How vividly alive the world seemed. Philip knew how to wreak pleasure from life, from the small things: a burst of sun, a cheeky ice-cream; the radio turned up loud. Being with him I felt like the teenager I'd never got to be. He was so in touch with small pleasures, and it was something I'd never been taught.

But that was then.

I'm starting to drift off finally, when I hear it.

The scratching sound by my door. I pull back the bedding, still blurry with sleep, and move clumsily to the door. I fling it open. I'm expecting an empty corridor again but - what's that? A shape, a shadow?

'Hey!' I call out.

Something near the stairwell moves. I run. I chase down the corridor, round the corner and down the stairwell, racing after the person I'm almost sure I saw. My steps aren't that loud, but they're loud enough to block out slippered feet below me. I grab the banister and run faster, breathing hard.

A breeze comes through the side door, cracked open onto the quad. The door's moving in the wind - or from whoever just went through it. I seize it open and scan left, right. The cobbles shine like teeth. The sky is clear, and it's very cold. I step outside. Stone like ice under my bare feet. I take a few steps, out past the circle of light from the East Wing.

My ears are listening so hard they almost ring. Is it just my imagination? There's something… some hitch in the darkness. A shadow in not quite the right place. An absence of noise.

When I hear a sound behind me I spin on my heel, gasping. I see a flicker of movement by the wall of the chapel. Quickly I spin the flashlight up. No one.

'Who's there?' I call out into the night.

'Sadie?' a voice says. Someone steps into the beam of light.

Ned?

'What are you doing out here?' Ned has campus accommodation too - outside the main dormitories, of course, as housing a man in the same building wouldn't be 'proper'. But why is he out and about at night?

It's starting to drizzle, slicking his hair to his forehead. He looks up at the sky and back at me.

'Sorry if I scared you. I can't sleep - I thought some air would help.'

'Oh.' I lower the flashlight beam.

'It's just, the meet today,' he says. 'It kind of got to me.' He pauses. 'What do *you* think, Sadie? Is she coming back?'

'I wish I knew.'

He's quiet; we both are. For a moment it's like we're

listening together, waiting.

Where are you, Devon?

But the wind says nothing. Devon Hundley is silent.

I crawl into bed for the second time tonight. I touch the locket around my neck - it's cold from the outdoor air, tapping my chest-bone like a small icy hand.

Nobody made this much fuss of me, did they? Fiona's voice echoes in my mind.

I'm sorry, Fiona, I think into the darkness. *God dammit, I'm sorry.*

Then the exhaustion takes me over and pulls me down, down, into a welcome black nothingness.

*

In between third and fourth period I jog up to the vending machine on the third floor and get two cereal bars to substitute for the breakfast I missed, and head into the staff bathroom to rinse out my coffee flask.

'Oh!'

Simone startles, quickly dropping her phone back into her bag and swiping at her eyes. She's turned away from me, but I can see her in the mirror. I stand another awkward moment before she turns around, sheepish and red-eyed.

'Simone, are you... okay?' Who was she talking to, or texting, that has put her in this state?

'I'm fine, Sadie.' One eyebrow raises like she doesn't know what I'm talking about. She does a great impression of having nothing wrong - except for the blotchy eyes.

Well, if she wants to keep secrets, that's her business. I'm not one to talk.

She sniffs, and turns on the faucet.

'Did you get roped in to do a study hall today?'she says as she washes her hands, obviously eager to change the conversation. 'Thorpe told me Ned's down with food poisoning, so gym's canceled. So guess who gets to supervise a bunch of restless freshmen for an hour?' She grimaces.

'Food poisoning?' I say. That's weird - he seemed fine last night.

'I know. Do you think it's secretly a hangover?' Simone grins at me, and the teary person I walked in on has vanished completely. She switches off the water and reaches for a towel.

'Hey, Simone?' I say, hesitating. 'You haven't had anything of yours go... missing, recently, have you? '

She rolls her eyes at me. 'Just my will to live'.

*

I'm finishing classes for the day, packing up the room when my phone pings. My chest does that too-familiar squeeze, somewhere between dread and excitement. *I've told him no.* I hit the locked screen and the message flashes up. Sure enough, Philip.

Sadie, please. I need to see you. It's not what you think. I'll explain when you get here. I'm sending a car. It'll be there in 20.

Then another message. This one just says: *Please come.*

He's not giving me much choice about this, is he? What does he mean, it's not what I think? I lock the classroom door behind me, hurry to the East Wing and change. I'm down outside the gates in fifteen minutes, standing on the road so I can stop the car before it turns in. The less visible, the better.

I wave it down once I see the indicator flicker.

The driver is quiet as an undertaker. His hands grip the wheel and dappled shadows fall across them as we go up the tree-lined drive to the Hundley house.

Philip was the first person I rang after Thorpe called me into her office for our "discussion" that day. I was sure her reasons for asking me to leave weren't about Philip. If she'd known about *that*, she wouldn't have been able to keep the rage out of her voice. As it was she'd been crisp, impersonal, cool. She'd talked about "fit": in other words, how I wasn't one. I'd held it together till I got back to my room, and then I'd fallen apart. I wiped my eyes, pulled up Philip's number. It rang out, I had to dial again before he picked up.

Sadie? he'd said, his voice full of a strange caution. Not at all like his usual self. When I told him what happened he was full of concern, but still his tone was strange. Distant. The concern you'd show for a colleague or a friend you haven't seen in a while. I was too upset to notice at first. I worked my way through the tears and into anger. *Who does she think she is,* I'd fumed. *Telling me I'm not good enough.*

He asked me if I needed money. And I did, the 'handshake' Thorpe had suggested wasn't going to tide me through the season. But something in the way he asked it made my hair prickle.

No, I'd said. *I don't need money.*

I waited for him to say *can I come see you* or *I'm here, what do you need?* but instead he cleared his throat. Said he felt really bad for me, but in the circumstances, it seemed like as good a time as any to-

He trailed off. *To what, Philip?* My defenses were rising. I told myself I was wrong. He wasn't about to do

what I thought he was about to do.

And then his voice started to shake. It all came out in a rush, garbled, like it was choking him. How Angela had come to him a couple of nights ago. That she'd told him some things. That he was sorry but-

But what? What could she possibly have told him now to make him change his mind?

Everything's starting to feel different, he said.

I held my breath. He'd been so sure. He'd made it sound like the divorce was a done deal. *You filed the paperwork,* I said. *You made the decision. Both of you.*

He said he was sorry. Sorrier than I could imagine.

And he asked me not to call him any more.

I stir myself, and realize the driver has already turned into the driveway. If there were any cop cars on the road I didn't see them. Thank God for tinted windows. Gravel rattles and crunches below us, and ahead the house rises up like a trophy.

I shouldn't be here.

Of course it's not the first time that thought has crossed my mind. If I knew what was good for me, I probably shouldn't have been here that night in July either. Or that weekend in August.

I shouldn't have snooped in the living room, examining the silver-framed photos.

I shouldn't have kissed Philip in the kitchen.

Or let him hoist me up on the marble kitchen island. The cold of it under my thighs. My shoes falling to the floor. His hands on my bare skin. His thumbs hooking under the hem of my skirt-

I shouldn't have done any of those things.

But he said he needs my help, so here I am. What is it

about this man that makes it so hard to deny him?

'You can leave me here,' I say, once we reach the parking bay. I wait for the car to circle around and crunch back down the drive, before I go to the door. I have practice at being discreet here. I lick my dry lips, then reach out and ring the bell, and wait.

'Sadie.' He swings the door open and it hits me again how ill he looks, how pale and drawn. 'Thank you for coming.'

He ushers me in, and the cool air of the house closes round me. The chessboard tiles are so shiny I can see my silhouette in them. It's all just as I remember. The heavy smell of lilies greets my nose. I feel a rush of memories coming back, involving me in skimpy underwear Philip bought for me, presented in a perfumed, beribboned box, him smiling a sly smile as I unwrapped it.

Try them on, he'd said, standing here in the hall, almost in this exact spot. *Try them on right here.*

I blush ferociously.

'Let me take your coat,' Philip is saying smoothly, removing it from me so deftly I almost don't feel it. I half expect him to keep going, to remove the rest article by article, but no. The time for that is over. Through an open doorway I see the "hunting room". Deer heads mounted on the wall. Shining rifles in cases. Philip isn't into it, but hunting runs in Angela's family, and the guns are heirlooms. I shiver.

'Why did you ask me to come?' My voice sounds small as it echoes off the marble tile and high ceilings. I try to make it stronger. 'You said you couldn't explain on the phone.'

Philip nods. His eyebrows draw in, looking even

127

more serious.

'I trust you, Sadie. You know that?'

I nod. *But do I trust you?* comes into my head, but I say nothing. Trust isn't the point. Philip could ruin me, my career, my reputation, everything, with the snap of his fingers. Logically that should ruin him too, but that's not the way these things tend to play out. The men get a finger-wagging and *boys will be boys*. The women get dragged through the muck until they bleed. Although, believe it or not this isn't the secret I'm most scared of. If the world finds out about me and Philip Hundley, I might never teach again. But that's not the worst thing I've done. The worst thing... well, if that gets found out, it could destroy more lives than mine.

'I didn't know who to show this to,' Philip goes on, leading me towards the stairs with a *you first* gesture. He explained to me once before that men are supposed to do this, in case a woman falls down the stairs. But it unnerves me, having him walk behind me, watching me. Watching me look at this house. Angela's house. The place he chose to stay.

We reach the top of the staircase. It's a steep, shiny cascade down to those hard marble tiles. I swallow, imagining what it would be like to fall from here.

Why am I having these thoughts? What's wrong with me?

Philip gently takes my wrist, and leads me to what looks like the master bedroom. Philip goes to the nightstand on one side and opens the bedside drawer. I sneak a glance around me as he's doing it, noticing how empty the room looks, how drained, like it isn't really being lived in. The closet is open. I see Philip's shirts all hanging side by side, and an empty space - where are Angela's clothes?

'This.' He lifts an envelope out of the nightstand, puts it in my hand. The envelope has his name on it. It's stamped, addressed in careful block letters. No return address.

I unfold the sheet inside, and exhale.

'What is this? Who sent it?'

It's just one sentence. *This is all your fault.*

Philip looks at me, his cool blue eyes unreadable. I look back at the nightstand, then around me at the empty room. Hair prickles on my neck.

'Is this… Have you shown this to the police, Philip?'

He clenches his hands into fists then releases them.

'Philip, you have to show them.'

A frown crosses his face. A man who doesn't like being told what to do. Then it passes and his shoulders release.

'It's not a ransom note, Sadie. It's not like-'

'But you don't know, Philip. This person -' I wave at the note. 'This person might know something. They might have *taken* her.'

He looks at me. 'Nobody took Devon, Sadie. She *left*. She took her bike, her wallet, her phone. She ran away.' His voice sounds tired, bitter. I wonder how many times he's said these words to himself already.

'And Angela? Did you show this to her?'

Philip sighs, sinks down onto the bed, cradling his head. 'You don't understand, Sadie. Angela is… I mean, since Devon disappeared. She's not right. Anything can set her off. And she gets these, these *fantasies*. She's so paranoid. She thinks I-'

That's when we hear it. A car on gravel.

Philip blanches.

'*Fuck*. She shouldn't be - don't move,' he says. 'Don't go anywhere. I'm just - I'll come back and get you, okay?'

Before I can say anything he's racing down the stairs, leaving me on the landing. Outside the car stops.

Anywhere but their bedroom. I dart through the nearest door on the landing. I realize it as I turn the handle, see the chipped marks where a kid's stickers have been peeled off - even before I close it behind me and see the wall covered with trophies. Devon's room.

I pace across the room, stand to one side of the window and tweak the curtains just enough to see down into the sweeping driveway. But peering down I don't see Angela, or anyone.

I turn back around, listening out for voices downstairs. Nothing. I let my jelly-legs give way under me, and slump down the wall until I'm a human puddle on the thick-pile cream carpet.

I listen for the sound of the front door. Nothing. That doesn't stop me from lying down on the ground, wriggling myself under the single bed. My eyes widen. On the wooden slats under the mattress, written over and again in black permanent marker:

I hate you I hate you I hate you.

I draw a sharp breath. What does it mean? Was she writing to herself; was this depression? Or was it something else?

Maybe it's old, from years and years ago. Kids have hot tempers. Maybe I shouldn't read too much into it.

What happened, Devon? Tell me.

But she's silent. So silent, now. I hear feet on the stairs.

I force myself to stand. I remember Philip telling me on one of those perfect sunny days in his car how he'd always wanted kids. How Angela had been older than him when he married her, and was clear that she didn't want any more. But he'd married her anyway, because obviously he was smitten.

'Sadie?' Philip calls from somewhere on the stairs. 'You can come out. False alarm.'

I cross the room and open the door. He spins around, obviously thinking I was still in the other bedroom. He frowns when he sees me.

'What are you doing in there?'

'It was better than hiding in *her* room.'

He sighs.

'Well, sorry about that. It was nothing. A neighbor with a casserole.'

I glance out the windows behind me again.

'Come on.' He holds out a hand and with a twinge of misgiving I take it. There's still a jolt at the contact. The things my body shouldn't feel, it still feels. We walk down the stairs.

'Maybe you should call me a car,' I say. My nerves are still jangling.

We're back in the hall, winter sunlight creeping from the kitchen doorway across the checkerboard tiles. I step through almost automatically, even though I should be moving towards the front door instead. I can almost see us - Philip and me - in the kitchen, a vision of us from before, like ghosts. A shiver goes down my spine, but this time it's a warm shiver. Remembering.

'Your cabinet,' I say.

There's a thick spiderweb of cracks spiraling out from

the center of one glass panel.

Philip sighs.

'Was there… were you guys fighting?'

I shouldn't ask, but it spills out of me. There could be other explanations, but the tension in this house says otherwise.

'She's gone,' he says.

'Angela?' I stare at him. 'What do you mean, gone?'

'She's… she hasn't been herself since Devon - you know - since she disappeared. Angela's always been pretty, well, volatile. She needed help. Proper care,' he says lamely.

I try not to show my shock. Angela's in some kind of psychiatric care? So that's why Lucy won't come home. Because she can't. Because her mother needs to be cared for, and can't care for her.

Philip looks at me intently, probably wondering if I'm going to tell anyone about this. Of course I won't. I look past him, out at the sunlight, its winter gold on the lawns. We've walked out those doors, Philip and I, we've walked on that grass. I'd like to say I didn't pretend it was really my life - the house, Philip, everything; I'd like to say I didn't let it all rush to my head in a fit of *what ifs*… but of course I did.

I turn back to Philip, standing just outside the patches of sunlight. He's watching me. His eyes look tired but still hungry. He's not the groomed, public-facing man I'm used to.

He reaches out a hand, and I take it without even thinking. He pulls me closer. His thumb rubs small circles on my wrist.

'Stay a while,' he says. He waits a beat, eyes locked on

mine. *Please,* the eyes say.

I hesitate. He leans in.

The kiss is soft but hungry. So terribly hungry. There's a moment of quiet, blissful darkness.

'Philip.' There's a warning in my voice, but it's myself that I'm warning. 'I have to go.'

When I get back to Horton from the Hundley estate it's late. I walk up through the cold, the East Wing looming in front of me, a hulking monster in the dim light. I'm back where I told myself I wouldn't be. Back entangled in Philip Hundley's problems.

You got entangled in more than his "problems", didn't you, Sadie? Fiona's voice prods, sneering a little. I pull the hood over my head and square my shoulders into the wind.

Fifteen

When I wake, I know immediately from how bright it is that I must have slept through my alarm. I check my phone. Slept through my alarm and the breakfast gongs, first *and* second. But I can still make it in time for class. I fling back the curtains, and freeze.

Across from my window is the gym, its floor-to-ceiling glass windows facing onto the quad. And today on those windows are painted tall red letters.

Omar the janitor is already out there with the powerhose, starting to soap down the final "S". But I have no trouble reading it.

CONFESS.

Confess?

I shiver, stepping away from the window. So perfectly positioned, right there across from my window. Like the view was made just for me.

I'm quick-stepping down the hall, about to make it to first period with seconds to spare, when there's the sound of Thorpe clearing her throat just feet from me. I jump, my hand flying to my throat. When I turn, she's staring at me with something like distaste.

Wimp, I hear Fiona say. *Sadie, you wimp.*

'You weren't at breakfast today, Ms Kelly -'

Is *that* what this is about?-

'-So you'll have missed the whispers. However, I take it the - the *decoration* - of our new gymnasium has not passed you by?'

I swallow. 'Yes, I noticed. Do you have any idea-'

'I certainly do not,' she cuts me off. 'But it is a prank I plan to get to the bottom of, you can be sure. Coach tells me he locked the gym round nine p.m. and was the first to discover it this morning at seven.' She pauses. 'Your room overlooks those windows. I assume you saw nothing, shall we say, out of the ordinary, last night?'

I hope I'm not flushing. *I drugged myself to sleep again, so no, I didn't see anything.*

'I was sleeping.'

She looks at me like I'm an idiot. Because *sleeping is what people do at night, Ms Kelly.*

'Well, I'm sure it goes without saying, but if during lessons today you find this is becoming a - a topic of interest, among the students, please do your best to shut it down. This is a very delicate time for the school. Stunts like this are the last thing we need.'

I force my most agreeable yes-of-course-face, and hustle down the corridor to first period.

Confess.

It's not for me. It can't be. But all the same I know the truth; I know I'm not innocent.

I offer up a silent apology. First Fiona. Now Devon. The night I try not to think about - that I've spent ten years trying not to think about - surfaces in a flash of freeze frames. Fiona in the garden, laughing. Fiona on the stairs, lipstick smudged.

I'm the reason she's dead.

And that's not even the worst part.

But I get through the day until last period, when the ninth-graders are making their way through the Burnham Wood scene in *MacBeth*. I look out the window at the trees that border Horton's well-groomed lawns. I picture a moving forest, slowly advancing, swallowing everything in its path.

The bell rings.

Heloise Ryder, a tall girl in the front row and the closest the sophomores get to outspoken, has her hand in the air, getting my attention.

'Miss?'

I nod.

'Is she... was Devon... do they think someone's killed her, Miss?'

I can feel the blood draining from my face.

'*No*, Heloise. She wasn't - there's no -' I let out the breath and try again. 'There's absolutely no evidence of that.'

'So she *might* have been.'

Large eyes stare at me, rows upon rows of them. The desk that used to be Devon's - third row, by the window - sits empty as it has every day since I got back. No one dares sit in it.

'Heloise, let's not sensationalize. All we know is that Devon is *missing*. We're still trying to get to the bottom of where she went and why she hasn't returned. *Yet*. If you want to talk to me about this after class, please do.'

But she doesn't stay after class. Instead, they all shuffle out together in a pack, huddling, whispering. I use the internal phone to reach Omar and explain I want a desk removed.

'Be there shortly,' he says.

The school is quiet now, that down-time between the end of classes and the dinnertime gathering. I hear no footsteps in the corridors.

I take my phone out, release it from silent mode.

Philip: *When will I see you again?*

I feel that tug inside, that inconvenient tug. I remember how betrayed I felt, before. When he said he needed to stay, that something had 'changed'; that there wasn't going to be a divorce after all. How dirty it made me feel, because despite myself I had to wonder if there had ever been a divorce filing or if I'd just been another cliché, tricked into being the 'other woman' I'd never wanted to be.

I'd asked him once how he met Angela. He'd told me how his dad used to work for the Hundleys as their gardener. How Philip used to help him out sometimes in the summers. How he was infatuated with Angela back then, an eighteen-year-old boy who saw her as a princess.

That was never how he saw me.

My phone blinks again, bringing me back to the present, and I realize I have a missed call too. But to my relief it's not from Philip: this one's from Jan. I go to voicemails - Jan always leaves voicemails, she says text messages are 'too finicky'.

Just me, Sade. I was, ah, just wondering if you've heard from your mother recently. If she's been in touch at all, you know. Give me a call when you can.

That's weird. Why would she think Mom was in touch? She knows how it is between us. But I'd like to chat with Jan, I haven't spoken to her in a couple of days. I check my watch. She eats early; she'll be having dinner now. I'll try her later.

I stand, looking out the window. The windows of the gymnasium are glistening again, freshly washed. It's not yet dark, and I can see the faint glint of the pool through the glass. I walk to Devon's desk, run my hand over the surface of it. I pull out the chair, and with a glance at the door to make sure Omar isn't already outside, I sit. I close my eyes for a second, aware of the oddness of what I'm doing. Then I blink them open, sharing what used to be her view. You can see the black entrance gates from here, the tree-lined avenue, and beyond it - freedom? Danger? The world outside this bubble?

I glance back down to the desk in front of me, and startle. The words are carved into the wood in vicious cuts.

Watch your back Ms Kelly.

I hear myself gasp. I whip around, as though my class might have filed back in to see this. Do they know this is here? They must. Perhaps it's common gossip now, the words on Devon's empty desk.

I run a finger over the sharp grooves. It's the work of a pen-knife, probably one of those wildly expensive Swiss ones whose price tag Horton parents wouldn't bat an eye at.

I run through the girls that sit here in my other classes. Rowena Harrington in eleventh grade. Wei Lin Min in twelfth. Iris Okoro in the ninth grade. I run a thumb over the carved letters and try to picture any of them writing this. Iris is loud, attention-seeking, disruptive sometimes, but she doesn't have the patience for this neat and precise work. As for the other three, there isn't a rebellious bone in their bodies. I know it in my bones, it was Devon who did this.

There's a rap at the door and I stand up so fast I almost fall out of Devon's seat.

'Sadie?' Omar always greets me with a smile. Today I can't quite manage one back. 'That desk you wanted moving?'

'This one,' I say, standing to one side of it. Not wanting to touch it. Suddenly wanting to be just as far away from it as possible. I look out the window and see a car cruising slowly through the main gates onto the road. Not Simone's car or Thorpe's or Hirschfield's. Wintry sun bounces off it, masking the color, but I think I see a flash of green, just before it turns the corner.

Angela Hundley drives a car that color, gunmetal green. But it can't have been her. *Remember what Philip told you.* Angela's in a clinic somewhere. Safe. Secure. *Not here.*

*

It was Devon Hundley who'd come to fetch me the day Thorpe summoned me to her office to suggest I look for another job. Thorpe had a way of poking her head outside the office and finding the nearest loitering student to send on a mission. I'd opened the door of my office to a careful tap and Devon was standing there, pristine as usual, her cool eyes on mine. *Mrs Thorpe wants to see you,* she'd said. I was in the middle of marking papers and though I had no idea what this was about, I thought I wouldn't mind the interruption. I fished my keys from my pocket and locked up as Devon hung about in the hallway, watching me. Always the observer. The rhythmic sound of verbs being conjugated drifted up from Mme Denoel's class a few doors away. *Je dors, tu dors, elle dort...*and as I walked away, over the sound of chorusing verbs, I thought I heard her voice follow me, light as a whisper.

I thought for a moment I heard those four words that I had always dreaded.

I know your secret.

But when I turned round, Devon hadn't moved. She just stood there, silent. And I walked on.

I told myself that day that I'd imagined it. I've told myself that many times since.

*

In the morning I'm hollow-eyed, half-dead. I'm not myself these days. I'm getting to be what Jan would call 'high strung'. It's no wonder if I've been imagining things. And yet when we're doing Jane Eyre with the sophomores I can't help shivering, thinking about Bertha Rochester in the attic. The furious, insane, rage-filled wife. Her nighttime "visits" to terrorize Jane.

But Jane wasn't just an innocent victim, was she? She didn't *mean* to steal Bertha's life. But she did.

'Miss?' Rachel Calhoun says and I jerk back out of my thoughts. She sits in the far back left, the same seat Lucy Hundley sits in.

'Miss, the bell just rang.'

I nod, like I knew that all along, obviously. 'Homework's on the board, girls. See you tomorrow.'

I have a free period after that, and I use it to swallow down more coffee than I should, then let myself out for a walk in the grounds. Some of the morning dew is still frozen on the grass, and it crackles beneath me as I walk. *Lost girls*, I think. So many of us. Fiona, dead. Devon - gone. Lucy Hundley, lost in her pain. Me, lost in the past. All our voices, all our secrets, silent.

Back when I was a student here, I existed mostly in a daydream, clinging to images of how the future would be, and to my imaginary friends in books. I read constantly. Jane Eyre, Elizabeth Bennet, Cathy and Heathcliff... I walked Horton's paths and lawns, finding quiet places from where I could look back at the elegant redbrick wings and pretend it was my home, that I was Lady Catherine de Bourgh or some other aristocrat in the stories I loved. Even though Horton was cruel, it was beautiful. It was all about seeing it from the right distance.

My phone buzzes in my pocket. It's Philip.

Sadie? It reads. That's all. I shove it back in my pocket but I've wandered too far, and it's starting to rain by the time I run back across the lawns, end-of-class bell ringing. I feel like a student again, late and about to be reprimanded, when I see Thorpe's dark figure standing in the doorway, watching me hoof it across the grass.

'Ms Kelly,' she says with a nod.

'Afternoon, Mrs Thorpe.'

She looks exhausted.

'Getting some air?' she says, and I nod, surprised at what appears to be an attempt at conversation from her.

'I'd better get to class.'

'Yes,' she says, still staring out, making no move to shut the door or hurry me along. I wait, feeling like there's something more she wants to say, but the girls are milling in the corridors. Soon my second-period will be taking their seats.

'I wish they'd never come to the school,' she says abruptly. 'Those Hundley girls. That whole family.'

I stare. Thorpe always acts like it's her honor to serve them all. I guess I thought she really believed it.

A classroom door slams open next to us, and a ninth-grader catapults out, missing Thorpe by inches.

'Oh sorry, Miss. I didn't realize -'

'Once more and it's detention, Bethany,' Thorpe says

without looking round. Then she strides past me, out through the open doorway and into the rain. A line of girls stand flat against the wall as she passes, watching her like trees who've just escaped a winter storm. The heavy door closes behind her.

We all stare after her. And then I feel a buzz in my pocket, and an unknown number lights up my phone. I hesitate, then pick up.

'Sadie?' a man's voice says. Not Philip's.

'It's Rob.'

Rob? Jan's weird neighbor? Why the hell would she give him my number?

'Oh. Rob. Um -'

'Look, I don't want to worry you, I'm sure she'll be fine, but, well, Jan's in the hospital. She had a fall.'

My heart beats once, hard - impossibly hard, as if to remind me what loss, the deepest kind of loss, feels like. *No*, my brain whispers. *No*.

Sixteen

'I'm sure - I'm sure she'll be fine,' Rob says again. 'But I thought you'd want to come.'

I think I stuff the papers in my bag but I don't really know, there's just the feeling of my hands being empty as I walk down the corridor, then run, then walk because the running frightens me, like it's admitting how bad this could be - and then I'm making an excuse to Thorpe, and then I'm in my car, driving. It occurs to me that I shouldn't be driving, because I'm probably in shock, but I'm on the road by then anyway. Then it seems like no time passes before I'm at St Joseph's Hospital, standing inside the revolving doors, squeaks of rubber soles on linoleum all round me like whispers. I want to do something, say something, to protect us, me and Jan, but it's too late for that.

Focus, Sadie. Calm down.

I get directions, the elevator pings, and finally I'm outside a door. I push it open. She's lying in bed, a pink-and-white hospital robe on. Her eyes are closed and her face is pale and I think, what if she's -

'Sadie.'

I whip round.

It's Rob, sitting in an armchair against the wall. He's yawning, looking disheveled.

'It's okay. Don't look so panicked. They've given her some pain pills and they knocked her out. It's her hip.' His expression grows more somber then. 'We're waiting for x-rays. At her age, if the hip's broken, it could be a while before...'

Okay. It's bad news, but it's bad news on a scale I can deal with.

Whatever she needs, we'll figure it out.

'Sadie? Are you okay?' Rob's watching me, looking concerned. I guess my face must be showing everything. I sink into the chair beside him.

'Did you find her? What happened?'

He winces. 'Apparently she fell down the stairs. She told me she was having a nap, and then she woke up when she heard a noise. She had this idea maybe there was someone in the house. And then she was trying to look down the stairs to see, and she fell...' He turns to me. 'I don't know, Sadie. Maybe she just imagined it? There was no sign of a break-in.'

My heart thuds.

'Did she say she saw anyone?'

Rob shakes his head. 'She was a bit confused, though. She was in some pain when I got there.'

Those words bring me back to what matters. The gratitude hits me in a wave. I'd formed a negative impression of this guy, just because he's a little awkward to me and because Jan seems to like him so much. But it looks like he's earned her trust.

'Thank you, Rob. I'm grateful - I'm glad you were there.'

He clears his throat and looks away. 'No problem. I just had some shopping to drop off for her and... well. It was lucky.' He checks his watch. 'But now that you're here, mind if I -?'

'Of course not.' I force a smile. 'Please go home if you need to. You've done so much already.'

I'm distracted, though, thinking about the noise Jan heard. Her belief that someone was in the house. A year ago I'd have assumed it was nonsense: Fiona didn't get her vivid imagination from nowhere and Jan has a pile of mystery novels a foot high beside her bed. But there are the other things. The disturbances in the garden. Henry the gnome. All those anonymous phone calls that led Jan to get that location-tracking app - I'd assumed they were just spam calls, but what if it there was more to it?

Rob glances at the bed. 'If you're sure you don't mind... Tell her I'll swing by later in the week.'

'I will.'

The door closes behind him and the little *click* seems to stir Jan. I hear a murmur, and I get out of my chair to perch myself on the edge of her bed. I touch her dry hand with mine. Her eyelids flutter but don't open. She opens her mouth.

'*Fiona*,' she whispers.

I can't help it. The tears start to roll down my cheeks, like they were ready, waiting. There's nothing I can do to hold them in.

'No, Jan. Jan, darling. It's me, Sadie.'

Her eyes slowly open. I wait for her face to fall, for the ten-year grief at her lost daughter to come back in a wave. But she turns her hand under mine, clasps it. She looks peaceful, which surprises me.

'What happened, Jan?' I lean over her. 'Rob says he found you, you'd fallen down the stairs.'

She nods carefully, her head must still hurt.

'I heard something, I thought maybe it was a burglar, you know? I suppose if I were a sensible woman I'd have stayed in my room, but I wanted to check, make sure, you

147

know, so I just tiptoed to the top of the stairs and looked over the side.' She clears her throat.

'And?' I prompt her.

She glances at me, then over towards the spot by the window where Rob was sitting before. Is she looking to see if he's there before she speaks? Her expression shifts, considering, reconsidering, then she smiles and shakes her head.

'There was no one there, love. Just an old woman's imagination.'

'You're not old,' I chide her, but the hesitation bothers me. What is she not saying?

She sighs. 'I have to be more careful. Those ratty old slippers. And I was a bit agitated, you know. My hands were slippery, I was sweating.' She winks at me. '*Perspiring,* I mean.'

One of Jan's old jokes: a lady never sweats, she perspires. But now doesn't feel like the time for jokes. I feel sure she's hiding something from me, but I can't say what. If someone really had broken into her house, she wouldn't want to conceal it. And she doesn't seem that anxious.

So I don't push her to report anything to the police. She doesn't want to - and I don't want her getting a reputation with them as "that" kind of lady, and not taking her call seriously if something really does happen one day. But still, it troubles me.

The hospital says the fracture is clean, so they don't expect there to be complications, but they remind us that recovery time can be unpredictable in older patients. They'll keep her for another few days to be sure there's no infection, but hopefully a week from now she'll be recovering at home. Jan takes all the news uncomplainingly. She seems oddly happy, serene, despite the circumstances.

I take over the chair I found Rob in, and after a while Jan goes back to sleep. I curl up in the chair, watching her peaceful breaths. That moment plays over in my mind: *Fiona*, she whispered, holding my hand, like for a moment she thought her child had come back to her.

I sit, and remember.

*

Everyone knew about Octavia Dennison's graduation party. She'd even put a sign up on the notice board in our dorms. It was supposed to be self-selecting: no one at the bottom of the social pyramid would put themselves through the misery of showing up. But that sort of thing didn't work on Fiona. She hadn't seemed to care about the Horton girls' approval in the last couple of months, since she'd been dating her new guy. She'd started acting superior, repeating to me the things he'd obviously been telling her: how the other girls were shallow, and jealous. I didn't think it was jealousy, I thought it was something crueler and colder than that, but I was happy to go along with whatever was working for Fiona's self-esteem.

It was May, still bright, almost warm. I saw Fiona's car in the drive and swallowed down the apprehension - I didn't want to go, but she'd talked me into it. But the minute I opened the door I knew something was wrong. Her outfit was fabulous but her eyes were red-rimmed, she looked dishevelled and shrunk down somehow, like she'd spent the day curled in a ball on her bed.

'What is it?' I dropped on the seat. 'What's wrong?

Are you okay?'

'He broke up with me,' she whispered.

'Oh, Fiona...'

I wanted to sound sympathetic but in all honesty I was relieved. I didn't like that she was dating someone I didn't know. Maybe I didn't like that she was dating anyone at all. I'd never liked her growing away from me.

'He was embarrassed,' she sniffed. 'Because he was dating a, you know, a "schoolgirl". He said his friends would judge him. I figured now that I'm graduating, we'd be a real couple. But he...' she trailed off, shook her head.

'Let's not go to the party,' I said. 'Let's just stay in. We'll get some ice-cream, watch a movie -'

Fiona's head snapped back up.

'No,' she said sharply. 'I want to go. We're *going* to that party, Sadie.'

And who was I to argue?

*

When Jan wakes again she's more alert, already more like her usual self.

'Let's not keep talking about me, Sade,' she says, in her kind, brisk way. It brings a lump to my throat. 'What about you? Tell me how it's going at the school.'

'Oh, it's... fine,' I lie.

'And your mother?' she says. 'I don't suppose you've been in touch?'

I'd almost forgotten her voicemail. I shake my head, feeling guilty.

'It's just she's always at church, but I haven't seen her for a couple of weeks. I thought she might be sick, and I called her, but she didn't pick up.'

I shrug off the faint unease. 'You know how she can be, Jan. Sometimes she's not very social.' I'm sure it's not the first time Mom has ignored a call from Jan. Their relationship can be a bit frosty, too.

'Yes, I suppose you're right.' Jan gives me a smile. 'Well, go on, you don't need to be hanging round here all day. Come and see me at the weekend, will you? If I'm still here?'

I plant a kiss on her cheek. 'You know it.'

I get back in the car and take the road out to Jan's. The afternoon's getting late, but I just want to check the place over. Jan and Rob both seemed certain there was no intruder after all, but I'd feel better vouching for that myself.

I pull up outside the house and already it feels lonely without her. I open the gate and walk up to the front door, checking for anything out of the ordinary. Nothing, no signs of forced entry. I rummage in my bag for keys and quietly let myself in. The house is silent, nothing but some motes of dust drifting in a beam of five-o'clock sunlight.

Footsteps.

I freeze.

The footsteps are coming from *my* room. The room above the living room. Jan's room is above the kitchen.

A door opens, closes. Someone at the top of the stairs.

'*Rob?*'

He flashes me that bland smile.

'Oh, Sadie, hi again. Hope I didn't scare you.'

'You did actually.' What's he doing here?

'I just thought it would be good to come by,' he says. 'Check on everything. Make sure it all looked normal.'

My heart rate starts to slow.

'Oh. I guess we had the same idea then.'

He smiles. 'I guess we did.'

He comes down the stairs, dusting his hands.

'Anyway, it all looks fine up there.'

I nod.

'Shall we go, then?'

He gestures towards the door. Part of me wants to stay, I don't know what for. But he's right: we've checked the place over. I've seen for myself, no forced entry. But I'm back in the car, hands on the wheel, before I let my body relax.

He's good to Jan, I remind myself. *You're very lucky he was there.*

I shake off the feeling and start the car. There's one more stop I want to make.

Seventeen

I take the car left out of Jan's road and keep going - past the minimart, the post office, the dry cleaner's, past my old school.

I don't really think there's anything to worry about. What I said to Jan was true. But maybe it's the lingering shock of today, the fear I felt hearing about Jan's fall... Maybe it's time to try and heal things with Mom.

It's over a year now since we've spoken. That's a long time, but there are reasons.

Jan became everything to me growing up, because Mom wasn't. Jan was the one who encouraged me, who hugged me, who told me all the time how proud and impressed she was by me: by the things I'd learned, the prizes I'd won, the tests I'd aced. If I ever brought home a piece of work that teachers had praised to show Mom, she'd go tight-lipped and tell me not to brag. She was always suspicious of me getting above myself, thinking maybe I needed taking down a peg or two. But what six- or seven-year-old needs that? As far as I'm concerned, Jan is more or less entirely responsible for me having any self-esteem at all.

And then when I'd called her from Hong Kong to say I'd seen a job posting for Horton and I was thinking of applying - of moving home - I thought despite everything she might be happy. That over the years, despite how fraught our relationship had always been, she might have actually missed me. But she just stayed silent. When I thought maybe we'd lost the connection, she finally spoke:

I thought you had more brains than that.

That was the last straw for me. *Almost thirty years of this,* I thought. *Enough.* So when I got the job I never told her. I left it to Jan to pass the message along. I stopped calling. And she didn't call me. I'd said some harsh things to her in that conversation too. I guess we were both too proud to try and pave things over.

The thing is, I admire my mother. I always have. She's so capable, so resourceful, always so in control. She doesn't make a list when she goes shopping because she never forgets a single thing. She's the kind of person who never burns rice and ends up having to soak the pot, and her stockings never have holes in them. If she says she'll do something, she does it, and she keeps every promise she ever makes. As a kid I just always wanted her to admire me, even a little bit as much as I admired her.

But now I turn in on Holly Crescent, a street that doesn't look all that different from Jan's, and which has changed almost as little over the last twenty years. I downshift to second gear. It's all so familiar. I have a sudden, vivid memory of Fiona, lodged in the scraggly tree in our front yard. She was wearing a Wonder Woman costume she'd got for her birthday - I had to play the baddie of course. I can still see it: me standing against the railing, its blistered paint rubbing against my spine through the thin t-shirt, Fiona swooshing her cape about on the tree branch as she prepared for her heroic leap. The smell of tree sap in the air.

I'm here. Number 35. I slow the car to a stop, look out the window, and gasp.

This is not right.

There's graffiti on the gate. The bins are tipped over,

trash strewn everywhere like a racoon got to it. The place is a mess. It looks abandoned.

And I know without a second's hesitation: Mom would never, *ever* let her house get like this. The weeds, the overgrown hedge - that might not be a telltale sign for everyone, but Mom... in the past I wouldn't have been surprised to see her out there with a nail-scissors and a fine-tooth comb. She is obsessively neat. Maybe it was something to do with the teenage pregnancy, with having to prove something to the world. But her house and yard are always *immaculate.*

I walk up to the front door. Weeds are starting to poke through the gravel. The hedge separating the neighbor's yard is raggedy with new growth. I ring the bell, but I already know no one will answer. I edge down into the grass, peering into the front room, but the lace curtains are still there, and I can't make out anything inside. I continue round the house, to the side window that overlooks the kitchen. There are pots and pans hanging up, but nothing in the draining rack, nothing in the sink, no sign of recent use.

I pull my phone from my handbag and call her, ankle deep in the overgrown grass. It rings out, not even going to voicemail. Is she ignoring it on purpose? Is she somewhere else, far away, watching my name flash on the screen, waiting for it to die? Or is it something worse?

I take a deep breath and go back onto the street and around to the neighbor's house. The neighbors have changed since I was a kid, I've no idea who's here now. When I ring the bell a gentle-faced woman in a sari opens the door. Her slight frown clears as I explain myself.

'Oh, you're her *daughter.*' She nods, as if pleased to

discover I really exist. 'I see it now, there's quite a resemblance.'

I ask if she's seen my mother around recently. I hear how strange it sounds that I don't know.

She bites her lip. 'I didn't hear many details. She just knocked on the door - oh, a couple of weeks ago, I suppose - and told me she was going away for a while.'

A weight lifts off me, though I'm more puzzled than ever. I guess it's the result of what happened to Jan today, but part of me was picturing Mom in the house, unable to come to the door, ill, or worse.

'She asked if she could leave a set of keys here in case of an emergency,' the neighbor continues. 'We do that for each other sometimes. Burst pipes, fire alarms, you know.' She trails off. 'She didn't say how long she'd be gone. I feel sorry, looking at the place though. How tidy she always kept it!' She eyes me. 'Some of the neighborhood boys have a bit of a thing against her, you know. I think they must be responsible for that graffiti.'

I'm not surprised. Mom loves calling 311.

'You don't know -' I hesitate. I can feel how she'll judge me. 'She didn't mention where she was going, did she?'

Sure enough, the eyebrows shoot up. 'I guess I figured she'd moved in with family.'

I make an apologetic, helpless face. *Family.* 'She's not calling me back.'

The neighbor looks uncomfortable.

'I wonder if... you mentioned the spare keys. Could I borrow them?' I say finally.

She hesitates, her eyes combing over my face again, perhaps checking that the resemblance really is there, that

I'm not some con artist. Finally she goes to a drawer in the hall, rummages, and puts a single key in my hand.

I let myself in, smelling the familiar smells of bleach and chamomile. I'm not sure exactly what I'm looking for. A note maybe, or a receipt for a bus or a train ticket somewhere. Signs of where she's gone. But there's nothing. I walk through the rooms and the house is like a stranger, like it can feel my presence and isn't sure about me. As if it isn't sure it remembers me, or doesn't like who I've become.

I put my hand on the banister, climb slowly up towards the bedrooms. Mom's room is on the left. I push open the door, and stop, letting out a little gasp.

Photos: so many of them. And all of me. On the nightstand, on the vanity, on the windowsill. Me at graduation. Me in kindergarten. I try to imagine her in this room, eyes drifting to all these different moments of me, frozen in time.

This wasn't what her bedroom looked like when I was here. This isn't anything like what I remember.

She misses you, I hear Jan saying. But if she missed me, why didn't she call?

'But where is she　?' I say out loud. The house doesn't answer.

*

Back at Horton, the hour is late and I'm exhausted. Questions about Mom keep me tossing and turning for a while as the wind drums against the windows, but finally they all give in to sleep. I wake feeling almost rested, and take a long shower and call Jan to check in. I don't tell her about Mom; I don't want to worry her. I get dressed and head downstairs, but by the time I'm approaching the dining hall it's clear something isn't right. There's a cluster of teachers and students all milling around, and one of the first-years is crying while a friend strokes her hair.

'It's, like, cursed,' she's saying between hiccups. 'This place, you know? I think it's, like, actually cursed.'

I look around for someone who's going to make sense of all this, and see Simone heading my way. I raise my eyebrows and she responds with her what-the-fuck face.

'It's the swimming pool,' she says, taking me to one side out of earshot of the girls. The stale smell of the morning coffee vats wafts over from beside us. 'It looks like somebody, well, dyed it.'

'*Dyed* it?'

She shrugs. 'Go and see for yourself.'

I walk down the halls to the door that exits onto the quad, Simone beside me. We go outside and stand there, looking across at the gym's tall glass windows to the pool inside.

'It's *red*.'

Simone wrinkles her nose. 'Creepy, isn't it? Hey, you kind of dashed out yesterday,' she goes on. 'Everything okay?'

I nod. 'Family stuff.'

'Girls, girls.' I can hear Thorpe from somewhere down the corridor, encouraging people to go in and get their breakfast, telling them to 'stop lollygagging' over some 'silly prank'.

Her no-nonsense tone does its work, at least for now. I spot Lucy Hundley in the corridors as Simone and I walk back to the dining hall. What must she think of all this? Meanwhile that hysterical freshman is still murmuring about Horton being "cursed".

In the middle of first period I look out the window and see a pool-cleaning team pull up in the quad and two men with a vat of chemicals and pipes get out. Simone says the pool filter would clean out the dye by itself in a couple of days - but I can see why Thorpe doesn't want to wait that long to get rid of Horton's giant bloodstain.

Simone finds me when I'm locking up at the end of the day. 'I think we both need to let our hair down after the day we've had.'

I know I could use a drink, and force a smile. Jan's accident, Mom's disappearance, all these nasty pranks - what does it mean? Am I going mad?

I check my phone as we walk over to Simone's cottage. Philip.

Sadie, are you ignoring me?

In the cottage, I wrap both hands round the wine Simone pours me. On top of the benzos I took earlier, it shifts everything into a hazy, manageable place, and I feel a weight lift off. I tell Simone about Jan's fall. I don't tell her about Mom though - I don't know how to answer the questions she might ask.

'Anyway, how are you?' I say. The cushions swallow me up, making me feel safe. The cottage doesn't feel so cold tonight. The wine is doing such a good job. I could fall asleep here.

But when I look up Simone's face is somber.

'Well, actually, Sadie...' She pauses. 'Actually, not that great. Richard and I, we're separating.'

I scooch myself up on the cushions. I have so much on my own mind it's hard to muster all the sympathy this deserves, but I can at least look the part.

'You are? Are you okay?' From what I saw, he wasn't a great husband - but I think sympathy would be more helpful right now.

'I've been better.' She looks away. She looks suddenly uncomfortable; angry almost. 'Sadie, forget I said anything. I don't really want to talk about this.'

Who am I to judge her see-saw mood?

'Anyway,' she says. 'Did you see that hatchet job the Daily Post did on the Hundleys?'

Hatchet job?

'Philip and Angela, I mean,' she goes on. 'No?'

I shake my head. 'What did they say?' What *could* they say? As far as I could tell Philip and Angela had done everything right.

Simone shrugs. 'Oh, you know. Dredging up all that old stuff. Her first marriage and everything.'

I've never thought much about Angela Hundley's first husband for some reason. I didn't realize there was much of a story to it.

'Was it a bad divorce or something?'

Simone gives me a look. 'Not *divorce*, Sade. He died. You didn't know?'

'I never heard about him,' I admit, feeling stupid and suddenly nervous.

'It was quite dramatic,' Simone says. 'Young guy. He fell down the stairs one night. They found his body the next morning. And then a year and change later, Angela ties the knot with Philip.' She looks at me. 'You can imagine *that* didn't go down well.'

I'm astounded. I'm not a gossip-hound, but Simone says this like it's common knowledge. How did I not know? How did I never ask?

'I - you know what, Simone? I'm sorry. I don't feel that well.' I put my glass down on the coffee table. Suddenly I wish I hadn't drunk it. My head doesn't feel right. 'I'm sorry. I think the last couple of days are hitting me harder than I thought.'

*

Back in my room, I pull out my laptop. The news article is easy to find, and I go down a rabbit-hole of tabloids after that. Angela's first husband was a man called Tony Hundley. I guess she kept his name and then Philip took hers. Philip's choice, or hers? To make them all look like a matching set.

All of what Simone reported is right here. Tony, a well-to-do guy from a military family. Marries Angela when they're in their early twenties. Twelve years later he's found dead in his home, a night-time fall, a fatal brain injury. And then a little over a year later she's married to Philip. The online comments are vicious and I can't help agreeing with some of them.

He never told me any of this. Did he think I already knew? Is that why he liked me - because I didn't treat him the way everyone else must have? He always said Angela's family and friends didn't like him, but he made it sound like that was because they were snobs. No wonder they don't like him. This is ugly. I slam the laptop closed. I feel dirty, tainted. I head to the bathroom, strip off and run the shower. I let it steam up the room, turning the water so hot it's barely bearable. But I can't stop my mind racing, running over all I've just read. How much of a fool I feel. All I didn't know. I step out and put on a robe. I can hear the hum of a television set from the girls' room next door. I'm patting my hair into a turban when my phone rings. I glance down at the bed and see the number.

Philip.

I don't touch it, just let it sit there on the bedspread, watching. Waiting for it to ring out. I don't know what I feel. Anger. Fear. A darkness that I can't place.

But it rings. And rings. And finally despite my instincts I pick it up, hit Accept.

'Sadie,' he says.

I lick my lips, hesitating. Even though I've already picked up, it feels like I could still backtrack now if I don't open my mouth.

'I know you're there, Sadie.' His voice is patient, gentle.

I say nothing.

'I know you're there.' He pauses. 'Alone in your room. Hesitating. Crossing your arms that way you do.'

I look down at my crossed arms, and uncross them. I step back from the phone on the bedspread, towards the window, staring at the chestnut trees in the dusk, as though they'll tell me what to do.

'Staring out the window,' he goes on. There's a hint of a smile in his voice now.

'Pretending to ignore me. Chewing your finger like you do.'

My finger drops from my mouth. My heart thumps.

'Sadie, come down.'

Eighteen

I can hear his breathing. Little hairs stand up on my arms.

'I don't want to.'

'Just come down, Sadie.'

He doesn't say it sharply, or pleadingly. His voice is quiet and simple, like he's placing an order in a café. Like there's no way I'll say no. I step back from the window and stand in the room a moment longer. Then I pull up my wet hair and take my key. My footsteps echo down the corridor. Outside the side entrance, I slink across the back of the East Wing, over the frosty grass to the main gates.

He unlocks the passenger door and pushes it open for me to get inside. I stand where I am and shake my head.

'No. I'm not getting in there.'

He watches my face another minute. I can feel it even though I'm refusing to look at him.

'What's going on with you?' he says at last. 'You won't answer my texts -'

'You never told me,' I say.

There's silence.

'You never told me about Angela's husband. About all that... about what happened.'

A pause.

'Well?' I say.

He sighs.

'I told you about Tony the first time I took you out. The boat, remember? I told you about my friend from the army. My friend who died.'

Him? Philip has no idea what that little mention did

to me that day. How I'd seen him as a version of me, someone who'd lost someone too.

'That friend was Tony Hundley? But you said he was killed in Iraq.'

Philip looks impatient. 'No I didn't. I said he was *in* Iraq.' He taps the wheel. 'Soldiers are people too, you know. They die other places besides the battlefield, just like anyone else. Why does it matter how he died?'

I fold my arms. 'It matters that you conveniently omitted how you jumped into bed with your *friend*'s wife before he was cold in his grave.'

Philip thumps the steering wheel. 'How *dare* you.' He glares at me. 'Don't talk like you know what happened.'

I swallow. His hands thumped the wheel so hard I couldn't help flinch.

'Tell me then,' I say, keeping my voice hard. 'If I don't know, tell me.'

Philip stares up at the roof, teeth clenched. Then he takes a deep breath.

'Angela married Tony the summer I left for college. I didn't see any of the family again until years later. My dad's funeral. I didn't expect to see them all there but they all came: Angela, her parents, her siblings. Tony was there too. I was in the army by then myself, and Tony said he'd put in a word. He had me moved to his regiment somehow I guess. Then we were shipped out to Iraq. I was going back to base with him one time, spotted an IED that we were about to drive over. He said I saved his life after that. Whether it was true or not.' Philip stops, runs his tongue over his lower lip. 'He had PTSD after Iraq, I hear. Some damage to his eardrums that probably threw off his balance a bit. I guess that's how he fell so bad.'

Philip sighs. He's been talking at the ceiling but now he glances my way.

'And then, afterwards. At the funeral, God - this beautiful widow, and those little girls, all in black. Lucy was only eleven, Devon was nine. Those big eyes. They knew he wasn't coming back. Smart girls, already. Too smart. You know Devon didn't speak for months after Tony died? Angela took her to see so many specialists.' He shakes his head. 'At the funeral she didn't say a word, didn't shed a tear. Just those big eyes. Big, silent eyes.'

I nod despite myself, because it's all too easy to picture. Devon and her watchful ways. The sphinx girl. The silent daughter.

'So yeah,' Philip says. 'I kept visiting them. I took them out on weekends. Tried to keep their spirits up. What happened between me and Angela... it just happened.' He looks at me again, and the nostalgic look settles into something darker. 'Of course, I hadn't bargained on Angela being... well, Angela. You can be so in love with the idea of someone, the idea of saving someone, that you don't see what they're really like. I'd fantasized about her as a teenager. It turned out she was... she was nothing like the girl I thought I saw. She has some demons of her own, I guess. And she didn't even really seem to want me, not after the first few months. Honestly I don't know why she married me, but I think maybe it was to spite her parents, or to shock them maybe. Marrying the pool boy, you know? I thought we were doing it in *spite* of what people would say, but now I think she got some weird kick out of it. She liked throwing that back in their faces.'

He looks at me. 'That's the truth of it, Sadie.

165

Angela's...' He turns to me. 'You want to know the truth? She scares me. She scares me, Sadie.'

*

I'm dreaming, and in the dream it's dark, I'm in my childhood house, all the lights are off and I can't remember where any of the switches are - I've been away too long - and without the lights, I can't find her. It's Fiona, that's who I'm looking for, I realize. I can hear her, somewhere in the house, but I can't see her. I hear the creak of her footstep on the landing, I hear a rustle... but when I crawl to the door, find the handle, fling it open, all I find is darkness and more darkness.

My mind pictures Tony Hundley lying on a stone floor, alone. Moonlight coming through the windows. Dawn breaking. Blood pooling round his head.

Philip said Tony Hundley's balance was bad with the tinnitus. Insomnia, PTSD; a tragedy waiting to happen.

But what if he's wrong? What if it wasn't those things at all?

She scares me, Sadie.

I think about the day I saw her in Thorpe's office. The same day that horrible note got swapped for my pile of class handouts. She was in the building that day. And other days? What about those letters, those envelopes that started turning up last term?

But no. I'm just fantasizing. I need to stop this, and try to sleep. I wait for my heart to slow again. As it does, I lift the photograph of Fiona and me from beside my bed. She was eleven when this was taken. So was I. Somehow, I look young but she doesn't. I look like a goofy kid but in Fiona's face I can see the fourteen-year-old she'll become, and the sixteen-year-old, the eighteen-year-old. I can almost see the other Fionas too, the ghosts of the woman she never got to become. Fiona at twenty-five. Fiona at thirty-five.

I reach out and put the frame back down and turn off the light. My heart is quiet now, although not in a good way. It's heavy, and tired, like the heart of an older person.

I think about Philip, his explanations. I believe him - don't I? I do. I *do*. And yet…

Come on Sadie. I close my eyes against the darkness. I plump the pillows, toss the duvet so the cool side is next to me, punch it into a comfortable mound beside me. And then I stop. Because cutting through the sounds of me rearranging bedding… did I hear something? I sit up in bed and turn on the light. My bathroom door's ajar. Was it open before? Or closed? I'm imagining it, I must be. And still, I get out of bed, push back the door. Check the bathroom over, snap back the shower curtain. I've seen too many movies. There's nothing, nothing at all.

I stand there in the cold for what feels like a long time, the breeze creeping round my ankles, before finally going back to bed.

*

I call Jan in the morning before class. The news is good, thank heavens.

'They're saying I can be home by Friday.' Her voice is its usual self now, determined and cheery - and then muffled, as though she has her hand over the receiver. I assume she's talking to a nurse or someone, but then I hear her call them *love*.

I pause, squeezing my feet into my pumps.

'Is someone there with you, Jan?'

'Rob came by. Brought me some things from home.'

I should be grateful, but despite everything I don't like the idea of him rustling around in Jan's place, looking through her stuff.

'That's nice,' I say, trying to put warmth in my voice.

Second gong sounds. 'Jan, I've got to get to class, okay? I'll be there on Friday to pick you up.'

'No need, love. Rob will do it.'

I try again to shake the feeling off.

'I'll be there,' I say, as firmly as I can, and hang up.

Morning classes are muted, and then in the afternoon Thorpe calls us into her office to notify us that we're losing another student, Bethany Goldstein. Apparently Bethany now believes Horton is haunted.

'Her parents will be coming to collect her after classes today,' Thorpe says stiffly, then looks at the rest of us. 'I think we all share the desire to be discreet about this.'

Around five o'clock I'm climbing the stairs and hear the slam of a trunk. I look out and see the flick of Mr Goldstein's trenchcoat as he gets into the driver's seat, and Bethany's red hair catching the sun as the car pulls away.

Another one bites the dust, Fiona's voice says in my head. I sympathize with Bethany. After all, I know what it means to be haunted.

I slip out of my pumps and take a Klonopin from the remainder of my supply. The shower is just beginning to soothe out the knots in my shoulders when my phone goes off. I left it on the sink, and the shrill ringing bounces off the bathroom walls. I duck my head out of the curtain to glance at it. It's vibrating its way to the edge of the sink but before it can fall I just make out the number calling.

Mom.

I lunge forward to grab it, but my foot squeaks across the tub and I go flying forward. I cry out and grab for something, but the nearest thing is the cistern cover, and it grates sideways and topples in my grasp. It smashes onto the tile and I just stop myself from landing wrists-down on cracked porcelain.

Jesus.

I ease myself back up, ignoring the pain in my bashed knee and wrenched shoulder, and pick my phone up.

'Mom? Are you there? Mom?'

'Sadie?' Her voice sounds strange, nervous, different.

'Mom, what's going on? Where *are* you?'

A pause. 'Can I meet you somewhere, Sadie? I have some things I... need to tell you.'

That's an understatement.

'Can you meet me at Trudy's?' she says.

Did she say that because she knew it would get to me? Trudy's is a diner we went to sometimes as a treat when I was a kid. It's been around forever.

'I can be there in forty minutes,' I say.

She takes a breath. She's nervous, it sounds like. 'Okay. Forty minutes. See you there.'

I drop the phone on my bed. I'm wet and shivering. What's going on? Where has she *been*? I guess I'll find out. I step back into the bathroom, pull my robe from the hook and belt it round me. I go to pick up one of the pieces of the tank lid, globs of shampoo trailing down my neck.

Wait.

There's something there. In the cistern.

A faint memory plays in my mind, Fiona boasting to

me how she'd hidden a bottle of booze in there. Safe from room inspections. Safe from roommates. The perfect hiding place.

I peer down. Inside, tucked into one corner of the tank - my heart thumps - is a Ziploc bag, a big one. I pull out the bag. Inside the bag, a large Tupperware, the waterproof kind with snap-to-seal lids. My breathing speeds up. I lift it out. Open it.

Bound together with two frayed elastic bands are a set of notebooks. I undo the elastic and let them fall into my lap. They're all the same. Little red notebooks. I turn one over and see the gold embossed letters on the front. *Diary.* My breath hitches and I take it in my hands, part the pages gently. Childish handwriting. I catch names here and there, standing out on the page. *Mommy. Lucy.* I breathe in.

Devon's.

It occurs to me that she could easily have left these at home, there was plenty of space to hide them in her bedroom. But instead she chose to hide them here. Because she liked having them with her? Or because she didn't trust her privacy at home?

I shuffle through the journals, trying to find the one that matters. She's kept them in order, I can see it even from flicking through them: her loopy, babyish writing of a few years ago transitioning to the fluent scrawl of a teenager. But the most recent one ends last Spring. I check them again, making sure. There are six in all - recording everything since she was ten years old - but if there was a recent one, it's not here.

I slip the most recent diary, the last before the missing one, out of the pile. I start at the beginning and page through it. I know what I'm looking for: my name. I want to know what Devon thought about me, what she *knew* about me; and I want to know if she had anything to do with those messages, those nasty *we don't want you here* notes. But as I comb through the pages, there's nothing like that. I'm not on her mind at all.

What jumps out at me is Philip. He's everywhere. Philip says this, Philip says that. Philip buys her the new dress she wants. Philip persuades Angela to let Devon get a piercing. Philip takes her shopping. Philip gives her books to read. There's suggestions of Philip and Angela fighting, and Devon takes Philip's side. She seems to think Angela is taking him for granted; that Angela doesn't deserve someone like Philip. From the diary a picture of the family comes out: Angela and Lucy on one side, Philip and Devon on the other. It seems like Lucy doesn't think much of Philip, and this hurts Devon's feelings. *She's always taking Mom's side. She doesn't understand.*

It makes me uncomfortable to read. But who am I to judge? Some girls just don't get along with their mothers. I should know. I check my watch - I need to get going.

Time to see Mom.

Nineteen

It's six-thirty, and Trudy's isn't busy. Mom orders a tuna sandwich, I just stick with coffee. If she were a different kind of mother she'd probably fuss and push me to eat something. But she doesn't.

She looks good, though. It still takes me by surprise sometimes, how young she is. When I was a kid she never wore make-up, never dyed her hair, and she looked older than other kids' moms even though she wasn't. Now, she looks so young. Just eighteen years older than me.

A plate with her tuna sandwich clanks onto the table and the waitress disappears. Mom cuts a triangle from the sandwich with her knife and fork, her usual fastidious way. But instead of putting it in her mouth she places her cutlery down again and folds her hands on the table.

'I'm sorry I didn't tell you I was going away,' she says. She's silent for a moment. 'I was in a clinic.'

I stare at her. 'A clinic? Were you... Are you sick?' My stomach turns over.

'A different kind of clinic,' she says, and takes a breath. A big one. 'A clinic for addicts, Sadie. A treatment center.'

I shake my head. This doesn't make sense.

'But you're not -'

'I am. I have an alcohol problem, Sadie.'

The radio is playing some tinny Top 40s. The booth's vinyl fabric sticks hotly against my arms.

'But I don't understand.' I shake my head again. 'You don't even *drink*.'

Mom just sits, looking at me, and it hits me. I always thought she didn't drink because she didn't want to. She was the teetotaller type, I figured. Against fun in general, my angry teenager voice said. But that's not the reason. That's not why we never had alcohol in the house. Why I never saw her so much as crack a beer or sip a white wine cooler.

'You never told me.'

She sighs, drops my gaze at last. She spears the piece of sandwich and puts it in her mouth, swallows before speaking.

'I didn't talk about it to anyone. I figured I had it under control. It wasn't anyone's business,' she says defiantly. 'And you're my daughter, Sadie. I didn't want you to see me that way.'

'So you were an alcoholic, and then you had me, and after that you got better?' I say, head spinning. I'm trying to straighten all this out.

'Addicts never get better, Sadie. They get sober. I was sober. For twenty-five years.'

Twenty-five years. And I never knew.

'But, what happened? Why did you... relapse?'

She licks her lips, eyes on her hands. 'I've been under a lot of stress, lately. Some... some reminders about the past that were hard for me to deal with.' She shrugs, slow and heavy. 'It happens. People slip up. I slipped up. Backslid. It was a very, very low point for me. Thinking that I'd thrown away those years. That twenty-five years meant nothing. I didn't think I was going to make it.'

I wait, speechless. I don't even want to think about *not making it*. What it could mean.

'I have a sponsor, I called them. Spoke to my doctor.

We managed to find a place that would take my insurance, something I could manage. I knew I needed something like that. Something radical. Staying by myself in that house, feeling myself go under... I couldn't do it.'

I take a breath. It's so painful hearing her talk about this. So much more painful than I thought this conversation could be.

'In the past,' I force myself to say. 'I don't understand. You said there were reminders. Reminders of what? What happened?'

Her eyes cut away from me for a moment. 'Your father, Sadie...'

I wait, a cold feeling running down the inside of my arms. I know this story. A summer fling. A boy she barely knew. No address, no way to track him down. I know this story - don't I?

'Your father,' she says. 'He... he wasn't a stranger. He was someone I knew. Someone I liked. But he did something one night he shouldn't have.' She examines her hands on the booth in front of her. 'I didn't tell him to stop, not out loud. But inside...' She stops. The chills move down to the pit of my stomach and lie there.

'You were...'

'In my day they would have called it *being taken advantage of*. They have other words for that now.'

I swallow, keeping back tears. *That was me?* That *was where I began?*

'When I realized I was pregnant I told him but he didn't want to hear. He was only young, too. Said it wasn't his, couldn't be. What was the point in fighting it? The best case scenario was supposed to be his parents making him marry me. But I'd been around women like that, women whose husbands resented them, figured they'd been trapped and could take it out on their wife with their fists, no questions asked. I wasn't about to become one of them.'

'And...' It's hard to say. 'You didn't think about... ending it?'

'I thought about it,' she says, glancing at me. 'I thought about it. But I didn't know where to go. Who would take me. How to...' She shakes her head. 'We didn't have the internet then, and I guess I wasn't a very resourceful kid.' She shrugs, locking her gaze on mine again. 'He married someone else, I heard. Went on with his life. Maybe he hasn't put a foot wrong since. Maybe he's a model citizen now. *Youthful indiscretion,* that's what they'd call it if they ever found out.'

'I'm so sorry,' I whisper.

'And then, when I had you,' she goes on, like I haven't spoken. 'It was so hard. Harder than I could have imagined. You were colicky, you cried all the time. Then you got ill. Ear infections every few weeks. I drank coffee all day to stay awake, and then I was too wired to sleep. I started drinking to take the edge off. I didn't realize I'd gone too far, because there was no one around me to tell me so. But it got bad. And then worse. You got out one day, you got lost - do you remember that?-'

I shake my head, though now that she says it, there's something there. A memory of a road, a maze of roads going on forever; my blue canvas shoes with yellow laces, the shoes I loved. I see myself looking down, then up at the sidewalk, the houses.

'The social workers were calling in. I knew I needed to change. Shape up. If I didn't, they were going to take you away from me. I could see it happening. I'd seen it happen to others, before. So I changed. I stopped drinking. Smoking. Everything. It almost killed me but I did it.' She looks at me. 'You were maybe three years old. You don't remember?'

I shake my head, slowly.

'It was a long time ago,' she says.

Somewhere in the back, one of the waitstaff drops a load of silverware. It clanks and rattles as they pick it off the ground. My head feels fuzzy. I feel guilty and betrayed at the same time. She must hate me, I think. That's why it's always been the way it's been between us. Because my father... I don't want to say the word. I can barely think it. Is it an excuse, to say it was a different time? A time when no-one talked about "consent", and boys were taught a different language?

'He's still in Providence?' I say. 'My...'

She nods. It's like neither of us want to say *father*.

'You could have told me you had a problem,' I say. Is that the right word to use? 'An addiction, I mean. You could have told me about the addiction.'

She gives me a tired look.

'You already thought so little of me. I could never compare to Jan. I wasn't going to throw away what respect you still had for me.'

Was I really like that as a kid, as a teenager? It's not how I remember it. I don't remember feeling scorn. I remember pain. But I can see from her eyes this is genuine. This is how she remembers me.

'But you didn't even tell me where you were going,' I say. 'I had to pull up in front of our home and see it deserted; ask a neighbor about you.'

She sighs, pushes away her half-eaten sandwich.

'I didn't know Jan would raise the alarm,' she says. 'She should have minded her own business.'

My confusion turns to anger suddenly. 'Jan was just being -'

Mom waves her hand to say *enough*, and I stop. She's right, it's not the time for this. She sips her water.

'They told us to cut out triggers,' she says.

'Triggers?'

'Habits from our daily lives, or from our past. Places, people, things that led us to destructive behaviors. That's why I couldn't - why I didn't call you, when I was there.'

'I'm your *trigger?*' The anger in my voice surprises me. Somehow this feels like the worst thing I've heard so far.

She takes a slow breath, looks at me. A cool, honest look, so honest it burns. She doesn't say yes. She doesn't need to.

I ball up my napkin, stuff a couple of dollars on the table.

'I need to go,' I say.

My palms peel from the vinyl seating. My vision blurs. Our table's near the door at least. A bell *ding-a-ling*s as I push out into the street.

Breathe.

Strains of music from inside the diner follow me out. A car honks. The light turns. I walk.

I drive back to Horton in the dark. I see my mother's face in the café: something about those hesitations. Something that's been scratching at me since I got in the car to drive back. That this is not the full truth, that something's left. Something she still hasn't said.

Something that maybe neither of us can afford to

hear.

My mind's on a tilt-a-whirl, the past mixing with the present. Dark things rising up. I take deep, steadying breaths as I make my way back into the school grounds. I hug my coat tighter and let myself into the East Wing, the quiet. In my room I grab my water bottle from the bedside table where it's still half-full, and drain it. It tastes strange, chalky on my tongue somehow - probably because the adrenalin and shock have left my mouth so dry.

I collapse on my bed, staring at the ceiling. My hand drifts to the locket round my neck, opening and shutting it. Snap. Snap.

They told us to avoid triggers.

*

I'm back outside Octavia's house: Fiona and me, parking along the driveway and walking up. How big the house seemed, and the shimmering green lawn in front. It smelled of jasmine as we turned the corner. The lawn was crowded with clumps of girls, boys too. Music was blasting. A bar on the grass. I picked my way across the perfect lawn as if I might hurt it. No one seemed to notice me. Maybe Fiona had been right - we wouldn't humiliate ourselves by being here. I'd just stay under the radar.

Like you usually do, Sadie.

We got drinks, and Fiona downed hers and started on another.

'Are you okay, Fiona?' I'd never seen her drink like that. 'Do you want to talk about it? About Peter?' I knew the boyfriend's name by then: *Peter Kagan* she'd told me, after I badgered her. She said it as if it were one word, *PeterKagan. PK*, she'd started referring to him as.

She shook her head. 'I'm allowed have a drink, Sadie. Don't badger me.'

It certainly seemed like everyone else was drinking freely. There were no parents here, I realized. I'd thought because Octavia and her friends were fancy their parties would be better behaved somehow. But now I was beginning to see that was a mistake.

I went to the bathroom and walking through the clusters of girls I could feel their eyes. What's *she* doing here, the air seemed to say. When I came back Fiona was talking to some boys who had their backs to me. They didn't pay me much attention when I appeared. They were more interested in Fiona, that much was clear, but I wondered what kind of interest it was. Maybe rich boys weren't as judgmental as rich girls. There was an energy in Fiona right now I didn't recognize. It was to do with Peter and the break-up, I was sure. She was feverish, dangerous, like she wanted to do something crazy, no matter who it hurt.

When the boys went to the bar again I turned to Fiona. Her eyes already seemed just a little out-of-focus. I wondered how many drinks she'd had.

'You're not going to... *do* anything with them, are you?' I said, nodding my head towards the boys. They were Octavia's people, not our people. It was against the rules, I wanted to say.

Fiona looked at me. I saw then what she was thinking. This was why the Horton girls hated Fiona and didn't hate me. I stayed in my lane. Fiona didn't see lanes.

Her eyes narrowed. The lemon bobbed around in her gin.

'Do you think I'm a slut, Sadie?'

'*No,*' I said. 'No!' I was rattled, stunned that she would ask me that. But did I hesitate for a moment, before I answered? Just for a moment, did I hesitate?

The boys came back with the drinks and Fiona straightaway took a giant gulp from hers. I'd never seen her like this before.

'Give me your keys, okay?' I murmured. I'd been drinking too, but I figured an hour from now if I drank only water, I'd be fine.

'In a minute,' she scowled.

'*Fiona-*'

She glared at me but started to fish in her bag. She flung the keys at me when she found them. The boys had drifted away.

'Way to go, Sadie,' Fiona said. 'Even they can sense you're a goddamned killjoy.' She thumped her glass down. 'I'm going to the bathroom.'

I stood there alone, felt the threat of tears gathering behind my eyes. I wasn't sure if people were watching, but I couldn't make a spectacle of myself now. I backed up to the patio, shielded by a sun umbrella.

It wasn't just today. It was a feeling I'd had for a while. Fear, and betrayal. Fear that we'd never get back what we once had. Why had Fiona changed like this? I knew I didn't have what she had - that effortlessness, that breezy way of charming people - but that had never seemed to matter before. It hadn't mattered to Fiona. She'd liked me just the way I was. She'd valued my loyalty, my kindness, my sense of humor. It didn't matter that I was the quiet one, the awkward one. Unless she'd just been lying to me all along.

Someone rang a dinner gong, shouting *pizza* out

through the French doors, and a cheer went up. On the lawn girls started tipping back the last of their champagne flutes.

'They're not really *friends*, though, are they?' someone was saying. They were standing near me, but from my vantage point behind the sun-umbrella I was well hidden.

'So *trashy*,' the voice went on. 'And the way she keeps that kid Sadie hanging around her, like a dog on a leash. Ugh, that girl needs to grow a spine.'

It was like I'd been punched in the gut. This time I didn't hold the tears in. I couldn't, there was no room in my body for them. The humiliation had already filled me brim-full.

Maybe that was the moment that changed everything. Maybe if not for that, the evening would have ended differently. Maybe we'd never have got the call the next morning that said they'd found Fiona's car, wrapped around a lamp-post.

*

I feel the weird spasms in my stomach, but all of a sudden they become intense. I don't even make it to the toilet before I'm violently sick into the sink. I can't think what I ate today that could have done this. My appetite's been so weak, I've barely eaten anything. My legs buckle under me and I have to grab the rim of the basin to make sure I don't fall and crack my head. I steady myself, wait for another wave to pass through me. Coach Ned had food poisoning last week. Could it be a bug, something going around? But surely I didn't catch it from him, we barely see each other.

I let my weight sag forward, forehead against the

mirror. I run the water cold, pat some over my face. And then it begins again. When it's over I curl up in a ball by the toilet. This is going to take a while.

I lie there, feeling feverish and dreamlike, for what seems like it could be hours. The stash of Devon's little journals is scattered on the floor still, beside me. Flashes, pictures, drift through my brain. Devon. Fiona. Angela Hundley. Nessa Rath. A parade of faces, resentful, betrayed, scared, furious. Every now and again a wave racks my body and I heave myself up and over the toilet bowl, purging out whatever's inside me.

After what seems like an age, I feel sturdy enough to drag myself to the door. I open it, casting my eyes along the corridor, and to my relief there's a girl on the stairs.

'Lucy,' I say, as her face comes into focus.

'Miss?' she says, not quite meeting my eyes.

'Lucy, could you fetch the nurse for me? I'm not feeling very well.'

She frowns, then nods and scurries off. I shut the door and drag myself to my bed.

My limbs are trembling. I think I have a fever. I moan, and stumble back into the bathroom. The retching starts again. The ceiling is the last thing I see before my brain shuts off, and the darkness takes me under.

Twenty

I wake up to a pounding on the door. I come to, face cold against bathroom tile, mouth dry. How long have I been like this?

Simone is standing outside my door, looking concerned.

'Sadie? Everything okay?'

'I -' My head spins.

'Sadie? What's going on?'

Slowly, I drag my gaze back to her.

'I - I think I have food poisoning.'

'You look like death.' Simone puts her hand out, feels my temperature. 'You're hot. You're probably dehydrated.'

Simone ushers me back to bed. 'I wondered what was going on - you never texted me back.'

She goes away to fetch me a Gatorade from the vending machine, and I stumble back to the bathroom despite my pounding head, gather up Devon's journals, and stuff them in a drawer. When Simone comes back she shakes her head, twists off the Gatorade cap for me and hands it over.

'Do you think you have what Ned had?'

'Dunno. Maybe.'

'You need some aspirin.' She rattles round in my bathroom looking for painkillers. If she sees my stash of Klonopin there, she says nothing about it. 'With any luck it'll pass in a few hours. You might even be through the worst of it already.'

'Simone?' I take a deep breath. It's time to voice this out loud. 'I know how this must sound to you. But... I think I need to leave Horton. I don't think I can stay here any more.'

This place doesn't like me. It doesn't want me here.

I put the Gatorade down, but it's already sloshed over the rim; my hands are trembling. I put them in my lap to try and stop it. And suddenly, outside in the corridor, there's a piercing, high-pitched scream.

Simone looks at me.

'What on earth-?'

She moves to the door, steps out onto the corridor. Some of the girls are outside their rooms, congregating. Someone starts crying. I go to the door behind Simone.

'They found her.'

It's Nessa Rath. She's ashen. The other girls aren't looking at us, it's like Nessa's the only one who sees us.

'Devon,' she says. 'They found her.'

For the briefest moment, my heart leaps. Then the truth sinks in. She doesn't mean Devon's safe; rescued. She means Devon is gone.

Forever.

*

The details come out. A girl's body has been found at the foot of cliffs at Bantam Lake. A rocky spot that's not that far from Milham; people like to go there in the summer and lie out. I've been there myself, though not since I was a teenager. A bicycle's been found in the trees nearby that matches Devon's.

So she's gone, she's really gone. She's not coming back.

I know your secret.

I shiver. I didn't wish it this way. I never, ever wished it this way. I'd rather she'd told the world than for her to suffer harm.

Simone's scrolling fast through her phone, filling me in on details.

At the foot of the cliffs. The media outlets haven't used the word yet, but you can feel them wanting to: *suicide.*

I know suicide is unpredictable, that people who don't seem troubled or depressed can be hiding all sorts of things inside... and yet. There was something so determined about Devon, ruthless even; something that said *I'm in it for the long game.* This is the last thing I pictured.

'*Lucy,*' I remember. 'Oh, God. Do you think she knows yet?'

Simone looks up from her phone, a look of pain on her face. 'Oh my God, poor Lucy. We'd better go find her.'

We hurry to the seniors' floor. When we turn the corner I stop short, seeing Thorpe there already, standing outside Lucy's door. My hand freezes on the banister. The corridor's empty otherwise - did Thorpe make the others leave? - and in the silence Lucy's voice seeps out from inside the room. She's on the phone, crying. Simone and I stand there, not knowing what to do. Thorpe doesn't meet our eyes.

Mom, Lucy's voice chokes out. *Mom.* The rest dissolves in sobs.

I stand frozen. I don't know how to go near a grief like this. A few feet from us, Thorpe turns and looks our way. I swallow. A tear-trail is running down her cheek.

*

Classes are suspended for the day. Ned's sent down to the gates to keep the journalists at bay. Thorpe's walking around dazed, like a zombie.

Simone shows me a news clip of Angela Hundley. She's coming out of a house, and screaming at paparazzi who are outside. She throws something at them - her handbag, it looks like - and they scatter. *Beasts,* Simone says.

Bedtime gets pushed back, because it seems cruel to send the girls to their rooms and tell them to sleep through this. When we finally call lights-out I turn the news on low in my room and lie there watching it. Out my window I can see the lights still on in Simone's cottage.

This doesn't feel real.

*

Back in Octavia Dennison's house, the gong had rung, the lawn had emptied. There was laughter and music drifting from inside. Standing on the patio, hidden, I was wiping my eyes with the back of my hand.

Was this really how everyone saw me? Fiona's feeble, spineless sidekick? A hanger-on? A doormat? A *loser.*

I didn't know how I'd face going inside, seeing all those eyes on me. Knowing what they thought of me. As soon as Fiona came back I'd tell her I needed to leave.

But she didn't come back.

I waited and waited, and then finally I took a deep breath and went indoors. And just as I got to the foot of the staircase there she was. Flouncing down the stairs, make-up reapplied, bolder than ever. Her warpaint. *We need to get out of here,* I thought again. Food was being handed round and the music was turned up high. I could see how she was having trouble focusing. I cursed Peter Kagan again for making her like this. Two years at Horton had·crushed something inside her, and whatever was left, she'd given to him. Now he'd stomped all over it and here was the result. A reckless, dangerous version of the girl I knew before.

Half-way down the stairs her eyes found me, and widened. And then she tripped, sprawling forwards, drunkenly clinging to the banister as she missed the last few steps. She let out an ugly sound as she fell, and the clatter of her tumble turned heads. I saw the frozen looks of distaste. Suddenly all I felt was shame. Shame, and anger. *Trashy*, they'd said.

'I need my keys,' Fiona said, and held out her hand.

I shook my head. 'Don't be crazy - you can't drive, not now.'

Stubbornly, she held out her palm. 'You always think you know better than me, Sadie, don't you? Just give me my keys.'

'I'll drive us,' I said. 'You can pick up your car tomorrow.'

One of Fiona's strappy shoes had come loose. She fumbled it back onto her foot.'You're so fucking *patronizing,* do you know that?'

'Well, you're a *mess,*' I hissed. 'You're *embarrassing.*'

Her eyes snapped up, onto mine. 'You don't get to talk to me like that. Who do you think you are? You're - you're' - she searched for the right thing to throw at me. 'You're *nobody.*'

I put my hand out to steady myself as though she'd landed a blow.

Nobody.

The boring, mousy one. I was just here to make Fiona shine brighter. Everyone knew it. Even Fiona knew it. But somehow I hadn't known it. Not till now.

This is the end, I thought. It was our graduation night. School was over for good - and suddenly, it seemed, our friendship was too. Our friendship, the one thing that had sustained me through these years. *I hate you,* I thought at her, like it was a feeling I was trying on for the first time. But I wondered how your heart could break over someone you said you hated.

'You know what? Fine.' I felt for the keys in my pocket and threw them at her. 'Go. See if I care.'

We both looked at the keys on the floor in a kind of shock. I waited to see if she would really pick them up, as if to tell which one of us was bluffing. But she did. She swallowed, then snatched the keys from the step beside her and put them in her pocket. The party continued around us; they'd stopped watching. Fiona broke eye contact first. She gripped the banister once more for steadiness and then let go, tottering to the front door. I watched her go.

You're not her mother, Sadie, I told myself.

I reminded myself of the things she'd just said to me. Told myself if she didn't need me, then she didn't need me. She could make her bad decisions all by herself.

She didn't look back.

And then at the door she wobbled again. I saw it - the way her heel skated sideways for a moment, the way she took a second to right herself. And a wave of remorse rushed over me. How could I let this happen? How could I have come so close, all because of pride?

'Fiona -' I pushed my way through the bodies in front of me. 'Please, Fiona. Don't.'

I saw her back stiffen, and slowly she turned around.

And then she burst into tears.

'I'm sorry, Sadie.' She shook her head through the mascara tears coursing down her face. 'I'm sorry. I didn't mean any of that. I didn't mean what I said. I didn't mean it at all.'

I was crying too, I realized.

'You're my best friend. My *best* friend.' Fiona gripped my arm, hugged it, then squeezed her own arm through it so we linked, the way we'd done for so many years.

'Come on,' she said. 'Let's get some air.'

*

We talked for hours that night, it seemed. It was a beautiful night, warm for the start of summer, and Fiona had the benefit of all those drinks to keep her warm. We sat in a far corner of the patio, looking out over the Dennisons' beautiful, perfect lawn, and forgot where we were, as the party forgot about us, too.

She told me how she'd been jealous of me, of how her mom treated me. How Jan always praised me and talked about 'how far I'd go', encouraging Fiona to adopt my habits and my ambition; be more serious, knuckle down. How sometimes it seemed like Jan and I were the real mother and daughter, and she was the outsider. And then at Horton, how she'd been targeted but no-one had bullied me.

That's because they don't care about me, I wanted to say. *It's because I don't threaten them.*

She shook her head when I said that. 'They respect

you. They don't respect me.'

We shared secrets, into the dark. It was wonderful. I didn't know how it had happened, or why we'd had to come right to the precipice in order to do it, but somehow I'd got my old friend back. I asked her about next year. She shrugged.

'I applied some places, but I don't know. Maybe I'll just stay here. Nisha Graham says she's making a boat-load in tips at the Olive Garden. They're going to make her a floor manager once she finishes school.'

I shook my head. 'But Fiona... you could do so much more.'

She laughed at me. 'You sound just like my mother.' She fished some cigarettes out of her pocket, lit one. 'I guess, if I could have anything I wanted... maybe I'd study drama. Be an actress.'

'You'd be a great actress.' I smiled.

After a while we fell silent. It was peaceful. It was night-time by then, and there was just the gentle burble of the party going on inside, and the golden light spilling out of the windows behind us. They had forgotten all about us, and I realized I didn't even wish them any harm, my schoolmates. I *wanted* them to enjoy their party. I loved everybody, right then. I leaned my head back against the side of the house, where the stone still held a little of the day's warmth. I felt peaceful, like we'd talked our way into a new place, a bright place. The future. I felt in a flash how young we were, how much life there was spooling out ahead of us both, long as a golden ribbon.

When I woke, it was cold.

I was alone.

'Fiona?' I said aloud. It felt late; much later than

before. The party was getting quiet. There were fewer cars in the driveway; people had left.

I stood up, and something rustled. I put my hand in my pocket and pulled out cash. Cash, and a note.

PK called. He wants me to come over! I'm sorry, Sadie. Can you get a cab home? Forgive me.

xx F

*

I draw the curtains, and hear my phone buzzing by the bed. I hurry over and check the caller, and shudder.

Philip.

I hesitate - I don't want to take this call. How can I possibly say the right thing? But the phone keeps ringing, imploring me to answer. To help.

I pick up.

'Philip? I - I heard the news.' The words are so inadequate. 'I'm so sorry, Philip.'

His voice catches, and I don't hear what he says.

'Philip?'

His breath shudders.

'My little girl. *My little girl.*'

I exhale. 'Philip? Where are you? Are you okay?'

'I'm home, I just - I just got back,' he chokes. 'Back from the morgue. I had to do it. Angela wouldn't. Couldn't.'

'Oh, Philip.' My stomach twists. 'I'm... I don't know what to say.'

Another shaky breath echoes down the line.

'It was just one time,' he says.

I wait, not understanding.

'When she and Tony were having difficulties.' He

gasps, swallows. 'It was just one time. I never imagined...I didn't think -'

My heart pulses, one slow beat. My throat is dry.

'Philip, what are you saying?'

'I never put it together - when Devon was born. Almost to the day. Angela let it slip, a couple of months ago.'

Oh my God.

My little girl.

He thinks Devon's his daughter.

'And I didn't tell her, Sadie. I never told Devon. She never knew.'

It dawns on me: *this* was what Angela told him. The thing she let slip. The thing that made him stay.

'Are you sure, Philip? Are you sure she was telling you the truth?' I barely hear myself speak.

'I made a mistake, Sadie.' His voice trembles.

'Philip? What mistake? What do you mean?'

But he's hung up. I call him. And call him.

But he doesn't call back.

*

My little girl.

Is it true? I think of Devon's diary entries, the way she hero-worshipped Philip. A crush, I'd thought then - or something more? Did she sense, deep down, when blood meets blood?

And Philip: I'd heard the pain - agony - in his voice just now. How much he regretted not having claimed Devon when he had the chance. Not having told her what Angela had told him. Maybe when Angela first let it slip it had seemed safer not to say anything. Safer to keep the secret close, tight. But he always thought he'd get the chance to say it all out loud.

Maybe deep down, we never expect our secrets to be forever.

Can it really be true? Was Angela lying?

I picture Devon in my mind - the yellow hair and even features; a Vermeer face with a thousand-yard stare - and then I picture her with Philip, side by side.

There's something there, I see it. Maybe Angela really was telling the truth.

And if she was? How do you measure loss within a deeper loss? How do you measure what goes deeper than human reckoning?

Ashes to ashes. Dust to dust.

I close the curtains, and go to bed, and it's a dark, dreamless sleep.

But in the morning when I wake, there's a strange noise filtering through my room. I go to the window. A buzzing, humming sound, like a nest of bees or a highway has suddenly sprung up outside the school. I push up the sill, and the noise takes shape.

There's a cluster of paparazzi outside the school gates.

What on earth?

My phone pings.

Simone.

Oh my god have you seen the news?

Cold trickles down my spine.

I coax my fingers to text back: *What news?*

The three dots quiver furiously then burst into words.

Philip Hundley. Police are seeking him for "questioning".
He's gone. Disappeared.

Twenty-one

I'm reeling.

Philip.

Philip?

I can't believe it. I refuse to. My skin is crawling, my insides are screaming. This is a mistake. It's some kind of horrible mistake.

But why would the police be searching for him? On what grounds?

No, the voice says again in my head. He can't have anything to do with Devon's death. I don't believe it.

He wouldn't harm his daughter.

But you didn't really know him, Sadie, another voice in my head says. *We never know what anyone is capable of. He had you wrapped around his little finger, too.*

'Ms Kelly,' Thorpe is saying. '*Sadie.* Are you listening to me?' Thorpe is ashen. She wipes a hand over her brow. 'We have to get Lucy. We have to prepare her. Oh, *hell.* Why didn't somebody warn us?'

Her voice is trembling. In the corridor next to me her fear could be a mirror, except what I know is worse than what she knows. I put a hand out to the wall for support.

Outside Mme DeNoel's room, Thorpe knocks and doesn't wait for the door to open.

'Lucy Hundley?' Can I have a word with Lucy Hundley?'

There's a hush, and then Mme DeNoel is at the door, flustered.

'Lucy's not here, Mrs Thorpe. Charlotte, you said

197

she'd gone to the infirmary, is that right?'

A girl's voice pipes up. 'I *thought* she might have gone to the infirmary, Miss.'

'Sweet Jesus,' Thorpe explodes, then turns on her heel. I'm scurrying to keep pace with her, brain swimming, heart sinking.

Sure enough, when we knock on the door of the infirmary, we're told the same. Lucy Hundley isn't here.

*

We end up corralling the girls on the second and third-floor student lounges, one teacher each to supervise, and the rest of us turn into a search party. I cover the grounds with Simone. It's raining. We call Lucy's name and all we hear is bird-calls and the splatter of heavy rain through leaves, the occasional thud of a horse-chestnut. Simone steps on a branch, and I jump when it snaps.

We've only been out maybe fifteen minutes when I see flashing red and blue lights through the trees.

Beside me, Simone's face is pale in the rain.

'What's going on, Sadie?'

'Your guess is as good as mine,' I say.

'Do you think he took her?'

Please God, no.

'But why would he take her?' Simone goes on. '*How* could he take her?' She looks back at the main building. 'Nobody's seen her since dinnertime last night.'

I look back where she's looking, and see police officers walking up the stone steps, Thorpe directing them - *this way, this way* - into the hall.

We arrive back at the school sodden. Coach Ned and Mr Hirschfield, the geography teacher, are in the hall, murmuring.

'They're in the office with her,' Ned says, nodding towards Thorpe's room. The door is closed but through the glass panel I see a flash of navy blue.

'Angela Hundley's been briefing the police. Apparently she's been staying at her sister's house so she doesn't know when Philip was last at home. All they know is that he was supposed to come down to the police station this morning, routine stuff, they need both the parents in to give interviews after they found, you know. The body. And he didn't show up.' Ned rubs his face. 'And then they called him, and his phone's off. And when they went to the house, there was no one there.'

Simone nods. 'Somebody leaked it to the press of course, and now they're all over it.'

I can't believe this is happening. The two things have to be related, don't they? Philip and Lucy, both vanished? It can't be coincidence.

'Maybe they took off to *avoid* the press,' I say. 'After everything with Devon being found. Maybe he took Lucy out of school so they could just lie low somewhere for a while.'

Ned looks at me.

'Without telling Thorpe? Without telling her mother?' I go silent.

'Girls still upstairs?' Simone asks, and they nod.

She looks at her watch. It's late. There's been no gong. Everything's falling apart. The cafeteria staff probably got roped into this hunt too.

'We better feed the kids,' she says, and the others look relieved at the idea of something useful to do.

Soon the girls are ushered down to the dining hall,

and while they eat, I'm back upstairs, alone, by the window in the common room, staring out at the rain. I can't eat. I can't anything.

Did Lucy run away because she heard that Philip was under suspicion, and missing? Has she gone to find him?

I don't know whether to hope that she does, or hope she doesn't.

Philip.

I picture his strong, tanned hands, the wrists with those golden hairs...

I picture Devon, her frail, slight little body.

When I throw up in the common room toilet, the little pink tablet comes up undigested. Which is a relief, because that means I'm allowed one more. One more to beat back the shadows in my mind.

*

We don't find Lucy. Everything is in a state of suspended animation. We can't pretend it's normal, we can't resume lessons, but we don't know what else to do. We concentrate on keeping the girls fed and calm, trying to answer their questions, trying to keep them together in a group for some sort of comfort.

It's another late bedtime for the girls, who congregate in their pajamas in the student lounge, talking in subdued whispers, checking their phones without pause.

'Want to crash at mine?' Simone says.

It's not just the girls who are feeling shaky.

It's cold in the cottage but Simone pulls an extra blanket from the closet and tosses it on the couch, along with the throw. She looks terrible, I realize. Her face is drawn and grey.

'Sadie?'

I look at her.

'I don't know how to… there's something I need to…'
She rubs her hands over her face.

'What is it?' I pull the blanket closer over my
shoulders.

She shakes her head. 'It's not - never mind.'

She doesn't finish, just shakes her head and
disappears into her room. She leaves the door open. I slip
off my shoes and wrap myself fully clothed in the blankets,
digging myself against the back of the sofa for warmth.
Next door, Simone's mattress creaks.

'Maybe by the morning they'll have found her,' I say.

She says nothing back. Maybe the exhaustion's
caught up with her too, and she's already asleep. I'm
exhausted myself, but sleep doesn't come for me. Instead I
watch the darkness outside, the shapes of trees against the
night sky.

Is that *Ned?* I sit up.

I can only see him from behind but I'm almost
positive it's him, walking down the drive. He gets to a car,
unlocks it; the lights flash in welcome and he gets in. The
tail lights flick on, and slowly, quietly, his car eases out the
gates and disappears into the night.

I check my watch. What was *that* about?

Maybe he's gone to stay with family for a while. I
guess I can't blame him if he wants to get away from
Horton right now. That's my plan too, except I don't plan
to come back.

I lie back on Simone's couch, and as the clock ticks on
her wall I toss and turn and don't sleep. I watch the
shadows of trees outside moving against her wall, as

memories pull me under.

*

It's summer outside. There's birdsong, and the shouts of kids playing under an open fire hydrant. The rhythmic bounce of a basketball. It's three weeks after Fiona's death. And here we are, Jan and I, in Fiona's bedroom, sorting through her things. Deciding what we can keep, what we should give away. Jan is a model of stoicism. She's silent but methodical, careful, sorting through everything piece by piece. When I break down, *she's* the one who comforts *me. I'm sorry*, I blubber into her shoulder. She pats my back, softly.

She thinks I'm apologizing for the crying. But I'm apologizing because I failed her. Because I didn't watch over Fiona. Because I let her drive away.

We fill bags of Fiona's clothes - bags and bags. Fiona loved her clothes. On top of one of the bags I see the bright velour hoodie that Octavia's friend sneered at that first day in Horton. I pull it out.

'I'll keep this.'

Jan just nods, blinks a couple of times, and goes back to sorting the drawers.

I stand up and walk to Fiona's desk. Photographs with push-pins, jammed all over a cork board. Books, magazines. No-one's been in here since she died. I lift a box of make-up - bits of eyeshadow dust spilt everywhere - and set it aside. Underneath is a sheaf of papers. I pick it up, turn it over.

An acceptance letter. I suck in a breath. *Yale.*

Yale? When I'd talked to Fiona she'd sounded so skeptical of that college world. *Olive Garden,* she'd said. I hadn't got into anywhere half as prestigious as Yale.

I turn over the next one. And the next. My whole body's trembling. Good grief. Was there an Ivy League she *hadn't* gotten into? Scholarship grants too. I root further through the pile and find other papers. A draft of an admissions essay. SAT results - perfect test scores. Why hadn't she told me?

Because she knew you'd be jealous.

I put the acceptance letters into my bag, quietly, out of Jan's sight. I read her personal essay in my bedroom that night. Her theme is *accountability*. She says I'm the one who's always kept her accountable. The person who carried her forwards. I don't cry; I can't. I've used up all the tears.

The next morning an impulse grabs me. I don't examine it. I don't fight it. I just do it: I sit down at the kitchen table and write back to Stanford. I write in Fiona's name. I accept the offered place.

I figured Stanford, because it was the very farthest one from Milham. No matter what Fiona said I thought deep down she'd wanted to get away, too. It would have been easy to picture her there, in the sunshine. Dating a surfer or something. I wrote it in a kind of dream.

My hand didn't even shake when I dropped it in the mail.

The funeral had been two weeks earlier. No-one called Peter Kagan had shown up. Another ghost, I thought, and wondered once more if Fiona had made him up.

I found a book on Fiona's shelf, a few weeks later. It was one Jan had put aside for the charity shop. Her old book of Celtic Myths and Legends. I flicked through it, and landed on one whose illustrations were familiar. A girl on a stony beach, long mermaid-like tresses of hair flowing all around her. A seal pelt by her feet. A man, standing to the side. The selkie story. I glanced at the title.

Peter Kagan and the Wind.

*

Sadie.

I hear the voice in my head so strongly, it's like Fiona's there in the room with me. My eyes fly open. I'm still on Simone's couch, bundled up. And that's when I see it. In the dark a thread of light, scanning the courtyard outside Simone's cottage, back and forth.

I bump the nightstand and the lamp clatters to the floor, but doesn't break. I wait to see if Simone stirs but she doesn't. I pull the blanket round me, move silently across the room to the window.

The cops? Someone on night duty?

But what cop would swing their light around like that? Like they're looking for something, stumbling?

Lucy? Did she come back?

Then I see it - a black shadow slipping inside the chapel.

Lucy? Or someone else?

I grab the flashlight by Simone's door - heavy in my hands, a weapon if it needs to be. I'm not quite thinking as I slip out the door, over the cobbles.

My heart pounds. I'm in my bare feet but I barely feel the cold. The sane, undrugged part of my brain says *go back inside* but it's not the part of my brain I'm listening to. I clutch the flashlight closer. Trails of water splash under my feet as I reach the door.

I have to know.

I push against it, and slowly the door yields open. It makes no noise, and inside the chapel is as dark as outside. Have they heard me? I stay where I am, picturing someone behind the doors ready to strike. Nothing. I sweep the beam of the flashlight up -

- and one pale figure sits on a pew, with her hand in front of her eyes, blinded by the light I'm throwing her way. She lets out a little breath, like a gasp.

I stop.

'Nessa?' I say.

Twenty-two

'I'm sorry, Ms Kelly.' She's frozen in place. She doesn't move an inch under the flashlight's beam.

Wordless, I drop the light down from her face.

'Are you alone?'

She nods.

Still, I cast the flashlight round the back of the chapel, briefly into the recessed alcoves. Nothing. Just the blank, stern faces of the paintings. I walk slowly up the aisle. Nessa is sitting three pews from the front. She's wearing pajamas and a coat over them. She watches me with her eyes like saucers.

I cast the light around once more before sitting down in the pew next to her.

I study her face, blotchy and swollen. 'What are you doing here?'

The question breaks her. Tears flood down her face, a sudden rush of them, silent at first, and then there's a thin wail, a strange, animal sound, and she clamps her hand over her mouth.

'I didn't mean... I never meant...'

Something dark shivers through my veins. She gasps in a breath and looks at me. Her whole body crumples in a sob.

'I was supposed to go with her,' she says.

For a second, my heart stops.

Slowly, very carefully, I say: 'Go with who, Nessa?'

I almost don't think she's hearing me. Her eyes are fixed straight ahead.

'Devon always liked me, you know. I don't know why. Nobody really does. We were going to go together.'

'Go where, Nessa?' I say, holding my voice steady, ignoring the ripple of dread.

She just shakes her head.

'I've always been scared of things,' she says. 'People said I was a wimp. A baby. But Devon said that that was smart; she said most people weren't scared enough.' Nessa looks at me. '*She* wasn't scared.'

Her words fall into the darkness around us. My feet are like ice against the floor. But I'm not shivering because of the cold.

'Nessa, do you know anything about Lucy Hundley? And Philip? Do you know where they are?'

She shakes her head, stares up the aisle ahead of us.

I take a deep breath. 'And Devon? Do you know anything about Devon?'

Nessa licks her lips, her eyes glazing over again. She looks down at her hands.

'You have a car, don't you, Miss?'

I nod.

'There's something I need to show you.'

*

In the passenger seat Nessa says almost nothing, just *left here* and *straight ahead*, and the night is quiet for once, no wind in the trees. The cars on the road with their lights on seem alien and empty, like there's no one inside them. It feels like the world is holding its breath. Moonlight filters over Nessa's pale hair.

'Here,' she says quietly, a few turn-offs before we get to Milham. One of the roads out to Bantam Lake.

My heart batters my ribcage.

'Why are we here, Nessa?'

She just looks at me. And without a word, I drive on.

The trees start to billow as we approach the lake, night breezes off the water shaking the leaves.

'Pull in,' Nessa says, and I do.

She gets out of the car. I follow. The wind whips back my hair. In the daylight it's just a bit of lakefront where people like to picnic in summer. But here, now, in the dark, it's a different place. The pewter-colored sea is vicious. There's nothing and nobody it couldn't swallow. I pull my hair from my face, already tangled from the wind, and tuck it in my collar. Round the bed of the river, lit up on the water, is the marina where the *Dolores* is moored.

My eyes lock on the white surf, crashing against the rocks below. The raw power that could end me in a second. Nessa doesn't have to tell me. This is the place where Devon died.

She didn't suffer. She died instantly. That's what the police report said about Fiona. Like they would know.

Nessa has moved to the cliff edge, looking down. I don't tell her to stand back. Surf crashes off a rock, spitting white into the darkness. To the right is the broad path down to the sea, with handrails and steps, signs telling you not to stray from the path: in winter the rocks are treacherous, often wet.

Nessa starts speaking.

'She hadn't been herself for a while,' she says. 'For a couple of weeks maybe. She didn't want to talk to me. I don't know how to explain it. It was like she was just sleepwalking through everything, like she was in shock or something. And then she'd started to get this determined kind of look about her, until that last night, when I asked her to tell me what was going on… she said she was leaving.'

I look up. I know how many times Nessa must have been asked about this. *Did you see anything? Did you hear anything?* She had us all convinced she'd just woken up one morning to an empty bed.

'Devon told you she was running away?'

She nods without looking back.

'I asked her where and she said she didn't know yet.' She pauses. 'Maybe New York. She said she just wanted to leave. That she was done with her life, she didn't want to be Devon Hundley any more. She had plenty of money - cash, not traceable. And she had credit cards if it came to it. I figured it wouldn't last that long - that she'd have enough and be home in a few weeks - but still… I didn't want to stay at Horton all by myself. Without her. She wouldn't listen when I tried to talk her out of it. So I told her to take me with her.'

The wind rolls through my hair, runs cold down my neck.

'We left before dawn. We were going to take the Greyhound from Milham. I was going to go into the town first - to get our tickets, and other stuff.' She fingers her long hair, but doesn't look away from the water. 'Hair dye. Pair of scissors. A change of clothes. She gave me the money, said she'd wait here for me. We put our bikes against that tree…' She falls silent.

'And then?'

'I bought everything and came back here, like we'd said I would. And then - then she told me I couldn't come.'

So Nessa was abandoned. That must have stung.

'Why, Nessa?'

She flinches. 'She said we'd be too recognizable together. That we'd be all over the news and people would remember me - buying the clothes, the hair dye. She said I'd give her away.'

She steps closer to the water. When she turns there's a strange look in her eyes, something adult, and it's as if for a moment we're the same age.

'I didn't know if she'd just been using me. Having me go buy everything first. She was so cold to me. She'd never been like that before,' she continues. 'She was acting so different. She was shouting, wouldn't look at me. I... I just wanted to get her to *see*. I asked her, I begged her just to *look* at me and she wouldn't, and I - I grabbed her.'

I don't know how Nessa can hear herself over the sound of my heart thumping but she must, because she keeps going.

'I don't really remember what happened then. She pushed me. She was - she was angry. She'd never been angry at me before. I -' her voice cracks. 'I pushed her back. I, I can't remember. I can't remember how it happened, not exactly. But I remember her falling. She looked so... surprised.'

She stops talking. The truth settles over us, over everything, like a terrible frost. For a moment, the world stops.

Twenty-three

There's a before, and there's an after. There's always that seesaw moment, the split-second where everything changes. Afterwards you long for everything that belonged to the Before, every second of innocence right up until your world fell apart.

That's what I think of when I glance through the panel in the police station's "family room" and see Nessa's mother, a grown-up version of Nessa, slumped in her chair, stunned and broken. Everything in her body says *no, it can't be. No, not my daughter. Not my daughter. Anyone else but not her.*

I think of Jan's face at Fiona's funeral, of the shovel of earth, the first handful of it hitting the coffin, a soft sound, like rain. Before, and after.

I think of the last time I saw Fiona. The first time I saw her.

I drove Nessa back to Horton first. I went with her to her room so she could pack a few things, knowing she'd never be back. I waited for her outside the bathroom, and truth be told I was listening, too, for tell-tale noises. For how long it takes for a girl to get a razorblade and do something terrible to herself. But then she came out, face clean and shining, that whitish hair over her shoulders, a strange calm around her.

'It's okay, Ms Kelly,' she said. 'Don't worry. I'm ready.'

On the way, I asked her for parents' number. I called it, told them to meet us at the station, to bring their lawyer.

There were so many thoughts whirling through me but I managed to ask her once more about Lucy and Philip. She just shook her head.

'I don't know. I'm sorry. I don't know anything about that.' She looked out the window. 'What will they do to me, Ms Kelly?' She stared as though the landscape passing us by could tell her something. 'Will I go to prison, do you think?'

I shook my head. 'You're not an adult.' *And you're not poor,* I didn't add. Even at a time like this, the world would be kinder to Horton kids than other kids. But whatever happened next, it would change her forever, that much was beyond question.

'I don't know what will happen, Nessa. I'm sorry.'

She nodded, and again it was like someone beyond her years.

Now I turn away from the scene in the family room, and walk out of the police station. I feel like a balloon that's been let go - a strange kind of vertigo, almost like being numb. I think back to my last glimpse of Nessa, that calmness in her eyes as she looked back over her shoulder, following her lawyer into a small, brown room.

I drive back to Horton just as the sun is coming up. I pull the suitcase down from the top of my wardrobe and start packing. Leaving is inevitable now. Thorpe will certainly never forgive me for discovering Nessa, for bringing her to the police station in the night, for not alerting her first. She'll see me as a traitor, and she's not wrong. Even if she let me stay, who knows what will happen to Horton now. This story won't blow over.

I'll pack first. Then I'll go tell Thorpe the news. It'll be morning by then.

I see a light on in Simone's cottage as I cross the quad, dragging my suitcase to the car, but I don't stop. I don't have the words right now. I don't want to have to answer questions. I load up the car, then walk back to the main building, up the stone staircase. Thorpe's office has a light on. I check my watch. 7 A.M. I don't think Thorpe sleeps much at the best of times - and today is not the best of times.

Philip, I think again, *where are you?*

I take a breath, and walk up to the door. I'm seventeen again, standing outside the principal's office, shoulders rounded, eyes down, the way Horton had already trained me to be.

Humans are so predictable, aren't we? The way we seek the same patterns over and over, even the patterns that hurt us the most. Sometimes especially the ones that hurt us the most. Horton was the place that ruined us, me and Fiona. And yet when I saw the teaching job advertized ten years later, instead of running from it I ran towards it, as if somehow, if I went back to the place where it all started, I could thread the needle differently.

The door's ajar. I raise my hand to knock.

'Come in, Ms Kelly,' Thorpe says, in her all-seeing way.

'Mrs Thorpe.' I close the door carefully, hear it click, and turn. I take a breath. 'There's something you need to know.'

*

I have to sit behind the wheel for a minute before starting up the engine. My hands are still trembling. I never thought I'd see Lucinda Thorpe like that. It was as if she could see the future projected right in front of her, like someone had struck a gong and told her *life as you know it is over*. It felt like watching an earthquake in slow motion. I turn the radio on. The news hasn't broken yet.

I shiver. Poor Nessa. She'll have to change her name when this is all over.

At that, Fiona's voice speaks slyly in my head. *Change her name? Is that right, Sadie?*

I push the voice away.

Out of instinct I glance at the phone in the cup-holder beside me. But of course there are no new messages. Philip has gone dark.

He didn't do it. He didn't hurt Devon.

But if he's innocent, why is he missing? And what about Lucy? Nothing feels clearer, even if it should. My heart ticks steadily, waiting for the other shoe to drop. Hoping it doesn't drop too hard. Hoping the impact, when it comes, doesn't hit like a bomb.

I dictate a text to Simone as I drive.

I left Horton this morning. You'll hear more soon. Call me.

My phone chirps, signaling less than half-battery. It's been up all night as well. I root around for the charging cable I threw in the car but can't find it. Damn it. That's the only one I have.

My ringtone blares suddenly, making me jump. Jan. I hit the loudspeaker and hear the rustle of hospital sheets.

'Sade, I've been listening to the news. Unbelievable. Do they really think he took her? Did he do something to the other girl?'

'I don't know what happened, Jan,' I say, trying to keep my voice cool. 'I just don't know.'

Please, I say to the universe. *Let Lucy show up safe.*

'Also,' I tell her. 'I have news. I left the job. I left Horton.'

My phone chirps in my ear. An incoming call. Simone. I reject it for now and hear Jan's long, slow exhale.

'You did? Because of this?'

'It's... complicated,' I say. 'I'll tell you tomorrow. You're still getting out tomorrow, right?'

'Yes, love.' I can feel the concern in her voice. 'Where are you now, Sadie?'

'Mom's house,' I say, because that's where I've been driving, almost without knowing it. I pull up and see its familiar shape, the garden where if I let my vision blur a little, I can still see Fiona clinging to a tree branch, calling to me to climb up and join her. I get out of the car and slam the door, phone to my ear.

'Your Mom's? Is she there?' Jan says.

That's what I'm about to find out. I ring the bell, then ring again and wait just to be sure, but she doesn't come. Sunday morning. She's probably at the stores, or at church. On the front step, I pull my jacket closer. Suddenly I'm so tired, so cold. The exhaustion of everything is hitting me all at once. *I want my mom,* I think. It's a thought I haven't let myself have in a long time.

'Sade, go back to mine,' Jan says firmly. 'Just go home, rest. You sound terrible.'

Despite myself I almost smile. *'You're* the one in the hospital.'

'Only till tomorrow,' she reminds me.

'I'm so glad you're coming home,' I say. 'I'll be there in the morning to pick you up.'

There's a pause.

'It'll be fine, you know, Sade,' she says, her voice gentle. 'Everything will be fine.'

I nod, even though she can't see me. And even though she's wrong.

I sit there in the driver's seat for a moment after we hang up. The effects of not sleeping for a night, combined with everything that's just happened - reality feels a little hazy right now. Everything *should* feel better, safer. So why doesn't it?

I look down at my phone. Simone's ringing again.

My voice is scratchy when I pick up.

'Hello?'

'Sadie?'

She sounds tense, on edge.

'You heard,' I say.

I hear her swallow. 'About Nessa? Yeah. I can hardly believe it. That poor kid.'

Which one? I don't say.

'She was always a bit... intense, wasn't she?' Simone goes on. 'But I just - ugh, I can't imagine. How will she live with herself, after all this?'

She'll find a way. I've learned that guilt, like grief, is something you metabolize over time. At first you don't think you'll ever be able to bear it. You can't imagine ever standing up under such a colossal weight. But then, over time, you learn.

'So you're really not coming back?' Simone says.

'I'm not sure Thorpe would ever forgive me,' I say. 'I brought Nessa to the police without consulting anyone. Without giving her a heads-up.'

Simone sighs. 'Yeah. It probably won't help her damage control.'

'And besides.' I lick my lips. 'I had to go. It's like I said, Simone. There's something about that place. I don't know. It just doesn't want me there.'

There's silence. A strange, charged silence on the other end.

'Simone?'

'*We don't want you here,*' she says.

A chill goes over me.

'What?' I murmur.

'*We don't want you here.* Right?' Her breath hitches. 'Sadie... I'm so sorry. I'm really, really sorry.'

There's a lump in my throat.

'What do you mean? That was - *you?*'

She sucks in a breath.

'Sadie... I should never, ever have done it. There's no excuse. None. But I... I was going crazy, during those months. Richard was cheating on me. And I found out in the worst possible way - it was *bad,* Sadie, I read the messages. The things he said to her... the things they were doing together. He had a nickname for her in his phone, and he swore blind that it was no-one I knew, just a stranger.' She exhales. 'But then I saw him - saw him and you - at our little end-of-term party, do you remember?'

'Simone -'

'I know,' she says. 'I know, Sadie. I know that now. That was just him, nothing to do with you. But I didn't know that at the time. I knew you'd been seeing someone, you had all the signs. I got the wrong idea. I became convinced it had been you all along. That you'd been flaunting it right under my nose.'

'So you tried to bully me into leaving,' I say. I can hear the chill in my voice. She has no idea how it felt. How it took me back ten years, to the torture of my teen years, of knowing I'd never, ever fit in.

'I'm so sorry,' she says again.

'Was it just the letters?' I say suddenly. 'The rock through my window, that other stuff -'

'No,' she jumps in. 'Sadie, I would never...' She stops. 'I found out over the summer, okay? The woman he was seeing, it was someone he knew from work. I realized how stupid I'd been. How cruel. I felt *terrible*. I vowed I'd make it up to you.'

We're both silent for a moment.

'So, what now?' I say. 'I forgive you?'

She hesitates. 'That's up to you. I understand if you don't.'

'I don't know,' I say. 'I guess I'll have to think about it.'

*

I drive to Jan's in a daze. So many things aren't what you think they're going to be. Philip's secrets. Simone's secrets. Even my mom had her secrets. And do those secrets keep anybody safer, in the end? Do they protect anyone from pain? Or do they just trap us deeper, and deeper, and deeper?

I pull up outside the house and turn off the engine. I need to sleep for a million years.

But when I go up the path and get my key in the door, it won't turn. I rattle the handle a bit, try it again, but it's just not budging. I take it out, rub it on my jeans, blow in the keyhole.

'Sadie!'

It's Rob. He's on the street, walking towards me.

'I just saw you pull up. Are you locked out?' He frowns. 'Did Jan tell you about the keys?'

I straighten up. My vision feels blurry from lack of sleep. I imagine waking up to a world that makes sense. A world where Lucy Hundley is back safe in her own bed, and Philip has a perfect explanation for it all.

'We changed the locks,' Rob says, pulling me back to the present. 'After that night - it seemed wise to be on the safe side.'

'Oh.' I stare down stupidly at the key in my hand.

'Just wait there a second, I'll get my key.'

I wait on the doorstep. Rob goes a few doors down to his place, then comes back, keys jingling. He stands beside me, close enough that I can smell his cologne. His key works all right, but it's freezing in here. I can see my breath in the air. Rob shivers, rubs his hands together.

'I turned off the heat, since she said she wasn't going to be back for a while.' He slips out of the room and I hear him flipping switches, the crank of the water heater turning on. Even *I* don't know where those are, but Rob knows his way around here like it's home.

'She's getting out tomorrow,' I call out into the back hallway. He reappears, rubbing his hands on his jacket.

'Yeah? That's great news.' He stands there, blows on his hands again and tucking them under his arms.

'Look, why don't you wait at mine for a couple of hours while this warms up?' I must look dubious because he adds, 'I'm just heading out. You'll have the place to yourself.'

I guess it makes sense. In a few hours this place will be as toasty as it always is.

Rob leads me a few doors down to his place, into a

house that is identical in layout to Jan's, just decorated differently - decorated with surprisingly good taste, for a guy who looks like he gets dressed in the dark.

'Tea. Coffee. Mugs are here. Help yourself to what's in the refrigerator.'

When he closes the door behind him I watch him drive off then sink down onto the couch. Reality seems to be flickering in and out of focus. I'm so tired, but jittery too. I pat down my pockets and find the Klonopin, shake one into my hand, lie down and close my eyes. It's only supposed to be for half an hour, but I wake up to the sound of my phone ringing, and somehow it's dark already. It takes me a moment to figure out where I am. I feel around me for my phone and turn on the screen. It's late. Rob's still not home. I check the news headlines. The news on Nessa and Devon has broken.

My phone chirps. Low battery. *Great*. Then I remember: Rob has the same phone as me, I've noticed the model. I glance up the staircase, hesitating. He's not back yet. And he probably wouldn't mind. He's already let me into his house.

I climb the stairs and open the door in the middle of the hallway, which in Jan's house is the master bedroom. I hit the lights. There's a tangle of chords and cables by the floor of the nightstand so I inch closer and pick out the one I need. My phone chirps happily as it plugs in. I rub my eyes, still groggy from sleep. I'll just wait another till it's mostly charged, and I can buy a new cable tomorrow.

From the window you can can see the road out front, all the lights telling you who's home, who's not. A car slowly cruising by. I ease myself into Rob's swivel chair while I wait for my phone to juice up. I glance down at his desk.

And see pictures. Photographs.
Of *me*.

Twenty-four

Everything feels very cold. There's a ringing sound in my ears. The pictures, they're printouts, all from my Facebook profile. But my profile's private, and I know I never accepted an invitation from him.

He works in IT, Sadie.

There's a word for this. But it doesn't make sense, I think, as my brain whispers *stalker*. I don't understand how, or why -

Pieces start to rearrange themselves in my mind. That noise that made Jan think someone was breaking in, even though later there were no signs of forced entry? Rob has a spare key, just like I do.

The disturbances in Jan's garden, the security camera she bought. And all the things that have been happening to me. Is it possible...? Rob works from home. Nobody cares where he drives off to in the middle of the day.

Or night.

But why?

I yank my phone from the cable, clatter down the stairs. I don't understand. I just know I need to get out of here. My purse is still in the living room, on its side by the sofa. As I grab it, through the frosted glass of the front door I see a pair of headlights right in front of the house.

Shit. *Shit.*

I turn and run. I know the layout of these houses, they're all the same. I hurry through the shallow living room to the kitchen and duck to the utilities room where the back door is. I turn the lock - Rob's is old, rusting, but finally it gives - and then I'm out in the freezing air, in Rob's back garden. I dig my toe in the brick wall - dry mortar tumbles out under my boot - and use my hands to haul myself up and over the sides. Then I'm in the neighbor's garden, my feet smashing heavily onto their camellias. I pick up the pace, run across the garden and through the gap in the wall that leads to the alley. I hide there as I hear a car door slam, then the quieter sound of a front door. Then I pound down the footpath, to my car.

I drive blindly, taking turns at random. I don't think Rob saw me leave - the light in his bedroom was still on, so he probably went up there first - but I drive until I'm sure I'm not being followed. I need to think. I need to understand what I saw. But the more I go over it, the less it makes sense. I hold my phone in my hand, staring at it, deciding whether or not to call the police. What would I say? What am I accusing him of, exactly? I need to speak to Jan first. I pull out my phone and try her, but it rings out. It's late. She always has her phone on silent after ten o'clock. I curse and throw my phone down in the passenger seat. I'll be at the hospital first thing. I'll tell her everything, and together we'll decide what to do.

I check the time on the dashboard. Past midnight. I could go back to Mom's, couldn't I? But the truth is I don't have the strength. I don't understand what's happening, so how could I be expected to explain it all to Mom? The Klonopin I took a few hours ago is still in my system, the heaviness kicking in as the adrenalin leaks away from me. Finally I crawl into the back seat and give in to the darkness.

*

I wake stiff and cold, just as a grey light is starting to filter through the windows. I shiver, and pull my coat tighter, but it's not enough.

My phone chirps. I look down, expecting the low-battery alert, but it's a text message.

Sender: Philip.

My mouth goes dry instantly. I click on it.

Sadie, I know what they're saying. I didn't hurt Devon. I never would have hurt her.

My heart squeezes. I knew that already, but Philip - poor Philip - hasn't heard about Nessa.

My phone pings again.

Sadie, I think Lucy and I are in danger.

I freeze. My fingers skid to the Call button, then stop. *He* didn't make a call - why? Who's with him?

We're staying on the boat.

I swallow. My phone battery's sinking low again.

We need help. Can you come, Sadie?

I hesitate.

Danger. What kind of danger? I glance at my 7% battery indicator.

I'm on the way, I text, and turn the keys in the ignition.

*

It's still mostly dark, the houses only starting to wake up. When I hit the marina, the dawn light is beginning to creep over the water, threads of electric pink. If my brain wasn't quivering with nerves, I could almost enjoy it. Instead I force my shaking hands to park the car, and swallow down the fear as I lock the car, pocket the key.

The *Dolores*.

I always thought it was strange to name your boat

after a word for sorrow.

I step down to the dock. The boats rock and bob. Everything else is silent. I'm shaking, and I don't think it's the cold.

Pier 3. There she is, the *Dolores*. I walk down the pier, boats clinking softly around me.

'*Philip*,' I hiss.

There's no answer. I glance round. It certainly seems empty out here. A bird calls nearby, and I hear a noise. Philip? I'm about to call his name again when I think better of it. Maybe he's not the only person coming this way.

I look around, but there's nowhere to hide except the obvious place. I breathe in, crouch, and put my hand to the mooring line. I put one foot over the edge, and then another. The *Dolores* sways a little beneath me. I must have imagined the noise; everything's silent again. I reach into my pocket and call him.

Faintly, his ringtone sounds. It's somewhere nearby. On the boat - I'm almost certain it's coming from the boat. Is he waiting below deck? My heart jumps a little.

But why isn't he picking up?

I swallow, flick my phone to silent, and pocket it. The hatch is open. Cautiously I make my way to the stairs, put my foot on the first tread. The phone keeps ringing. Otherwise, everything is silent. I step down; down another step, and further down. It's dark down here. Only the thinnest light from the hatch above me. What's he doing in the dark?

Oh God Oh God Oh God.

There's a scuffling sound, a chair maybe. I freeze.

And then the hatch slams shut.

I scream. I can't see. It's pitch black.

The scuffling continues. I back away from the noise - and my hand finds a switch. Light floods the room.

Twenty-five

'Coach - Coach Ned?'

My mind reels. Is this some sort of... prank? But the look on his face tells me it's not. His eyes are bloodshot. His feet are tied to a chair, his hands behind him, and his mouth is gagged. He shuffles closer to me again, moving his face, flaring his nostrils, shaking and shuddering like he's having some kind of seizure. It takes a nauseous moment before I can steel myself to close the rest of the space between us and reach behind his head, hands on his skull - it's sweating, greasy - and dig my nails into the knotted bandana. It comes free, and he spits out the wads of cotton balled in his mouth.

'*Fucking hell.*' His voice cracks.

'How...what are you *doing* here?'

'Just untie me, for Christ's sake,' he wheezes. His face is red, like the rage of being tied up is only now hitting him.

'First tell me what's going on,' I hiss. 'Where's Philip? What did you do to him?'

His eyes bulge. 'Are you out of your tree? I'm on *your* side. We have to get up there, before that crazy little -'

He's cut off by the sound of an engine switching gears, and that's when I realize. *We're moving.*

'Fuck, *fuck,*' he spits.

'Who's up there, Ned? What is this?'

He turns to me, eyes straining in their sockets. 'Crazy *bitch.*' Then he focuses. 'Not you, Sadie, not you. Now will you *please* untie me?'

I swallow.

'Hold still,' I say to Ned as I bend over his tied wrists, and start trying to work the knots.

'Who's "she", Ned? Who's upstairs?' *And what does she want with us?*

He groans. 'The older one.' He spits the name out like poison. 'Lucy.'

I freeze. 'Lucy Hundley? Lucy did *this*?'

I'm trying to piece it together, and failing. Why would Lucy tie him up? *How* did she tie him up? And where's Philip?

The knots aren't coming undone. Now two of my fingernails are bleeding.

'Ned, this isn't working.'

He snorts in exasperation, rage. He wasn't like this at Horton. He's like a different person.

Lucy, my brain repeats. *Lucy.* Why?

'Can you, I don't know, find a fucking knife or something?'

Right, I think. The galley. I stumble over, pulling out drawers. My phone bangs against my thigh. My phone - I make my hands stop shaking. I scroll, hit Jan's number. It rings once, twice.

Then the phone chirps and dies.

Fuck.

It takes all I have not to scream. How could I be so stupid? With a pang of foreboding I remember being out here with Philip. How bad the reception was. Even with my phone, maybe I'd already be lost. *Focus, Sadie.* I jerk open another drawer. It rattles out and there's the silverware, gleaming. Then suddenly there's a sound from inside, and a rush of cold lake air.

'Ms Kelly!' a voice calls. 'Come back where I can see you.'

Jesus. He was right. That's Lucy Hundley's voice. Hoarse and high, like she's been crying or screaming. It sends chills through me.

'*Ms Kelly.*'

I don't move. If she ties me up like Coach Ned, then my chances of getting out of here -

'I mean it, Ms Kelly. I have a gun.'

I swallow.

'I don't think Coach Ned wants me to use it, do you, Coach?'

Ned's voice rings out nervously. 'She's not kidding, Sadie. She has a fucking rifle.'

'And if I can't see *you*, I'll have to use it on *him*. So unless you want that on your conscience, do come out.'

Silently, I lift the biggest knife I can find out of the drawer and slide it down the side of my boot.

'I'm coming,' I say, loudly, to cover any noise. I can't close the drawer though, it rattles too loud, she'll know. I just have to hope she doesn't come into the galley any time soon and put two and two together.

'Well come *faster.*' Her voice is getting higher. I don't want her to panic. No one holding a gun should panic.

I put my hands in the air and walk slowly out in view of the stairs and suppress a gasp.

Pretty Lucy Hundley. Her hair is a wild, dirty cloud. There's oil on her clothes and face. And she's holding one of the Hundleys' hunting rifles.

Does she even know how to use it? I swallow. Does it make us safer, or less safe, if she doesn't?

'Thank you, Ms Kelly,' she says politely, her voice easy now, suddenly relaxed. 'Please take a seat.'

I do, looking at her, my eyes fixed on hers. I need to psych her out, I need her to feel she's not in charge, that she can't do this. I need to make her feel like a scared child. I keep my voice calm:

'Lucy-'

'Here.' She tosses me a rope. 'I'm afraid I can't put this down-' she means the gun '-just yet, so you're going to have to follow my instructions.'

Christ. She wants me to tie *myself* up.

'But I'm sure you'll be a quick study,' she continues. 'Dear old Philip must have shown you a few things, surely.'

My stomach turns. *She knows.*

'Is that what this is about? Lucy...'

'What do you think, Miss? Do *you* think that's what this is about?'

Her tone reminds me of someone. *Me,* I realize. Me in the classroom. *What do you think this poem is about, girls?*

'If you're wondering where Philip is, he's right in there,' she gestures through the door to the tiny sleeping area that I remember from before. My heart thumps.

'This wasn't his idea, don't worry,' she says. 'I told him to come here. I wanted him to see this.'

See this? What's *this?*

'Philip,' she calls. 'I'm going to open the door.'

She nudges it open and there he is. His hands are tied too. He won't meet my eyes.

'I'm sorry, Sadie, I'm so sorry.' His eyes swivel round the room, to Lucy, and back to me. 'I didn't mean to get you mixed up in this. When Lucy called and told me she needed me to meet her here' - he looks bewildered, like he still can't account for how it happened - 'I just got in the car and drove, I didn't even think. Then when I showed up…. And she had the gun and I didn't know what she was going to do with it, I thought she was going to hurt herself -'

 'And I made Philip give me his phone,' Lucy cuts across him. 'Enough. You can catch up later.' She gestures at me. 'You're going to have to use that rope, Ms Kelly. I can't keep an eye on all three of you at once. Please.' She points to the chair, and I don't see what choice I have. I guess I agreed to play her game the moment I came out of the kitchen, into her sight-line. But I had to. I couldn't just leave Ned there. Slowly, I bind my legs to the chair I'm sitting on. Ned's averting his gaze. Philip is still staring at the floor.

'Now hands.' Lucy shows me what she wants me to do, and when I've slipped the noose over my own wrists she leans in and jerks it tight.

I remember Philip laughing up on deck last summer, teaching me his rope knots. *The impossible knot, Sadie. Not impossible to tie - very easy, actually - but impossible to get out of.* I'd smirked at him.

'Better.' Lucy looks between her stepfather and me. 'You broke Devon's heart, you know. The two of you. She *worshipped* you, you know that, Philip? Adored you. You betrayed her.' She turns to me. 'And *you* made him.'

 I open my mouth but I don't know what to tell her. That Philip came to me as an all-but-divorced man? That I never meant to hurt anyone but myself?

Lucy tosses something on the table. A flash of red. A notebook. I recognize it instantly - the shape, the color. A perfect match with the rest of the set. It's Devon's diary. Lucy turns to me.

'I found it in her room. I went there as soon as they told us that she was - that she was gone. I knew where to look. I'd *taught* her that. I'd taught her all Horton's secrets. That's what big sisters are supposed to do. Protect. Help.'

She stops and looks at the diary - this small, dog-eared notebook that somehow seems to be sending a current of electricity throughout the room.

'Do you want to know what's in it?' She turns to us, looking over each of us in turn. No one speaks.

'Devon saw you getting into the car with Philip, Ms Kelly,' she says. 'She wondered about it of course, but the first time, she dismissed it. She really liked you, Ms Kelly, you know? I don't think she wanted to believe that about you. But then she saw it again, and she followed you. Not for long, she was only on her bike - but I guess she saw enough to suspect. She was always so possessive of you, wasn't she, Philip?'

He's silent.

'So you're punishing me for that?' I say.

Lucy glares. 'I'm punishing you for what happened *because* of it.' Then she turns on Ned, who blanches. 'And what about you, Coach? *You* know what this is about, don't you?'

He says nothing.

'Don't you?'

Slowly, he nods.

A little moan escapes Lucy, a sound of grief, like despite everything she had hoped he'd say no. I keep my eyes on the barrel of the rifle, holding my breath, waiting for this all to make sense.

'But it wasn't like you're thinking,' he says in a rush. He raises his eyes towards the gun, then drops them. 'I'm not a - I'm not one of *those*. I didn't make her do anything. I -'

'Shut up,' Lucy hisses. The gun jerks. He shuts up.

My brain whirs. I'm trying to process what I just heard. I feel sick.

'What did you - what did you do?' I hiss at him. 'What did you do to Devon?'

Ned raises his head just enough to give me a withering look.

I suck in a breath. 'You...' And there I was in the kitchen, worrying about putting him in danger. 'I should have *let* her put a hole in you. '

'She was sixteen,' he says quietly. 'Not a kid.'

He looks up, and sees Lucy's and my eyes on him. I feel a wave of disbelief at what I see in his. He thinks he's not one of the bad guys. That the newspaper headlines we see all the time are about *other* men. Bad men. Not men like him.

'Do you want to hear what happened, the night Devon followed you two?' Lucy glances at the diary, swallows. 'When she came back it was past curfew. Dark, raining. And someone saw her come back, didn't they Coach? Someone stopped her. Told her how *concerned* he was, how dangerous it was to be out there late, unsupervised, alone. Made insinuations until she begged him not to report her. He invited her inside to discuss it. *She seemed upset*, he told her.' She picks the diary up by a corner then lets it drop again, like she can barely touch it.

'Nothing happened,' Ned snaps. 'I gave her a towel to dry off, made her some tea. Listened to her. That's all.'

Lucy's face is grim. 'That was all for that night. But you sensed it, didn't you? How fragile she was. How mixed-up in her emotions, and angry and betrayed. You followed Ms Kelly too, didn't you - after that? Just to see if Devon was right.'

I stare at Ned. I'm nauseated at the thought of him watching me and Philip. Spying on us.

Lucy goes on. 'And once you had the proof you thought you'd kill a couple of birds with one stone. You told Devon you'd fix it, that you'd get rid of Ms Kelly for her. You went to Thorpe and made up something about, what? - inappropriate classroom behavior, bad language? - making sure Devon and our family wouldn't get dragged into it.' Lucy closes her eyes for a moment. 'And then once you'd done Devon such a favor you expected one back, didn't you? You decided she must really like you. She must really want to *thank* you.'

I think of the girl Nessa described, lying in bed, withdrawing into herself. *Like she was sleepwalking.* I can imagine now what happened to provoke it. Why Horton was suddenly unbearable to her.

Ned glares at me.

'It wasn't like that, and don't *you* look at me like that, when you know full well *you* should never have been teaching at Horton in the first place.' His eyes narrow. 'You don't think people know? I did my research on you, Ms Kelly, don't you worry. I told Devon everything I learned.'

He has the gall to smirk at me.

I know your secret.

I can't think about that now.

'Lucy.' I turn to her. 'I'm so sorry.'

She folds her arms. 'You wouldn't listen to me.' Her voice gets higher, sharper. 'You wouldn't listen to me when I tried to tell you. You *sent me away*. I couldn't protect her. I couldn't watch out for her. Because you *sent me away*.'

'Sent you -?' Jesus Christ. Lucy kicked up hell when she was sent away for a semester. I figured it was shame and denial, everything that tied into the eating disorder. But now her words cut through me. *You sent me away*. She wanted to stay at Horton to watch over her sister. She must have suspected something, felt something, even if she hadn't put it into words.

I remember suddenly how she quit the swim team in eleventh grade. I figured it was just because she didn't like being on a team where her younger sister outshone her. She'd come to see me - I was her homeroom teacher, I had to sign off on her dropping an extra-curricular. *I don't like the way Coach speaks to us,* she'd said. She'd stared at me as she spoke, with what I thought at the time was a kind of insolence. I'd thought she just didn't like being shouted at in the pool, being criticized. I'd heard Ned in coach mode, striding up and down the pool's edge barking at them, goading them to do better, and he didn't use delicate language. I thought Lucy just didn't like his tough-talk. Now my stomach lurches. That wasn't what she meant at all. Why hadn't I listened?

You were distracted, Sadie, the voice says. It wasn't long after I'd started seeing Philip. *Very distracted. Remember?*

'I hadn't *seen* anything, I couldn't *prove* anything,' Lucy goes on, voice rising. Her whole body is shaking now. 'I couldn't prove anything but I *felt* it, I knew he wasn't right, I - the way he...' She glares at me. 'I wanted

239

you to *do* something...' Tears roll down her face, but she doesn't lower the gun. She swallows. 'You gave them that speech at the beginning of eleventh grade,' Lucy says. 'The same one you gave to my class when you were *our* homeroom teacher. You said we could come to you if we had problems. You said you were there to help us. But you lied. And now she's dead.'

I can't meet her eyes. None of this was what I meant. None of it was supposed to happen - but it did. It did.

'She tried to get her own back, you know.' Lucy's voice sharpens, and I look back up.

'Both of you, ' Lucy nods. 'Devon was a believer in revenge. She was going to do what she could, before she left. But Ned's car only hit a little ditch. And you, Ms Kelly. You were the last thing on her list before she caught that bus. She doesn't say in her diary exactly what she had in mind, but Devon was always brilliant at starting fires. Aced it in Girl Scouts.' Lucy grimaces. 'So I guess you were lucky Nessa did what she did.'

'That kid's the one you should be blaming, if you're blaming anyone,' Ned bursts out. 'That little freak who killed her.'

Lucy stares at him. 'Nessa's life is already ruined.'

But yours isn't. Yet. That's the subtext of what she's saying.

I lick my chapped lips. They're so dry, like my throat. I didn't know nerves could do this. I feel like I haven't drunk a drop in days.

'Lucy -where are you taking us?'

She looks at me, her eyes dark. She doesn't answer.

'I get it,' I say. 'You brought us here for Devon. You wanted revenge for what happened to her.'

Lucy frowns. 'I *wanted* to protect her. It was my job to protect her.'

I remember the vigil, and Lucy's accusations. *You were supposed to protect her.* Guilt can unhinge people just as much as anger.

'That's not your job, Lucy. You did your best. But it wasn't your job to protect her. You're still a child.'

'No,' she says, coolly. 'I'm not.'

I see Ned nervously dart his eyes my way.

'Philip,' Lucy says briskly, moving to the stairs. 'You're coming on deck with me. We'll leave these two down here.' She eyes me. 'Don't get into any trouble.'

'Philip,' I say as he follows her. He flinches.

'Sadie, I'm sorry. I need to do as she asks.'

Lucy looks back towards me, wordless, and disappears through the hatch.

Twenty-six

'She's crazy. She's *crazy*,' Ned starts saying. And yes, he's right, but even though Lucy Hundley is the one with the gun, he's the one I don't want to be in a room with right now.

'What the fuck are we going to *do*?' he says in a strangled voice. I don't answer him, I'm busy seeing how far my tied hands will extend, and if I can lift my bent legs high enough to slide that knife out of my boot.

'Devon,' Ned says, raising his eyes to the ceiling. 'If you're up there, sweetheart, *please*, get us out of here.'

'What the fuck are you saying?' I momentarily forget the knife. 'You have no *right* -'

His nostrils flare. 'I miss her too, you know. And for the record, I know the optics aren't good here, but-'

'*She was a child.*' I feel a wave of despair. Of all the monsters out there, it's the self-righteous ones, the ones who *think* they're beyond blame, that are the most dangerous. Because if they have enough power, if they're loud enough or smooth enough, their voice can convince others, too.

'Maybe she changed her mind afterwards, but I would never, ever, have, you know, if she was *unwilling* -'

'Oh,' I spit. 'So you're above physical coercion. I can't wait to tell the police so they can give you a medal.'

'Look,' he snaps. 'She wasn't some *kid*, it was -'

I feel like my head is going to explode. 'Ned. I need you to stop talking now.'

I have to ignore the murderous rage he's stirring in

me. I have to concentrate. The knife is sliding out of my
boot. I can't use my thumbs, so I've got it pinched
between my middle and ring fingers, gripping it as firmly
as I can with my fingertips, which is not very firmly at all.
I'm sweating, which makes my fingers slippery and the
gap between my boot and my leg clammy and squeaky,
but it's working. I've got it out of my boot, and I'm trying
to maneuver it into a proper grip when the boat swerves a
little and I drop it.

Fuck. Fuck. Fuck.

'What was that?' Ned startles, and sees it. 'Oh shit,
yes. Just… just pick it up, Sadie, just pick it up, come on.'

I work the knot as far down the metal bar as I can. My
knees are in the way, I can't quite get my hand low
enough. But if I can get another inch - yes, and then one
more -

The hatch snaps open again. I straighten up.

'I heard that,' Lucy says. 'And *him* shouting about
something. You better tell me. I'm not leaving Philip by
himself up there.' And then she spots it. 'Oh. You dropped
something.'

No. No.

She reaches down and plucks the knife from beneath
the table.

'Let me just put this away where it belongs.'

She turns and takes it back to the galley, and hot tears
spring into my eyes. I will them down. If I show weakness,
I've already lost.

'Shit. *Shit.*' Ned thumps his head on the table. Lucy
ignores him.

I close my eyes.

'Don't worry,' she says from the galley. 'You'll be free

to walk around soon.'

Why does that sound like a bad thing, the way she says it?

'Was it all you, Lucy?' I say. 'Everything that happened at Horton. Those pranks. And my friend Jan. Did you go to her house, too?'

She sighs and looks at me. 'I looked up your home address in Thorpe's files one day when she wasn't around. That gnome is super ugly by the way.'

Other things fall into place too. That "food poisoning" that only Ned and I got. It's probably why Ned looked so exhausted all the time, and why I caught him creeping around outdoors at night - was she baiting him too, scratching on his door at night, luring him outside?

'And the photograph from my office?'

'I hadn't meant to take that,' Lucy says, her voice growing quieter. 'I'd just meant to mess things up a bit. But you looked so happy in it, you and your sister. It wasn't fair. I couldn't stand it.'

Sister. I feel a wave of pain. That's how I thought of Fiona once, too.

I glance over at Ned, who's glaring at us both. Lucy's looking out the window now.

'I want you two to take a look out there.'

I swallow, and turn my head. Through the narrow bar of window I can see a rocky coastline. There are a few trees at the top, and surf leaping at the bottom. I recognize it. I was there with Nessa in what already seems like another lifetime ago, looking down at the crashing waves. This is the spot where Devon fell.

'I wanted you to see it first,' Lucy says.

First. Again my stomach contracts. What comes after

first?

Ned raises his eyes to the ceiling. 'Devon, sweet selkie girl, I *told* you. I told you your sister was crazy.'

'What did you...' Cold sweat springs all over. *My sweet selkie girl.* 'What did you say?'

'I knew she was crazy,' he repeats. 'Lucy. She's always had it in for me.'

I shake my head.

'Selkie. You called her a selkie.'

His face flickers. He shrugs.

It's then that I think I feel my heart break. *Fiona.*

Fiona and I were eighteen then. Ned was what - twenty-five? The heart-throb teacher. My stomach turns. Were there others?

But Lucy just looks at Ned blankly, because what he's said means nothing to her. It's only me that feels like I'm falling - falling through darkness, deeper and deeper.

Lucy claps her hands together. 'Okay, I think we're far enough from shore now. Time to go up on deck. I'm going to untie your legs now. No funny business, understood? Who wants to go first? Coach?'

His jaw is locked in silent fury, and he doesn't say a word or look at her as she bends down to untie his legs. Right as she gets the last chord loose he jerks a leg back, aiming a kick at her head, but Lucy is too quick for him, and in a second she's smashed the barrel of the rifle across his skull. He roars in pain.

'That's what you'll get!' Lucy yells, though I can tell it's more panic than rage. She's red in the face now. 'That's what you'll get if you don't listen to me!' She draws in a long breath. 'Okay. Let's try this again. Go up the stairs, Coach. Open the hatch, but don't walk through it yet.'

This time he does what she tells him, then she instructs him to stay there while she unknots my legs. I barely breathe, I'm trying so hard not to make any sudden movement.

Fiona.

Sweet selkie girl.

She was on the swim team too back then. And an outsider. Someone he could pick off from the herd.

'Okay.' Lucy's voice brings me back. 'I'm right behind you. Both of you, walk through and up onto the deck. Slowly.'

Ned in front of me, Lucy behind, we do as she asks.

Sadie, what's a selkie?

The wind and rain hit me like a wall. We're further than I thought from shore. Everything is grey, the sky, the sea, the rain. Surf splashes round the hull of the boat. The cold rain pelts down, mixes with the sweat on my skin. At least it gives me a reason to shiver that isn't fear. *Focus, Sadie.* Fiona's gone. Fiona's not here. And if I want justice, I need to live. I need to get out of here to see justice done.

Philip's at the tiller. It's like a mockery of all the times I've been here before, him steering us laughingly out on the water on a sunny day. A couple of days of this have left his stubble longer, his face thinner; he looks like an actor playing the part of a handsome hostage. But I don't want to look at him. I don't want to look at him ever again.

Meanwhile Ned's face is starting to show pure terror. I tell myself not to let it get to me, I can't afford to have his fear contaminating me.

The rain's getting thicker, really pelting down now. Even Lucy must feel it. Philip's eyes rove over us, stopping on me. I can feel his voice: *sorry, Sadie.* But sorry isn't enough, sorry won't get us home.

'We shouldn't be out here, Lucy,' Philip says. He sounds weirdly calm. 'The bilge pump isn't working properly, you know. Without repairs...'

She darts a glance at him. If this rain gets worse we could be in trouble, is what he's saying. I know from his rudimentary lessons with me that the bilge pump is what flushes water out of a boat, if heavy rain or overboard wakes starts to weigh it down.

I'm thinking about what Philip just said. *If the rain gets worse.*

An idea starts to form in my mind. It may not be a great idea, but if I don't take the risk, whatever comes next is going to be worse. I look at Lucy, two hands on the gun. She seems taller now than before, not so easy to overpower. But she needs to control this ship, keep us afloat in what's starting to look more and more like a gathering storm - and there's only one of her and three of us.

I see her glancing up at the rain, assessing how heavy it is. If I get to the drain plug... I'm probably crazy but it's all I can think of. I just wish I knew more, so I could calculate how much damage this will actually do. All I have to go on is what I picked up from Philip last Spring. But I look at him now, glassy-eyed and eerily calm, and I know he's not thinking about how to get out of this. I have to do something.

I laughed when Philip told me that all boats come with a plug. Wasn't it the last thing you needed on a boat, I said. He told me if the boat's moving fast enough, pulling the plug creates a vacuum to suck any rainwater *out* of your boat. But right now Lucy has us holding steady. That means if I can get to the drain plug, start letting the water in...

We'll have a different problem then. But at least it'll force her hand. She'll need to get help then.

'Okay,' Lucy says. The rain has plastered her hair against her head in a matted, dripping tangle. Her pretty features are wet and distorted with anger. She looks like a crazed porcelain doll. 'Okay, here's what happens next: you swim.'

Twenty-seven

This, it turns out, is Lucy's plan. She's going to unshackle our hands, and then make us jump in the water, and attempt to swim to shore.

'You, over there,' she directs Philip. 'And you,' she points to Ned. 'There.' She spaces us out on the deck, making sure we're not close enough to help each other. But she's positioned me right by the controls.

'Lucy.' I look over the side of the boat, into the thrusting waves. 'It's winter. It's freezing. Even if we could swim that far...'

'I'm giving you the chance,' she says.

Ned lets out a tight laugh. 'And what if one of us does get to shore? You really don't think we'd go straight to the police with this? You don't think you're going to spend the rest of your life in some juvenile detention centre, or better yet, an asylum? Why don't you just shoot us and get it over with?'

Ned, stop. Stop.

Lucy blinks at him, shrugs.

'That's not the same. It's not what I want. I'm not an executioner, Coach.' She looks up into the sky, squinting into the furious rain. 'You think I care where I wind up after this? I don't. It doesn't matter now.'

I look at Ned. At Philip. Ned's the swimmer, the athlete. The idea that one of us might make it, and that that one of us might be Ned, makes my blood rise up. I need to do something. I *will* do something. I just need -

And then Ned gives me the opportunity. He turns a

251

few shades paler and runs to the side of the boat, retching over the edge. Lucy takes a few paces after him and I seize the moment. She's yelling at him, and I know by the way her voice carries that she's turned away from me.

I go straight for the drain plug. I will my hands not to shake. I've never done this before.

No sane person has done this before, Sadie.

Rain smashes down all round me. Breathing fast, I grip it and twist.

Nothing.

Come on, come on! I breathe in, try again. I can't get a good grip with my hands bound like this. It feels like I'm straining harder than I've ever done anything in my life. My hands are screaming with the pressure.

Nothing.

I picture Jan's face, what it would be like for her to visit me in the cemetery, next to the daughter she already lost. I picture my mother, and never getting to show her she was wrong about me.

I push with my freezing, shackled fingers, with everything I can, and something gives. *Come on.* One more rotation. *Yes.*

God, I hope this wasn't as stupid an idea as it feels. I look over and see Philip's face. He's seen it all. And he looks pale.

'Get up!' I hear Lucy saying. 'You better not be faking it.'

She nudges Ned away from the sides, back to where we're standing.

'Okay,' she says, glancing back in the direction of land. She looks around at the three of us 'Get ready.'

'You're not really going to make us do this, Lucy?'

Philip says, pleading.

Lucy shrugs. 'I heard *him* appealing to Devon earlier.' She jerks her chin at Ned. 'Maybe try that when you're in the water. Ask her to help you. Maybe she will.'

'Lucy,' I say. I'm out of time, I have to tell her. I keep my voice steady. 'I did something to the boat.'

She looks at me.

'The drain plug. I took it out. You're going to have to radio for help.'

'You did *what?*'

She checks it, and sees that I'm not lying.

'Where is it?' she demands, and I think I see the flash of fear in her eyes.

'I threw it away.'

Ned is staring at me, mouth open, and Philip looks even paler than before. I know what I've done will sink us, but what I don't know is how fast. When Lucy looks at me, her face is grey.

'Are you crazy?'

Ned has started to laugh hysterically. 'You fucking crazy bitch. This - this - was your idea?'

I ignore him and hold Lucy's stare. 'You have to call the coastguard. We're sinking, and a storm's coming.'

'No,' she spits.

I stand firm. 'Call the coastguard. You know we can't ride out the storm, not with the amount of water we're already taking on.'

I see Lucy's mind working, eyes darting from me to Ned.

'No,' she says. 'I'm not calling anyone.'

'So what, we're *all* going to die?' Ned snarls.

'Just shut up!' Lucy yells.

The words are barely out of her mouth when a huge
surge of water hits the boat, and a wave smashes over the
side and Lucy loses her footing. In the second she takes to
right herself Ned sprints forward, knocking into her, and
they both hit the floor. I freeze, every hair standing on end
for the sound of the gun going off. It doesn't, but there's a
sickening thwack of something heavy hitting bone, and
Lucy shrieks in pain. I race forward. Ned pulls himself
from the ground, limping, the gun dangling from his
hands. The rope still clings around one of his wrists but he
must have managed to work the other free while we were
standing here. I pull at my own, but if anything, the rain
has only made the knot harder.

'You bit me, you little bitch,' he's saying. 'You crazy
little bitch.'

'Ned.'

He wheels round to face me

'Keep calm, okay? Don't do anyth--'

He laughs in disbelief. 'Me? I'm the one you're
warning? I didn't hear you saying that to her.'

'Ned, just call the coastguard, okay?' I point to the
little radio device on the dash. 'We just need to call the
coastguard and we can all get out of here.' I keep my voice
calm, reasonable. 'We can all make it out of here. You can
keep the gun. Just let Philip sail the ship. We need to get a
little closer to the shore. Please.'

'You,' he nods his chin at Philip. 'What she said. Get
us closer to shore.' He rummages in his pocket, takes out a
pen-knife. I guess that's how he freed himself before. He
tosses it to me.

'Just free his hands so he can steer the boat properly.
Then put it back on the floor.'

I do as he says. Philip looks to me, then at Lucy. There are so many emotions crossing his face at the same time. Then he drops his eyes, and starts working to turn the boat around.

I put the knife back on the floor, and scoot it towards Ned. He pockets it.

'What about the coastguard, Ned?'

He looks at me.

'Well, I don't think that benefits me, Sadie. I don't think that benefits me at all.' He looks toward Lucy, who's still hunched on the rain-slick deck, soaked through. 'Why would I want her to be rescued? And you...' He shrugs. 'I'm sorry, but I can see where this is heading. You've already made it very clear what *scum* you think I am. We're not in this together. We never were. I'm not letting you two crazy bitches put me in jail.'

I stare at him.

'Ned, come on.'

He blinks at me, gun still trained at my head. 'Be honest, Sadie. Be completely honest with me. If you get off this boat, and the police pick you up... are you going to leave it be? Are you going to just let me get on with my life?'

I hold his gaze, I can't help it. And even though every instinct of self-preservation in me is screaming *say yes! Just say yes!*... I can't do it. Because it's not true. I couldn't live with myself, to watch him go back to normal life after this. Watch him go unpunished and go back into the world and do what he did again.

'That's what I thought,' he says grimly.

Ned gestures to Lucy. 'Take that off.'

'What?' She stutters from where she's still lying on the

ground.

'Your life jacket. Off with it.'

'But --'

'Now.'

She unclips it, slides it off, puts it on the floor beside her.

'Back away.' He waves the gun at her. 'Where are the others?'

'What?' she stutters.

His eyes swivel over the deck, looking for something. And then his eye lands on them, the life-jackets by the seating area, folded up and glowing dully in the storm-light. He aims the gun, fires. I scream. He fires again.

They're useless now. He's put a hole through every one of them but for the one Lucy had on, which is now lying at Ned's feet. He looks at Lucy.

'Where'd you leave that rope?' he says.

He eyes the shore. And I see what he's thinking. He's going to leave us here. He's going to leave us, maybe tie us up, and now that Philip's taken us further into land, he's going to swim for it.

I look down at my feet. The deck is coated in a film of water. More than just rain water, or the spume of the waves. We're riding too low. The waves are finding it far too easy to come over the hull. There's a couple of lines at my feet, all coiled up, heavy steel shackles at the ends.

'Bring that to me,' Ned says to Lucy, and nods at a coiled-up rope on the deck near Lucy. Is that what he wants to tie us up with?

She doesn't move, and he barks it at her again. She crouches, and picks up the rope. She walks towards him, very slowly. Then a couple of feet from him, she springs. He bats her with the side of the gun, and she topples back onto the deck with a cry.

'Stand up,' he says, his voice icy. I don't think Lucy hears him at first. She looks dazed.

'Stand *up.*'

Slowly, Lucy rises to her feet. She's dripping like a wet rag doll. Her hair hangs in strings down her back.

'Ned -'

'Shut up!' He yells back at me without turning around. I look down, at the coiled rope beside me, the thick metal claw at the top. The one good thing Coach Ned ever taught me was shot-put.

'Come on,' he calls in Lucy's direction. 'Stand up straight.'

He flicks the safety. *Jesus.* He might actually do it. I can't - I *can't* let this happen.

They say your life flashes before your eyes at moments like this. What I see is Fiona, eight years old, running down the street towards me, chubby knees pumping, her long shadow in front of her, sunset behind.

I draw back, hurl the tether as hard as I can, and watch the metal claw clock him in the back of the head.

He stumbles.

The gun discharges.

I hear a shriek but I don't stop to think.

I skid on my knees across the watery deck, pick up the gun in one fluid motion, and hurl it into the water.

When I look back, the rain almost blinds me. Lucy's on the floor. So is Ned.

'Lucy?' I slither across the deck towards her. She's breathing raggedly. I look for blood but don't see any.

I hear a howl as Ned flings himself at me. 'You stupid bitch!' I barely see him, he's such a blur on top of me. All I feel is my head snap back, slam onto the deck. Philip's running towards me. There's a humming sound, getting louder and louder. Is it my head? Or something else?

My eyes stare up, out to the water, the fog. The humming gets louder. And then something emerges from the mist.

A siren. A boat.

I don't feel the cold or the rain, or anything from my body at all.

It's going to be okay, I think.

And then everything goes dark.

Twenty-eight

I don't remember much of the ambulance ride. Maybe the shock wiped out the memory or maybe it's the sedatives. I come to in a mostly-white room, where a nurse whose name tag says Ignacio is asking if I'd like another glass of apple juice. Images flash through my brain.

'Where's Lucy?' I ask. 'How did they find us?'

Ignacio looks blankly at me.

'Lucy,' I say. 'The girl on the boat. Is she okay?'

Strange that's she's the one I'm thinking of. That she's the one I ask about.

Ignacio gives me a careful look, either because he doesn't know much or he's been told not to upset me. 'Everyone made it off the boat,' he says. 'No critical injuries. A gunshot wound to his shoulder, that's being seen to. The police are taking statements now. They'll be in to see you once you feel ready for it.'

I look for the door, as though Ned might be about to burst in, still holding a weapon, even though I felt it slip from my hands, saw it hit the waves with my own eyes.

'Where are the others? Are they here too?'

Ignacio averts his eyes. 'I believe one of them was taken to the station already. He, uh, reacted violently and was put under arrest. That's what I heard.'

Ned, obviously.

When the officers come in to see me, I tell them what I know. I don't try to protect myself from any of it. It's a strangely liberating feeling.

'You have your family to thank,' one of the officers

explains. 'They said you vanished last night, and didn't show up at the hospital this morning.'

Jan. And... Rob? I still haven't figured that part out.

'I tried to make a call when I was on the boat, but it cut off...'

The officer nods. 'Your aunt had some app on her phone, apparently, so her friend was able to track your location with GPS. Which was lucky. You weren't technically a Missing Person yet, and I have to say, we wouldn't have been able to do so usually - but what with the red alert for the Hundley girl....' She gives me a grim smile. 'We were committed to doing all we could.'

The officer looks over her shoulder, towards the door. 'We'll have more questions for you in due course, Ms Kelly, so please don't go anywhere. But I gather there's someone here who'd really like to see you. Can I send her in?'

I just nod. Right now, my throat's too tight to speak.

*

Mom holds my hand. Her palm is cool and soft. I feel like a child again, those rare times when I'd be sick in bed and a kind of tenderness flowed from her that she didn't usually show. She scoots her chair a little closer to the bed.

She's told me all about it, how Rob had been concerned when he saw my car speed off like that, and then I hadn't turned up at the hospital the next morning. Jan had called Mom, and then after Jan got that strange call from my phone, but couldn't call back, they really started to worry. Apparently Rob had an old friend who was in the police department. Between that and the Horton connection, they were able to start the wheels turning.

'I'm so glad you're okay,' she says again. 'I just - it's hard to believe. That one skinny little girl... that she could do all this. She's just a child.'

I don't know about that. Lucy has more steel in her than many adults I've known. But Mom is right too. She's also still just a child, grieving her sister. I look up at Mom, those serious eyes that are so similar to mine. The shock's starting to recede and questions are fluttering back to me.

'Rob,' I say. 'I still don't understand. I thought he was stalking me. He - he had pictures. He'd been on my Facebook page...'

She winces.

'Sweetheart -'

The word sounds so foreign on her tongue, so gentle.

'Sadie, there's something you need to know about Rob. He came looking for me.'

'For you?' I frown. My brain feels heavy. Thirsty - so thirsty - for answers, but heavy.

She nods. 'Remember when I told you about your father - that he married, started a new life?' She swallows. 'Rob is his son.'

I absorb this slowly, my post-shock brain drinking it in.

'I got such a shock when he contacted me,' she goes on. She smooths the hospital sheet, as though erasing the wrinkles can fix something bigger. 'I suppose I assumed he'd have had kids, but I didn't think... I never expected one of them to show up on my doorstep. To contact me.'

'How did he know about you?' I say. Even as I say it the reality is sinking in. *Rob is your half-brother.*

No wonder he always seemed so awkward around

me. Mom must have told him about me, and he was trying to get to know me without giving anything away.

'Sadie. There's something I've never told you...'

I push myself to sit up straighter. I can hear it in her voice. Something's coming.

'I told you I knew Jan from back in Providence. But there's a reason she came here. To Milham.'

'Her job,' I frown. 'She got the job at Milham High.'

'No.' Mom attempts a smile but it's more a grimace. 'She came here for you, Sadie.'

For me?

'Damien - your father - he was Jan's brother.'

'He's...' I arrange it in my mind. 'Wait. You mean Jan is my - my aunt?'

'She believed me, although the rest of his family didn't. She came to see you after you were born,' she smiles faintly, like the memory is a long-ago wisp that's hard to grasp. I blink, trying to get my brain to keep up.

'We stayed in touch,' Mom goes on. 'I sent her photos over the years - she asked for them. And then after her divorce, she decided to move, and there was an opening here.' Mom sighs. 'Jan and I weren't close. We were never close, really. But I think she felt guilty - about her brother, her family, how they'd treated me. I suppose she thought if she was here she could, you know, watch over us.' She plucks at the sheet again. 'She and Damien don't speak these days. Haven't really spoken in decades, so I hear. She told me she tried to show him the photos one time, the ones I'd sent her, and he refused to look. Rob would only have been a small boy. I suppose when he grew up he remembered Jan and got it into his head-'

'-To contact her,' I say slowly.

Mom nods, watching me put it together. I wonder how it must have been for Rob. He probably thought he'd connect with his aunt and fix the estrangement with a few warm words. Instead, he gets a story about his father doing something terrible, a lifetime of denial, and news of a sister. I'm starting to be impressed that he could look at me at all.

I lie back on the pillows.

'But... why didn't you tell us? Why didn't I know I was related to Jan?'

She winces again.

'I didn't want you knowing that story, Sadie. It was too dark, too hurtful. You'd want to know why we couldn't visit your father, or his family. Why he'd chosen not to believe you were his in the first place. I didn't want you to think you'd come from a place of pain and fear. So I told you about a summer romance, instead.' Her voice falters. 'I thought it was the kinder thing to do.

'And Fiona,' she goes on. 'I couldn't ask a little girl like Fiona to keep that kind of secret. Imagine her seeing her cousins, her grandparents back in Providence, and having to hide from them all that in the new town where her mother had moved them, she lived just a few roads away from a cousin they didn't believe in. It wasn't possible.'

I close my eyes. 'So you just lied to us?

'Lies of omission. It was easier to just keep things the way they were. You and Fiona were already more like sisters than cousins. What could it have changed?'

Fiona's voice drifts back to me, our first sleepover. *Sarah's my name too.*

'I used to pretend we were sisters,' I say to Mom.

'Even our names almost match, don't they? Kennedy. Kelly.'

Mom shakes her head. It's a sad smile.

'I sat beside him in school.' She looks at me. 'Damien Kennedy. That's how I first got to know him.'

I let that sink in. You could say it was fate, I guess. If so, it was a mixed-up, sorry kind of fate.

I lie back in the bed. It's going to take me a while to wrap my head around all this.

'So Rob was what happened,' I say. 'The thing that made you start remembering. And drinking again.'

Mom shakes her head. '*I* let myself start drinking again. I don't blame Rob. But yes. It was a shock. It threw me. It was a long time since I'd felt so… off balance.'

Mom squeezes my hand. I look at her, and there's a softness in her eyes, a gleam that makes me think that she might be on the verge of tears. I can't remember the last time I saw my mother teary-eyed.

'Sadie, I'm so grateful, so very grateful you're safe.' She shakes her head. 'I have so much to say to you. The way things have been between us, and how I hurt you the other day in Trudy's when I told you…' She breathes in. 'I haven't been fair to you in the past. I know I've… I've pushed you away sometimes. But I was afraid -' she looks away. 'I was afraid you'd end up like me. I didn't know how to be a mother, how to model the right behavior for you. Jan… it made me furious how much you loved her, how easy it was between you two, like she was the real mother to you and I was some kind of stand-in. But… I let it happen that way. I encouraged it even. Because I knew she was better for you than I was. It made sense that you would leave me behind.'

I stare at her. How could she have got it so wrong? How could such an intelligent woman understand so little?

'Mom-'

She cuts across me.

'I'm sorry I was so harsh to you when you came back to teach at Horton. I shouldn't have acted that way, or said those things. I was angry at you for coming back here, to your past. I thought, in Hong Kong you could really get away from it all at last. Make a life for yourself. One that had nothing to do with me, with us.'

'*Mom*,' I say, and this time she falls silent.

'That's not how it works. Don't you see? You can't run from the past. You can't. *I* can't.'

She looks away from me, towards the window. 'I thought you would spoil it all,' she murmurs. 'That if you came back you'd lose your chance to get away.'

'Away from *what*?' I say. 'What was so damn *terrible* about Milham? What made my life so awful that you and Jan needed to catapult me into a different one?'

Because I can't help but wonder. Was the problem really Milham? Could we have made ourselves a world we wanted to live in, without cutting ourselves off from the past; from each other?

But maybe in Mom's head, it wasn't Milham I was supposed to get away from. She thought I would be better away from *her*.

'I'm sorry, Sadie,' she says, finally. She says it in a flat voice, and if you didn't know her you mightn't think she was feeling much at all. But I look up, and her eyes are wet. She opens her mouth and nothing comes out. She squeezes my hand.

And I squeeze back.

*

The Halloween decorations are already appearing in the stores. It's two weeks since we all got off that boat. I've been spending the time at home, in Mom's house. Jan's still recovering at hers, but sounding quite sprightly, and insists she'll be gardening again in no time.

A trial date has already been set for Ned. He still hasn't confessed to having a relationship with Fiona, even though I've told the prosecutors my suspicions - but three other girls, all alumni from over the last ten years, have come forward since Devon's diary was entered into evidence. I mourn for Fiona, for what I didn't know then.

Back then, when she and I were seventeen, eighteen, Ned was only twenty-three. I'm sure he'd wave that fact in my face if he were here, telling me how mature Fiona was; he'd probably claim that *she* seduced *him*. That he was the adoring man, totally in her power. It's the story he's built for himself. It sickens me that Fiona never got to see him for what he was; that she was flattered by the person he showed himself as. That she believed in him right up until she died. And yet, isn't it better that she died believing she was loved, than believing she was preyed upon?

I don't know. I still can't find the answer to that one.

It's unclear what will happen to Lucy. She might end up in a residential facility for a while, but a lot of that depends on Philip, on how much he's willing to testify against her. I've thought about it a lot, and for my money Lucy isn't crazy. She just felt like she had nothing to lose. That's a dangerous feeling. I think she'll probably get off pretty lightly, given the family she comes from. I read a couple of days ago that nearly three out of four kids in detention centers across the United States suffer from mental health or substance abuse issues. But those kids aren't born to wealthy and powerful families like Lucy's. I'm glad she has this chance to get better. She deserves it. I just wish more of our sons and daughters had that chance.

I think about second chances a lot now.

Seeing how close Rob has come to feel with Jan has made me think a lot about family, too. I'm happy he's found her again.

I've started to realize, too, how much my mom missed out on. She and I have been talking more, recently. The more she opens up to me about her past the more I can see how she never got what she needed from her parents - how for so much of her life, even when she was raising me, what she was craving was to be someone's baby, not someone's mom. That doesn't make everything okay between us, or smooth. But we're both trying. She said I love you out loud a couple of weeks back. Those are words that don't come easily to her. If I'm honest, maybe they don't come that easily to me either.

I've been thinking about Philip, too. About my choices, and what happened there. It was Rob, actually, who made me question whether there was another way I should be looking at it. I told him the story, about Philip and me, and he sort of squinted at me. I asked him not to judge me too harshly and he said it wasn't me he was judging, it was Philip. And then I realized what Rob was seeing, and that he had a point: a man fifteen years older than me, who had the power to get me fired with a snap of his fingers, had come onto me in the workplace. I wasn't an unwilling victim - but the truth is I wasn't truly free, either. Even as I told Rob *I could have said no,* I wondered how true that really was. What the risks of rejecting a man like Philip Hundley would have been. What would have happened to me if I'd reported him for inappropriate behavior. Was it the deep-down knowledge that there *was* no simple way out, that had caused me to lean into it all so recklessly? To convince myself that I *was* in control?

Maybe.

Maybe I trapped myself.

Maybe I've always been drawn to what could drag me under.

Angela Hundley came to see me in the hospital, just before I was released. I was there for a few days, in the end. The concussion, plus a couple of cracked ribs from where I hit the deck. She apologized to me for what I'd been through. I could see the turmoil inside her: her love for her daughter, her fear of what her daughter had done. Her loss. She'd been staying at her sister's, it turned out. Not at an institution, as Philip had seemed to imply. She wanted to tell me that she was paying for all hospital costs, and any costs associated with my inability to return to teaching. She looked me in the eye and told me it was not a bribe, and if I wanted to sell my story to *News of the World,* or bring a lawsuit against her daughter, there was nothing preventing me from doing it.

I don't see myself doing either of those things, though.

Instead I asked her the one thing I still wanted to know. I asked what had happened to her first husband. I'd lain awake picturing it too much by then - picturing crazy Angela Hundley, and the tumble in the middle of the night. I couldn't stop myself from asking. She just blinked at me. I guess she knew everybody wondered, but maybe nobody had ever asked her straight out before. Then she sat back in her chair and rubbed her chin. She told me she'd come out of her room that night to see Devon on the landing, crying. It had been a bad day, Angela said. A very bad day. Without saying it word for word, she told me how Tony used to be physically abusive towards her, and once or twice - including that day - he'd hurt the kids. He seemed to resent Devon in particular. And that night Angela had come out on the landing and seen Devon weeping, and then looked down the stairs and there was Tony, just lying there. She'd told Devon to go back to bed, she said. And then she'd looked down at Tony, and she'd thought she should go down and check if he was alive. But she didn't. She didn't call an ambulance. She went back to bed, set her alarm, and called it in in the morning. She didn't know if Devon had pushed him, or just found him. She didn't want to know. She'd decided it would just lie there, unasked, forever.

I stared at her. She told me she'd deny it if I ever breathed a word.

'Don't worry,' I said. 'I won't.'

'I know Philip liked to paint me as "unstable",' she mused, and I looked away, not wanting to think I'd been manipulated by him. Because it had been convenient for me, hadn't it? To assume Angela Hundley was the enemy.

'But sometimes it's a fine line, isn't it?' she went on. 'Between stable and "unstable"?' She gazed out the tiny window. 'Aren't we all just trying to keep our balance any way we can?'

She surprised me, Angela. She looked so normal,

sitting there. With her hair a mess, and not a Vera Wang pantsuit in sight. She looked like someone I might know.

I come back to reality now when I hear the slam of a front door, and Jan's coming down the steps and out her front gate, still hobbling a bit but not too bad. I'm inclined to believe her when she says she'll be "right as rain" in no time. She has a fierce willpower, Jan. I snap the locks on the car and swing open the passenger door. Jan gets in, a little mist of rain on her hat and scarf.

'Thanks, love,' she says, rearranging herself in the seat, turning up my heating like she always does.

When we pull up at the cemetery I root around for my umbrella but Jan shakes her head.

'It's only a little drizzle.' I remember how Fiona liked that too - the fizz of light rain on her face on these damp days. How she'd turn her chin up as though to catch it.

I start to shiver. Jan looks at me.

'You need more meat on those bones,' she tuts.

But that's not why I'm shivering. I've resolved that today is the day. Jan needs to know what I did. The thing I said I'd never tell her, I'll tell her today.

How I took something of Fiona's. Her future.

I never got accepted anywhere half as good as Stanford: it was Fiona who did that. I dropped her acceptance letter in the mail like I was in a dream. I pictured Fiona coming back. How glad she'd be to find the future we'd built for her.

But she wasn't coming back, and the dreams started to blur. Sometimes it was Fiona I saw in those California hills and winter sunshine, and sometimes it was me. That other world where everything in Milham would be just a memory. If Fiona didn't take the place, who would?

I checked Jan's mailbox. She kept forgetting to; of course she did, she was busy with her grief. I asked myself if I could really do it - if I hadn't lost my mind just imagining it. I kept expecting someone to stop me, but no one did. So I told everyone I'd got in. I booked a flight. And then the day came and I showed up with Fiona's I.D. Nobody batted an eye. I had them change my correspondence address to a P.O. box. I told professors I went by my middle name - Sarah - and to my new classmates I introduced myself as Sadie, short for Sarah. I didn't become too friendly with anyone. I kept a low profile, and stayed away from social media.

The thing is, nobody really checks your references these days. Nobody has ever asked to see my degree parchment. If Mom had come to my graduation she would have heard them call the wrong name as I crossed the stage, but she didn't. It was expensive, far away, and, I did my best to discourage her. It wasn't hard.

I became Sadie Kelly again when I got my first job. And if some second-degree connection had ever come up in conversation, someone who remembered me from the Stanford years, I guess a Sarah Kelly and a Sarah Kennedy sounded pretty alike, anyway. My old professors and 'friends' would just think they'd misremembered, if they remembered me at all.

Funny what you can get away with in broad daylight.

This is what I tell Jan - every last detail of it - as we stand here in the crisp autumn air. Somewhere overhead birds are migrating. Leaving us behind. It's a possibility, I realize, that Jan would never want to see me again. The sun is behind her, which helps in a way, as it means I have to look away, rather than look her in the eyes.

'Maybe you won't believe me when I say this, but... somehow I thought, if I could just do the job of being her, at least for a while, it would - I don't know - make room for her to come back. And if I kept everything going then her life would be ready for her. I thought I could make up for it somehow.' I stop. I search her face, squinting into the sun.

'I'm so sorry, Jan.' I draw breath. 'I tried to do it the way she would have wanted. I know it sounds strange. But when she was little she used to talk about going to Hong Kong one day, so that was where I went...' I don't list all the other things. How I studied Drama because it was what Fiona used to want to do. How I began adopting small habits of hers, things that kept her alive.

'I thought instead of *her* life disappearing, mine could be the one to disappear.'

When I stop there's silence. I'm trembling. I feel frozen all over, like I'm waiting for an axe to fall. I'm being judged, and not just by Jan, but by something bigger. My heart flickers like a plug has been pulled and it's about to go out. But I take a breath, lean into the honesty of the feeling. I'm not running from it any more, like I was before. Whatever the cost of telling the truth, I've told it now. I'll bear the consequences.

When her hand reaches out I think for a half-second she's going to push me away from her, hit me or something - but it just lands limply on my shoulder. I can feel that she's trembling too. And then she moves her hand to my locket, and snaps it open. I know what she sees inside. The photo of Fiona, ten years old, hair in a pink scrunchie.

We stand in silence for what feels like a long time,

nothing around us but the bird-calls. Finally Jan looks at me.

'You're right. What you took was stolen. It was never yours to take - or even borrow.'

I nod, letting the truth sting. It's right that it stings. But maybe I'm strong enough to hear it.

The birds call again.

'But you brought her with you.' Jan says. 'At least you carried her with you.'

I bring my fingers up to touch the chain at my neck. She's right. She means the locket, but more than that, and it's true. Sometimes I've felt almost like two people in the same body - Fiona's voice so close, too close, a voice I have never quite been able to shake.

I look at her. Jan's face could be carved from stone, except for the tear running down it.

'You're not her, Sadie. You're not my daughter.'

The words land like a blow. I can't believe how physical it feels, almost like being winded. The truth of them is so obvious. Undeniable. And even though it's cutting, it's also permission of a kind. *It's time to stop trying.* I close my eyes. *You're not her.* Shame. Relief. I feel it all.

I'd tried so hard. I'd tried to be that daughter.

Jan's voice continues. 'You're not her, Sadie, and you never will be. You'll never make up for what I lost.'

It feels hard to open my eyes again - I'm scared, still, of what I might see on Jan's face. But when I do, there's nothing cruel there. She looks lined, and wise, and very tired.

She reaches over to brush my cheek. It's damp, I realize.

'Sadie, nothing will make up for what I lost. I don't

expect it to. You shouldn't expect it to either.' She takes her hand away, folds her arms, and takes me in with that level gaze once more. 'You're young. You'll learn.'

We don't speak then, for a while. I think neither of us knows quite what to say, where to go from here. But strangely, I feel something like hope. Something I haven't felt in a long time - like there are still new chapters ahead, something still to be written. Something good.

'I guess I'll go,' I say finally. 'I'll wait in the car, if you want some time alone.'

I pull my coat tighter, and go to leave.

'Sadie?'

I turn.

'Remember that night when I fell?'

I nod, confused at the quick switch of tack. Why does she want to talk about this now?

Jan fidgets, pulling at the pocket of her coat.

'Remember I told you I thought I heard someone? That I thought there was someone downstairs?'

'You said you'd imagined it,' I say. 'That you got to the top of the stairs and looked down and there was no one.'

She nods. 'That's what I said. But it's not true. The truth is... I know how this sounds. But the truth is, when I got there and looked down, I saw her. Fiona.'

I just stare. This doesn't sound like Jan at all - she's the last person I would have pegged to believe in ghosts.

She just shrugs. 'I know how it sounds. That's why I didn't tell you. Call it what you like. I'd been sleeping, of course. I'm perfectly prepared to believe it was my imagination. A mother's wishful imaginings. A hallucination. But it doesn't change what I saw. What I *felt.'* She looks at me.

I remember the hospital then. How I'd held Jan's hand, and when she woke up she'd looked at me and murmured *Fiona.* I thought she had us confused; that she'd thought I *was* Fiona.

'Did she... did she say anything?' I ask. I feel stupid for asking. Of course I don't believe in ghosts. But somehow... I have to know.

Jan's smile is soft and bittersweet.

'She didn't, love. She just... looked at me and, well, smiled. Not the way she used to, not one of those big, cheeky grins. It was... peaceful. And that was it.' She swallows, makes a gesture with her empty hands. 'Then she was gone.'

I look at the headstone. A robin stops, perches on it. It trills, hops forward, then back.

Goodbye, Fiona, I think. I mean it this time, in a way that I haven't before. Like it's taken me all these years to learn how to say goodbye.

The robin cocks its head to one side, looks at me with those bright black eyes, and trills again. Jan watches it and smiles.

'Remind you of anyone?' she says.

We stand there for a while in silence, watching, until with a last flurry of song, the robin flies away.

Epilogue

I pull up to the old warehouse space, and pull the door that's been spray painted with flowers and green tendrils, and Shakespeare quotes. Inside there's the hum of space-heaters, and of kids talking. They're boys and girls, ages nine to sixteen, and most of them are from pretty poor backgrounds. Bunmi's Bards is an afterschool group founded by a local woman, Bunmi Jackson, a grassroots non-profit that recently got a bit of federal funding to expand its amazing mission. I was lucky enough to be their new hire. The salary isn't much, but it's enough to live on for now. Meanwhile it's making me laugh and think, and pushing me to teach in a way I never taught before. Every second I'm here I'm fully present, and as far as I'm concerned it's the best therapy money can buy. Just as well, since my income won't stretch to the other kind of therapy, anyway. I've been tapering off the benzos for the last three months now. I'm not all the way there yet, but I'm doing a lot better.

'Sadie, what's up.' It's Brandon, one of the other group leaders here. He winks at me, then gets pulled away by one of the kids, Rory, to hear a new monologue Rory and his friends have set to a rap beat.

It's almost the holidays now, and Jan's bouncing around like her hip never broke, busying herself with baking and accumulating a collection of poinsettias. The doctors say her speedy recovery is unusual at her age, and said probably it was good genes and a lifetime of good eating habits. I'm tempted to believe it's more about attitude.

I have to admit it - Rob has been good for her. It's still strange to me sometimes, putting all the pieces together, remembering that we're connected in this web that runs deeper and darker than I knew. He's shown me pictures of his father - of a man who looks enough like me that there's no mistaking it. I guess if he ever looked at a photo of me he'd see it too, and that's what he's scared of. Rob's asked me if I would ever want to meet him. I don't think so, but I can't say for sure.

Rob has a lot of his own stuff to work through, finding me and Mom and hearing her story. He says his dad always seemed to him like a really good guy, and it's obviously painful for Rob to have to square his version of his father with this dark chapter, especially when it's something his father still denies, still refuses to face. But Rob thinks change is coming. Maybe he's too much of an optimist. Or maybe he's right to hope. I'll admit, Rob's grown on me a lot, although the word *brother* or even *half-brother* isn't something I can really see myself using, not yet at least. But now that he's come out of his shell and isn't hiding anything, he's a lot more fun to be around - his wicked sense of humor totally took me by surprise.

And meanwhile there's Brandon, my new co-worker at Bunmi's, who has started to treat me with a special kind of warmth that I think is more than regular friendliness. He's nice - easygoing, good-natured. The kids love him. But I don't feel quite ready for anything like that yet. I have some things I need to work through first. For now, it's just nice to have a friend.

Simone and I still talk a bit, though not a lot. I've forgiven her for the part she played in things, but I don't know if she's forgiven herself. Thorpe has retired from Horton. She emailed me the other day. It was completely unexpected. She says she's going to take a trip - to Alaska. She's always wanted to see Alaska, she says. When I told her about my new job at Bunmi's Bards, she said she'd come to our next performance - it's in two weeks, the night before her flight leaves. It's weird to say, but I think I could actually grow to like Lucinda Thorpe one day.

I still hear Fiona's voice a lot, but it's different, these past weeks. The things she says are kinder. She laughs more.

'Ms Sadie, Ms Sadie!' Tanisha catapults across the room to me and bobs up and down, grinning widely. I focus again, seeing the bright room, the hand-painted children's art-work on the walls, the calls and shouts and the other adults trying to encourage but keep order. We're preparing for *Midsummer Night's Dream*, and Tanisha's been cast as Puck. Mischievous, bright-eyed, energy for days - she'll be perfect for it. I follow her deeper into the room of children.

'Want to hear my monologue, Ms Sadie?'

'I sure do,' I tell her.

She hops up on a bench and throws her head back, reveling in the attention. For a moment she reminds me of another little girl. A little girl from long ago, who wanted to grow up and be an actress too.

'Think but this, and all is mended —

That you have but slumbered here

While these visions did appear.'

It's the final monologue she's reciting. Puck's closing words. A couple of the kids nearby stop what they're doing, and turn to watch Tanisha. She's that good.

She reaches her last line and with a flourish, throws her hands wide:

'And so good night unto you all. Give me your hands, if we be friends,

And Robin shall restore amends.'

I close my eyes.

Thank you, Robin.

Thank you.

The End

A Letter from Claire

Hello,

I can't thank you enough for choosing to read *The Silent Daughter*. It's such an exciting thing for me to share it with you - putting a first novel out into the world is scary, but also what a thrill! I am so appreciative that you decided to pick it up, and I really hope you enjoyed it.

As a kid, I *loved* boarding school stories (although I never wanted to go to one - my wonderful parents are nothing like Sadie's and I never wanted to leave them!), so I was probably making up boarding-school fan fiction in my head even then. But I'm older now, and reminded that there is often darkness in beautiful places, and that dangerous things can go on behind closed doors.

Although I don't believe that society alone can "make" a monster of the kind we see in this story, I do believe we enable them wherever girls and women are coaxed into silence or have their voices tamped down. Although this is a suspense novel, with twists we don't necessarily see in real life (hopefully!) I've tried to treat this important, difficult topic with the sincerity it deserves. I hope with each new generation we'll have fewer and fewer silent daughters.

Besides Devon Hundley herself, the characters that captured me most in this book came to me as a trio: Sadie, her best friend Fiona, and Fiona's mother, Jan. I wanted to explore how two very different - but in their own ways, both lonely - young girls like Fiona and Sadie could

281

become close friends, and then become driven apart as they grow up.

Sadie's relationship with Jan is a huge positive influence for Sadie, but it also becomes a source of jealousy for Sadie's mom and Jan's daughter - what brings one character solace ends up being a source of pain for someone else. Our relationships can be so full of misunderstandings, even when we're all just trying to do our best. Writing these three characters made me think a lot about the family we're born with, and our other family - the family we choose. I'm so grateful that my life is filled with loved ones of both kinds - those who share my blood, and those who don't.

I hope that you connected with Sadie, Fiona, and Jan, and that their stories led you to remember some of the important relationships in your own life.

If you enjoyed the novel, I would be deeply grateful if you could take the time to leave a review on Amazon, or wherever you post reviews. I read all of them. It's the most uplifting thing in the world for an author to hear that you found something to like here - and for first-time authors like me (new kids on the block!), it's simply invaluable.

If you would like to continue being part of the journey, I'd be thrilled: you can sign up to my mailing list and connect with me on http://claireamarti.com, or follow @claireamartiauthor on Facebook. I'm always happy to connect with readers!

Thanks again for reading,
Claire

Acknowledgments

My dear friends and family -

I am warm right down to my toes when I think of the support and infectious excitement you've so generously offered to me on this adventure. When I announced I was going to publish *The Silent Daughter*, it was your chorus of "hurray"s, "go for it"s and "we can't wait to read it"s which made me think, hey, maybe this *is* a good idea! So thank you, thank you. Special mention to Margaret Gales, Natalie Butlin, and Réachbha Fitzgerald for advance reading and life-coach skills/practical advice/pep talks.

Thanks most of all to Mum and to Dad - my cheerleaders, biggest fans, picker-uppers and duster-offers, guiding lights and lifelong companions, as well as to Manuel Dudli Betrán and Frank Lowe, my second-time-around family.

Much love to you all,

Claire

CPSIA information can be obtained
at www.ICGtesting.com
Printed in the USA
BVHW072308230920
589459BV00008B/774

9 781087 889481